Who Killed Leeanne?

MIRA GIBSON

ISBN-979-8-9901812-0-5

For all the dreamers whose dreams are more real than reality.

LEEANNE HESSINGER

Wednesday, January 4, 2017

I WATCHED AS a seagull pecked at a crushed pigeon in the slushy parking lot outside of the local ShopRite. I had just moved to the small town and had bought a few groceries to tide me over until the incoming snow storm had blown through. The pigeon, broken as it appeared, wasn't dead yet, but that didn't stop the gull.

One bird eating the other alive.

Me, bearing witness from my idling sedan, foot on the brakes, windshield wipers squeaking across glass, exhaust fumes billowing up around the car and seeping through the window I had cracked open to help clear the condensation. I kept staring at the seagull as it tore into the ratty pigeon that was fighting it less and less.

I had never seen anything like it.

In that moment, I learned everything I needed to know about Liberty, New York…

…but it wasn't until my murder a year later that I understood the significance of what I had seen that day; what God and the world and nature had tried to warn me about…

It wasn't until I was fighting for my own life that I realized—fully—what I should've known all along.

SHERIFF JUDY KAVLESKI

Thursday, January 4, 2018

I KNEW THE DEAD woman, not personally, but by face and name like I knew most everyone in Liberty.

It was a small town. Sleepy all winter. Teeming with tourists up from New York City come summertime. Whenever a new face showed up and stayed, the residents took notice, and Leeanne Hessinger had quite a face.

She lay sprawled inside the entryway of the house she had been renting, knees collapsed at a twisted angle, one limp hand draped over the bloodied slash in her sweater near her sternum as if, in her final moments, she'd tried to nurse the fatal wound. Her head was tilted to the side. A pool of her dark hair spilled across wooden floors. Jeans intact and no signs of sexual assault. Woolen socks on her feet. No boots. Coat hanging on a rack deeper in the foyer. There was a warm kettle on the stove. The empty mug beside it on the kitchen countertop had a dry tea bag inside.

Dispatch had gotten the call from a coworker of hers, Trip Turner, who I also happened to know by appearance only. A clean-cut type. Fancied himself an actor, but he worked as a teacher over at Bethel Woods. He was slumped outside where my deputy and the responding officer were also waiting.

Murder was rare in Liberty. Crimes amounted to pot smoking and sometimes selling, petty misdemeanors at best, and when they occurred it caused more excitement than the department could handle.

I decided not to admit to myself that this time I was probably in over my head.

I needed to control the crime scene and the only way I knew how to do that was to keep everyone but myself out. My deputy was itching to be included. Didn't help that I'd left the front door wide open, winter wind cutting through the entryway, foyer, and the kitchen straight ahead, bringing Curt with it. I had instructed the one officer on the scene to stick to Turner, but not question him. He was better at orders than Curt.

"Sheriff?" He filled the doorway, a slippery stack of evidence bags in hand.

"Suppose I could use one."

Curt hadn't been my deputy long.

He cracked an evidence bag open for me, passed it over, as he absorbed the unbelievable sight of Leeanne Hessinger's body, both of us slow and constricted in our thick winter coats.

I made careful work of lowering to my knee in front of the murder weapon—a fixed-blade hunting knife that wasn't uncommon around these parts. It rested, blood drying along its sharp edge, next to Leeanne's thigh. I exercised balance and accidentally let out a grunt as I scooped the plastic bag around the hunting knife and slid it in.

I was pregnant. Being eight months along as I was made for trying maneuvering, but I had been managing just fine without accepting the help that was constantly offered.

"Run it for prints?" asked my deputy.

It was a bit of a struggle getting to my feet, but Curt knew better than to take my arm and hoist me up. He looked lost, confused by his own question, and I wasn't in much better shape. Wouldn't even know the lab to send it to. Never had such an occasion, in fact. This was serious. Daunting. We both knew it would likely be the most important case we'd ever investigate.

"Let's get a number on it," I suggested, because that's what it was, a suggestion, an educated guess at how we would have to proceed. "You got a box in the cruiser, right? We'll bag everything we can, number all of it, get it back to the station. I've got to get a forensics team on over," I frowned.

"Yes, Ma'am," he agreed before mentioning, "Trip's in a real state."

"I imagine he would be."

Curt lingered, sucked back into the sight of Leeanne.

"Wilcox," I said, urging him to get on task.

I heard his boots crunching through snow as I neared the body and angled over the dead woman's pretty face. She had been known to turn heads around town.

I wasn't much older than her, but I knew my looks hadn't held up like Leeanne's. Of course, death had dulled her beauty, turned her skin gray, veins blue under her pallor. Her features remained youthful. Eternally twenty-four, though I knew she was inching towards her mid-thirties. High cheekbones. The kind of delicate, button nose that celebrities often paid for. A wide, dramatic mouth.

Leeanne had a willowy physique. Long limbs and a slender waist. Swimmer's shoulders, a tall woman who didn't so much walk as glide. That's how I remembered her, gliding through town like some otherworldly creature that didn't belong; she'd drink in the scenery around her as if all of life was a wonder…

…and this was what had become of her.

It was a shame.

Outside, I made my way down the shoveled walk towards Trip Turner. He was sitting in the passenger's seat of his car, his boots in the snow, and the door open. A mile-long stare had come over him. The cruiser was parked beside him, my pickup truck behind it.

Curt lumbered between the police vehicles, tending to that box I'd put him on. He was doing a soldierly job with a Sharpie, but the grimace, the long face gave him away. His movements were solemn. It was sinking in.

Trip sensed me approaching, but didn't lift his eyes. He swallowed as though preparing to speak, but I realized when he said nothing, that he was only choking down emotions that were threatening to surface. He looked ill.

"I need to ask you a few things. Sorry to have made you wait." I slipped my mittens on and rested a hand on the icy hood of the car, looking down at him. "You worked with Leeanne?"

He nodded as though something deep inside of him was trying to pull him under, then he managed, "Yes. She teaches with me at Bethel Woods.

Taught," he corrected himself in a small, bewildered voice.

"Right," I said gently. I had known that, as I was familiar with the majority of employees over at the Performing Arts Center. "What were you doing over here?"

He sounded shaky and raw. "She was having car trouble. Her car's in the shop. I had been giving her rides."

"You came to pick her up?" When he nodded, I asked, "Could you walk me through everything that happened? What time did you get here?"

Trip cleared his throat, swallowed hard, chin quivering. He mustered some semblance of control and explained, "I pulled up at a quarter to nine or so. Texted her. She didn't come out. I called. It rang through to voicemail. Then I went to the door and saw it was open." Emotion rose up in his boyish face and he pressed his mouth into a bitter line, determined to hold it together. "When I opened the door, I saw her on the floor." Trip cut his eyes up to me and insisted, "I didn't touch her, just saw her lying there, saw the blood, the knife. I called the police." After a moment, he added, "I sat on the front steps and waited."

It jibed with what my deputy had told me, reporting what the responding officer had come upon when he had pulled in—Trip sitting on the snowy steps in a stupor. That's how Curt had found him as well, nearly catatonic in a shivering heap out front when he'd arrived not five minutes later.

"Were you personally involved with Leeanne?"

"No. Not at all," he said. "Not outside of giving her a lift to Bethel Woods when her car was acting up. I think I'm going to be sick," he warned as he pushed out of the passenger's seat, barreling past me to get some air.

I thought he might keel over and make good on his threat, but he held his hand against his mouth instead.

I gave him a moment before nearing him. Came around to face him, had to squint, the sun glared against the snow so badly, a sky of blinding haze to contend with. Trip was much taller than me, taller than most men and I had to crane my neck to meet his gaze.

"Why don't you go on home?" I offered. "I'll get these vehicles out of your way. We can write up a statement later."

"Thanks," he breathed through his hand. When he lowered it from his face, his jaw was clenched.

I joined Curt at the side of the cruiser and handed him the keys to my pickup. "Get these cars down the drive, would you, so Trip can get out of here?"

"You're letting him go?"

"He's in no shape to talk," I told him as I glanced back at Trip and wondered if I was right or not. "I'll write up a statement for him, have him look it over and sign it later."

Curt seemed thrown by the decision and reminded me, "He was with Leeanne."

I didn't need a reminder.

"You think he killed her?" I questioned, "and hung around to call the police?"

The look on his face told me that that's exactly what he thought.

"Move the cars, Curt."

As he did, I pulled my cell phone from my pocket and called the station to have a forensics unit come on out to the house. I would like to get back inside, myself, but Trip had piqued my curiosity and it wasn't because of my deputy's doubts.

I had seen Trip on stage once or twice. If recollection served me, he'd played Stanley Kowalski in *Streetcar Named Desire* some years back, bringing a seductive edge and boyish charm to the role, and daringly abandoning every brutish mannerism that Marlon Brando had sewn into the character. Trip had also starred in another classic stage play, the name of which escaped me, but his performance I had never forgotten. The subtle tears. The quaking rage that had turned his voice to jagged glass. My husband, Mitch, and I had been sitting in the front row and my skin had broken out in gooseflesh when Trip pleaded, desperation percolating just under the surface of his calculating façade, for his lover to run away with him. I had believed him.

The baby was kicking, a demand I had come to regard as hunger, so I pulled the egg salad sandwich Mitch had made for me that morning out of my coat pocket, peeled the cellophane back, and began munching to appease my unborn boy, as I idly watched Trip.

If anything, I was really examining my own susceptibility to buying his performances. I challenged myself to question if that's what his statement had been—another brilliant performance.

Was he one hell of an actor, or had the shock of discovering Leeanne dead in her house delivered such a blow that the raw emotion I had just seen—his vulnerability and baffled articulation—genuinely amounted to the real deal?

Studying him now, I couldn't help but notice that he looked irritated and impatient, gnawing on his thumb as he glared at Curt's slow work of backing my pickup truck down the icy driveway, careful not to spin out into a skid.

Was that a guilty man I had locked my sights on?

Could Trip Turner have killed Leeanne?

TRIP TURNER

Monday, January 16, 2017

I HAD BEEN FUNCTIONING in a cloud of loneliness for longer than I cared to admit. It had permeated all areas of my life—my office at Bethel Woods, the grand theatrical stage I had fallen in love with, my little cabin where playbills and scripts sat in stacks, and even my car—but I wasn't in denial about it.

I felt the weight of my aloneness. I had acknowledged the isolation it brought with it. I'd accepted it. I'd even tried to make friends with it, indulging it with more alcohol than was probably healthy.

The winter storms weren't helping. They came at the town sideways and always at night, forcing residents to stock up on food then steal away to their homes, fortified against the elements with their families, children readying the candles in case the electricity was blown out, as was often the case.

I had no family, no wife, no woman, though I had made my fair share of attempts over the years. For some unknown reason—I didn't know when or why—it had been starting to get to me. I wasn't *just* single anymore. I wasn't *just* alone. I was unfulfilled and bored with myself, with my routine, with my profound lack of spontaneity.

Reading plays and practicing monologues as I paced in my living room, whiskey sloshing in my glass to help conjure captivating emotions that would satisfy the character I was aiming to embody no longer entertained me as it once had.

At first, I had chalked it up to age. New York City was only two hours away, but I had less and less energy for it. Making the trip down to audition seemed, more and more, like a waste of time since I rarely got cast. The fiery optimism that used to drive me—foot heavy on the accelerator, wind whipping my face, and the car radio blasting some song I knew only half the lyrics to—had burned out.

I wasn't *resigned* so much as *content* with what had become my life at Bethel Woods. I taught acting in an afterschool program. I often starred in plays on their main stage, for which big time directors would fly in from all over the country. But the joy in even that much had run dry.

I had begun to long for someone who might fit me.

I wished I had never latched onto the idea, but once I had gotten it into my head that I would like a woman in my life, I couldn't let it go.

It was then, however, that I began to truly notice how small Liberty was. It wasn't quite a one-horse-town, but in terms of dating, it certainly felt that way.

That's when I began wrestling with what soon became my dark friend—loneliness.

My wants and needs were at odds against a circumstance I found I couldn't control. I told myself I had done well for myself. I'd find her. But then a small voice would rear up from the back of my thoughts, reminding me of my shortcomings. I had a roof over my head, but I couldn't take full credit for even that. My mother had left the cabin to me in her will. What, exactly, did I think I could provide to someone special?

I forced myself into my work, selecting monologues for scene study, picking plays for the main stage, creating acting games the kids might like, all the while refusing to believe that at thirty-seven I had missed my window for romantic love.

Hope coiled through my heart. At times, it stung. At others, it got me out of bed or into the next bar after hours. The result had been fruitless…

…and then another snowstorm hit town.

It took NYSEG six days to restore the power, which pushed the first returning day of work at Bethel Woods since the turn of the New Year back by a week.

I had already spent nearly all of January analyzing the state of my probably failed life. Why had I never moved to the city? What had possessed me to set my roots down in the same town where I'd been born? What the hell was wrong with me that I'd never ventured out to conquer the world? How could anyone in their right mind be satisfied with this?

It had taken three bottles of Jameson, a carton of cigarettes, and every Tennessee Williams play I had in my bedroom to accept precisely how far I *hadn't* come in my life, and by the time I strolled into the Performing Arts Center that most likely had been and would always be the pinnacle of my underdeveloped career, I knew I looked exactly how I'd spent those snowy days holed up in my cabin—rough, dehydrated, and oscillating between determination and desperation.

At least I'd brushed my teeth.

I kept my head down as I started through the lobby, heading straight for the stairs that would take me to the lower level where the Teaching Artists' offices were located near an art exhibit space.

The Bethel Woods museum wouldn't officially open until the spring so the exhibit room was white walls and air conditioning and nothing else.

Sometimes I smoked in there, but Carol didn't like it.

Bethel Woods was an interesting place. It was the home of the legendary Woodstock Music Festival. Its main museum upstairs contained a wealth of relics that I'd honestly never connected with. Hippy stuff wasn't my thing, but I appreciated its existence, both the festival and the museum.

Upstairs also held the theater where I'd performed more times than I could count.

There was a bandshell on the massive lawn outside where the summer concert series took place every year.

Of all the places in Sullivan County I could make a living doing what I loved, well, Bethel Woods had literally been the only option. Good thing I had convinced them to hire me a decade ago, and good thing I had been here so long that I could mess up, marginally, from time to time without any real risk of being fired, though I had to keep my eye on Carol. She was a scowler.

I slipped into my office, unscathed, and set the playbooks I had brought with me down on my cluttered desk, each one dog-eared and marked with Post-Its where I'd pinpointed a juicy monologue or two-character scene. Nothing racy. No swear words. I worked with teenagers who could come up with curses I'd never even heard of before in combinations that would make a felon blush, but Bethel Woods' policy mandated that none of the students could say any four-letter words under my supervision. Good looking out, Carol.

I had barely settled into my chair and gotten used to the fluorescent lights I hadn't missed—there weren't any windows in my office to smooth out the harsh overheads—when there came a knock at the door.

"Trip? Got a newcomer," said Carol, peeking her big head into my office.

Carol was a squirrelly woman who wore a smile that I'd learned not to trust. The deep grooves between her eyebrows told me how she really felt.

Best to stay on her good side.

I returned the smile and waved her in. "Happy New Year."

"Yes, happy New Year," she told me as she stepped inside with a tall woman who followed in after her. "I wanted to make introductions before the meeting. This is Leeanne Hessinger. She's going to teach creative writing down here in one of the conference rooms."

I was already standing and rounding out from behind my desk to greet her.

At first, she reminded me of Popeye's Olive Oil—a bag of dressed-down bones—but that was before I had a chance to really take in the sight of her.

I did a clumsy job of extending my hand. Hers was cool and slender, and I probably held on a bit too long, as I absorbed the full magnitude of the woman I was looking at.

She was gorgeous.

Long, blackish hair against a fair complexion, a vulnerable glint in the eyes and expression, both of which now reminded me of Laura Wingfield, though the impression could've been influenced by my having read The Glass Menagerie only days ago.

What struck me in that moment about Leeanne was the breathiness of her mannerisms. It was as though life had taught her to proceed with caution yet hadn't hardened her into someone bitter and jaded like I had been questioning myself to be.

"Leeanne, it's nice to meet you," I said, releasing her hand, which she quickly captured into folded arms. "I'm Trip."

Carol kept the formality in place. "Trip Turner teaches acting and makes *loud* use of the theater upstairs."

Leeanne smiled, graciously assuming that Carol had meant to be good-natured about the implied complaint.

"I'm so happy to be here," she said breathlessly. "I was starting to get worried with that last storm that the roads would never get cleared. I'm eager to start. I've never worked with kids."

"Teenagers can be vicious," I joked, but Leeanne took it seriously and looked intimidated. "You'll be fine. This isn't school and they know that. They want to be here. They might goof off, but it isn't hard to wrangle them back on task."

"I'll take your word for it," she said, coming more fully into herself.

"Any advice I can offer," I invited as open-endedly as I could.

Carol steered Leeanne towards the door, mentioning, "The staff meeting will be in the conference room in about ten minutes. I'd like you to meet the rest of the Teaching Artists, get you settled in your office, show you the supply closet…"

As they left my office, Leeanne glanced back at me over her shoulder.

For a split second, I thought I caught a glimmer of the same loneliness I'd been wrestling with myself lurking behind her dark eyes. But then her whole face lifted with optimism and she flashed me a smile that I knew was meant to break whatever spark of connection had just taken place between us.

With my hands in my pockets, I gave her a nod.

This was one meeting I was certain I wouldn't be late for.

THE CONFERENCE ROOM was frigid and windowless. I knew to bring my corduroy jacket and wrap a woolen scarf around my neck even though it made me look pompous. Leeanne didn't know the lay of the land, that the maintenance boys at Bethel Woods kept the central air set at sixty-eight degrees year-round, a subtle form of torture I had been contending with for ten years.

I had gloves in my pocket, ready to do battle.

Leeanne had nothing but the thin, clingy sweater she wore and her knee-length skirt.

As soon as she settled rigidly into one of the chairs around the table, she eyed the door, debating whether or not she should dart out quickly to grab her winter coat, but the many T.A.s piling into the room held her back from acting on the urge.

I sat across from her.

Leeanne twisted her arms together, not quite crossing them, and fixed her mouth into the shape of a pleasant smile.

To me, she looked nervous and overwhelmed. I tried to steal a touch of eye contact to reassure her, but she seemed to avoid my gaze, those dark eyes of hers meeting each Teaching Artist as they filled the chairs around the table. Sometimes she glanced at the notepad and pen she'd brought with her.

It was an eclectic cast of characters, our little Teaching Artists brigade who managed, against all odds—including Carol's oppressive tyranny and the students raging hormones—to inspire and empower the kids in our select programs.

Mary Roberts, practically a teenager herself who dressed in all black, wore platform shoes, and rimmed her tight eyes in smoky liner, taught photography and always seemed disgruntled until the snowy weather let up and she could bring her clicking cluster of hipster students outside to take photos.

Seated next to her was Cassie Davies, a fifty-year-old woman who taught painting and drawing in every medium one could dream up—watercolor, oil, acrylic, sometimes colored pencils. She'd retired from the local high school a year ago where she had spent well over three decades wrangling teenagers and yelling at them to 'produce something that could even loosely be described as art', a phrase I'd come to know and resent when I'd had her myself in ninth grade.

She barely tolerated my existence at Bethel Woods since, in my day, I had practically given her an aneurysm from grief. Cassie was still working on loosening her skepticism that the twelve kids in her program actually *wanted* to be there, little devils that they were.

On either side of Leeanne were Nora Graham, the sculpture teacher, and Carol Patterson, my nemesis.

Nora was happily married with six children, a fact that seemed to defy her petite anatomy as well as her age. She was bouncy and liked to thrust her iPhone under everyone's noses, boasting how cute her kids were—*kids say the darndest things!* She was also extremely active on Facebook. *Extremely.* I'd blocked her. I made a mental note to advise Leeanne to do the same before Nora would have a chance to 'like' and *comment* on literally every post Leeanne might have made since signing up for the social media site.

"Doesn't he look like a bunny rabbit?" Nora asked Leeanne, barely angling her cell phone enough for the newcomer to make her own determination, as she laughed, nose wrinkling, into Leeanne's personal space.

Not the bunny rabbits again, ugh. Nora and her husband had given their children five rabbits over the years and, incidentally, a rash of ringworm.

She had ambushed me with the same photo before the Christmas break. "Sammy doesn't resemble his rabbit," I told her dryly.

"But those *teeth*, though." She wheezed out another soundless laugh as Leeanne politely nodded and murmured something agreeable.

Then Carol breezed into the conference room with an official-looking binder. Closing the door, she announced, "I've reviewed everyone's proposal." She sat, stiff and scowling, and opened the thick binder, which I knew she wouldn't need to reference.

Whatever new rules and regulations had filtered down the pipeline, she already had them memorized.

"Once again, I see we have to start the new season going over the *Output Goals* section."

Uniform grumbling ensued. Mary looked especially deflated. Leeanne looked lost, her eyes widening, as she sat up and pressed the tip of her pen to her notepad.

"*Output* Goals are markedly different from *Outcome* Goals," she reminded us. "Leeanne, you're forgiven, but the rest of you have no excuse. Reference the 'Important Definitions' section, people. Outputs should answer questions like 'what will your program produce?' 'What will your program accomplish?' 'What activities will be completed?'"

Leeanne wrote down every word as though her ass was on the line.

"There was similar confusion with the 'Assessment Tools Used' column on the fifth page of all your proposals. We've gone over this, but I see I'll have to be more thorough in defining it for you," she complained. "It's not about *your* tools. It's the tools *that the students will acquire* as a result of taking your course. Mary, you've written, 'I will assess the kids' grasp of contrast...'. Clever use of recycling the term 'assess' by the way," she said a bit snidely for my taste.

Mary shrank. "Thanks."

"It wasn't a compliment," Carol informed her. "What I need you to note is the tool the student will acquire," she repeated. "Something to the effect of, 'Having been taught such-and-such technique, they will be able to assess their acquired skill of such-and-such by referencing the rule-of-whatever.'"

In order to move the persecution along, I guessed, "You want us to re-write the Outputs and Assessment Tools sections and resubmit our proposals?"

"I would," she confirmed, "and remember people, the 'Intent of the Program' field is a simple copy-paste job!"

Mary had an epiphany and made a strange groaning sound and Nora chuckled at herself as if she was a bonehead. She'd made the same error.

"If you don't have the verbiage for that field, I can email it to you."

"Would you?" Mary asked and the rest of the T.A.s nodded that they would need it emailed to them as well. I refused to nod my head and remained stubbornly stoic, secretly knowing I'd receive the verbiage via email as well.

Carol made note and allowed, "I know this type of administrative work can be tedious—"

"*Torture*," I corrected.

"Trip," she warned. "This is how we get grants. Everything needs to be just-so."

"I don't see how I could've possibly messed mine up," I argued. "I keep my proposals identical from season to season. I only swap out the names of the stage plays."

"Well, Mr. Turner, I might venture to guess that you've been cutting corners using an old proposal that was wrong to begin with."

"Good looking out, Carol," I said with a wink.

She frowned.

"Leeanne," she went on, "let's you and I have a sit-down in my office and I'll help you revise yours."

"Thank you," she said as she shook out her cramped writing hand.

"Oh, Mitch!" Carol exclaimed, rising out of her chair and waving the Director of Arts & Humanities into the conference room. He had skirted past the closed door and I'd barely caught sight of him myself through the narrow window. "You weren't in your office earlier," she mentioned as he gave a subdued nod to the Teaching Artists around the table. "This is Leeanne Hessinger, our newest T.A."

Leeanne awkwardly scraped her chair away from Nora. Carol hadn't given her much room to work her way out, but she managed and met Mitch, connecting their hands in a formal shake. She smiled breathily.

"Great to have you, Leeanne."

Mitch Kavleski rarely acknowledged my presence. I sensed it was because he assumed I had applied to work at Bethel Woods so I could sleep with the many female Teaching Artists in the program, as if the Performing Arts Center were synonymous to your run-of-the-mill yoga class.

Cool in his regard for everyone, Mitch had a regal presence that preceded his high standing in the county. In addition to being the Director of Arts & Humanities at Bethel Woods, he also served on the Board of Trustees.

He was distinguished and polished—a silver-fox who had a look that belonged on the silver screen—and though I had never been in his home, I imagined it was decorated with rare Matisse paintings or perhaps a daring Basquiat piece. He looked like he could host one hell of a cocktail party and yet boredom seemed to cloud his demeanor. Or maybe what I'd been picking up on was an air of self-importance. Who knew?

I didn't like how he was looking at Leeanne. The lingering handshake made me feel protective towards her, but I reminded myself Mitch was married and tried not to glare.

"I'll let you get back to it," he told Carol before excusing himself.

As the meeting unfolded, Carol prodding each of us to share the curriculum of our individual programs, I couldn't keep my eyes off Leeanne. Couldn't stop myself from hunting for the glimmer of loneliness I thought I had seen in her eyes before.

But she never lifted her gaze to meet mine.

"How was your first day at Bethel Woods?" I asked as I filled the doorway of her barren office hours later. I'd hoped to catch her at lunch, but she'd slipped out of the building and had spent her forty-five minutes somewhere that had required her car—I had watched her start through the parking lot as I'd smoked a much-needed cigarette outside.

"Not quite what I expected," she admitted, as I invited myself in.

"It can feel like it's more 'teaching' than 'artist'," I commiserated. "But you'll feel differently once you're with your kids."

"The paperwork is… staggering."

I laughed and shoved my hands into my pockets. "If you stay on top of it, it's not so bad. Also," I went on, nearing her with an air of confidentiality, "Carol never tells the new T.A.s, but you're going to want to keep a head count for each class."

"To note absentees?"

"Not quite. See, the higher ups don't actually care about who's in attendance and who isn't, because that would make sense. They just want to know that 'ten out of twelve kids' learned some skill or what have you. Try to quantify as much as you can in your class reports. 'Eleven out of twelve kids grasped the concept of past tense'. 'Seven out of twelve kids understood omniscient narration.' That kind of thing."

"You know a lot about writing," she pointed out, impressed.

"I know those two things."

She narrowed her eyes, sizing me up. "I suspect you know more than that."

Shrugging, I admitted, "I read."

"Thanks for the heads up."

Unwilling to let the conversation lull, I asked, "When did you move to Liberty?"

"Just after the New Year," she said, but folded her arms.

Guarded.

I eased in. "Winter can be deceiving."

"Oh?"

"The town is dead all winter," I told her, "but as things warm up in the spring, there's quite a bit to do around here. Lots of hiking and fishing if you're into that kind of thing."

I couldn't gauge her interest, so I kept going.

"There are a number of restaurants along Main Street."

"I noticed," she allowed.

I knew when a woman thought a guy was a creep, but I was well within my limits and wouldn't dare cross that line.

I tried my hand at flashing a little of my renowned boyish charm, mentioning, "There's always the casino over in Monticello. Brand-new place, Resorts World Catskills. Tons of restaurants and shopping. Bands often play there, and of course playing the slots can be entertaining. I'm not bad at Black Jack," I boasted with a sense of humor.

"I'm not much of a gambler, but I'll keep that in mind."

"Why Liberty?"

Her smile faltered and she didn't immediately answer. "I liked the name."

"Where did you move from?"

The second I had asked it, I knew I was prying, but I didn't backpedal or apologize. My palms got sweaty, though, and I hoped she would say something I could riff off of. I could then segue into a change of topic to meet her comfort level.

"I moved from Upstate."

"We're already Upstate."

"Farther Upstate," she barely clarified. "It was a city. I didn't like it."

I smiled good-naturedly. "Well, I'm sure Liberty is happy to have you."

"Thanks," she breathed.

I was dying to ask her out for a drink, offer to show her around town, but I'd already pushed my luck. "If you need anything..." I mentioned, backing away. "A second pair of eyes on your class reports or a Black Jack partner..."

"I'll think of you."

It didn't sound like a promise, but I left it at that and returned to my office where I feared concentration would elude me. It did, and I attempted to chase away my intrigue in Leeanne Hessinger that evening, and many evenings to come, with the help of a single-malt and full flavored cigarettes, as well as my dark friend who didn't hesitate to remind me that loneliness wouldn't be so easily escaped.

LEEANNE HESSINGER

Friday, January 27, 2017

I DON'T THINK I EXISTED except for in the stories I wrote.

Maybe I was a ghost or a shell of someone, hollow and brittle. Empty. Never fully realized. Nothing had filled me up. I didn't even have fond memories to cling to. My life had become mundane and unmemorable.

I had felt that I had nothing to lose by moving. I had built nothing of value. I'd accumulated nothing worth keeping, though there had been much to escape and abandon and flee from—that dark place far Upstate where I couldn't stand to live any longer.

Complicated emotions had come—the guilt and freedom of having stolen away down south without warning.

Liberty was a brand-new town to me, mysterious and uncharted.

I had promised myself I would write a Pulitzer Prize winning novel. Not only would I revel in my beautiful imagination and exist—*fully!*—within the characters and pages I crafted, but the novel itself, the product of it, once published at some future date I was determined to realize, would connect me to the world.

Finally, I would be alive, filled up, and fulfilled!
Whole.

I would autograph my novel at book signings. Give smart interviews. Pose for pictures with fans and attend writing conferences where I would be a guest speaker, invited there to inspire emerging authors. I imagined becoming close friends with my editor, getting into heated debates with my publisher, experiencing all the guts and glory of having authored a great piece of literary fiction.

It was ambitious. I was a decent writer, but not especially practiced.

I had been stifled and discouraged and distracted by those two people who had trapped me in a world—their world—where I had never felt I belonged.

Teenagers should never make decisions that impact the course of their adult lives. Should never commit. Should never think they won't grow and change and want out.

No one had told me that in high school. I'd had to learn for myself the hard way. In my heart of hearts, I doubted I would be able to accomplish realizing my dream of making my mark as a gifted author, but I was intent on trying.

Writing was my first love, the most important relationship I had ever had. To claim a few quiet hours to myself, typing away and exploring my vivid imagination, would be satisfying, in and of itself, whether or not the result happened to be very good.

I would try my hand at it here, in Liberty! I would welcome the snowstorms, embrace the wildlife, and open myself up to be inspired by my surroundings. I would let the world pour into me and fill me up with ideas then I would send them out through my fingertips, keyboard clacking, onto the page.

It didn't matter to me that I had no education, though that fact nagged at me from time to time. I had never gone to college or grad school, which was a method I understood the majority of published authors out there used to garner agents as well as hone their writing voices.

I had managed to grasp the basic tenets of grammar, though, mainly because I was an avid reader, and felt confident enough in that department.

I was allowed to have big dreams! No one had ever told me that growing up. Throughout my adult years, no one had encouraged me to take hold of and seize that possibility. I had never been allowed to be grand and spirited and wishful.

All of that would change in my new home. It had to.

The snowstorms had kept me tucked away in the little house I had been renting during those initial few weeks in Liberty.

The first miracle of my new life had been signing a lease despite my dismal credit and inability to pay the full security deposit. I had one of those faces, I guess. People trusted me. I seemed responsible. I sensed my landlord preferred a single, tidy woman to rent his place rather than a sprawling family.

He had asked several questions, though, the wintery evening I moved in, wondering where all of my belongings were, would I need help with the furniture?

I had lied and invented a cousin who would drive down at some later date with all that in a

U-Haul. Blamed the weather, the non-stop storms when my fictional cousin still hadn't been able to make the trip. It had made enough sense to him.

I had been avoiding the landlord ever since, uncomfortable with the lie I would have to keep adding to and elaborating on.

There was no furniture, but I had already plotted that my fictional cousin—Marcus—would be held up with gallstones or perhaps tonsillitis.

I estimated I could develop the story further and if I crafted the lie just so, I could milk the twists and turns of cousin Marcus' ailing health, stretching the developing fib clear through the entire spring.

If the landlord checked in about it then, I had already decided I would mention that cousin Marcus had in fact made it down with the U-Haul. Speedy as cousin Marcus was known to be, he had unloaded everything I owned while the landlord was out at the grocery store.

Then, of course, I would never be able to let the landlord inside the house, but that suited me just fine. I could fix leaky sinks and tighten cabinet screws myself if need be. I had always been handy around the house.

The second miracle of having moved to Liberty was that I had found the gumption to submit a proposal to teach creative writing at Bethel Woods.

I'd had absolutely no plan in terms of making money in Liberty when I had transplanted myself here.

The morning after I had settled into my rented house, I had woken up from the stack of sleeping bags I had slept on, bursting with optimism, and had scoured the internet for a job, hoping to get hired at the local paper or maybe work remotely writing marketing copy, not that I had any experience with either.

My expertise revolved around stocking shelves at Walgreens since my resume had been repeatedly overlooked at several bookstores as well as the library farther Upstate.

I had done a soldierly job of not letting my spirits sink all those years, but even now it was hard for me to think about. High school diplomas didn't amount to much, and I had known that.

It was kismet that my Google search had pulled up the Performing Arts Center.

Curiosity and a thump of excitement had brought me to the 'Get Involved' page of their website. When I had discovered the corresponding 'Teaching Artists' page, I was filled with such a surging wave of elation that I nearly choked on my tea.

My stomach had tightened with worried knots as I had skimmed the position description, praying that it wouldn't require formal teaching credentials. It hadn't!

Next, I had made doubly and triply sure that they didn't already have a fiction program in place, and confirming that, I had gotten to immediate work drafting a proposal to run a creative writing workshop.

I had nearly jumped out of my skin when I had gotten the call inviting me in to have an interview.

When Carol had hired me days later, I hadn't been able to contain my excitement. It was, hands down, the happiest moment of my life. I would teach creative writing and write my own fiction during my down time.

I would live and breathe stories, and finally be who I had always imagined I would become!

My first week at Bethel Woods was nerve-wracking and exhilarating all at once.

There was a huge learning curve and I took my administrative responsibilities seriously, staying late to dot the 'I's and cross the 'T's on all of my reports.

Getting locked in a room with Carol as she had gone over my work with a red, felt-tipped pen hadn't been enjoyable, and if I could help it, I would never find myself in the same predicament that my evidently botched proposal had earned me.

My workshop classes with the students—*my students!*—felt, by comparison, *right*.

Teaching had never occurred to me before, but I took to it naturally. It didn't feel like *teaching*, in fact. It felt like a conversation, one in which my students often impressed me with their keen understanding of both storytelling and symbolism.

Of course, eighty percent of the time my classes felt like a real zoo of unbridled hormones, flirtatious assaults, and a chorus of swear-words that had me gaping and blushing, my eyebrows pitched clear up to my hairline, as I stuttered to assert my authority and calm them down.

My mother would've used a bar of soap and a firm backhand, but that didn't seem like a politically correct way to go.

Trip had given me a stern heads-up about Carol, and I was afraid to so much as raise my voice at the kids, not that I was the sort to do such a thing.

All of the classes met three days a week on Mondays, Wednesdays, and Fridays from 4:30pm to 6pm.

I tried to establish a rhythm for myself, get a feel for how I would like my weeks to play out. I decided my routine would be to allow my creative writing class days to be just that, Bethel Woods all day. Reading my literary favorites at night over a protein-rich dinner and exactly two glasses of pinot grigio, my favorite, would follow.

Once the weather let up and I could see pavement again, I devised I would start jogging, but for now filling my head with the stories of published authors during my down time felt like more than enough.

On my off days, which were Tuesdays and Thursdays when I left the Performing Arts Center at 4:30pm because there were no classes, I would use the extra hours to work on my novel, the idea for which I hadn't yet decided on, though I was honing in on a fantastic title—<u>Pulse</u> or <u>Pulp</u> or <u>Pumped</u>.

Intuition told me I was onto something.

The weekends would be dedicated to exploring Liberty and the surrounding towns, and of course plugging away at my book.

Trip had been persistent.

Though he kept to the periphery of my working hours, it wasn't lost on me that he had been finding ways to sidle me at the watercooler, prowl around my office door or peek his head in to crack a private joke at Carol's expense, and linger in the lobby before heading out in case I was on my way home as well.

He might have been dashing and charming and undeniably funny—a confident mix of self-aggrandizing and deprecating humor made for one hell of a one-man show!—but I kept my guard up around him and suppressed my laughter so as not to encourage him.

He seemed the type who, if I were to let him in, would never give up the ground he had won and would continue to forage deeper into me.

I wasn't sure I wanted anyone getting close. Personal alone time was territory I had fought hard for. That's what moving had been all about, and I didn't want to relinquish the only positive outcome of the nervous breakdown I'd had up north.

Trip was starting to feel dangerous.

I collected my laptop, notepad and pen, and a file folder in which I had been keeping my students' short stories—I had scrawled my thoughts and feedback in the margins of the printed prose they had passed in at the end of Wednesday's class—and started through my sterile-looking office.

Like my rented house, I had brought nothing personal to Bethel Woods to cozy up the place. I was almost ready to feel self-conscious about it, but reasoned I could put embarrassment off at least until I had cashed my first paycheck.

By then, I might be in the market to buy a comical mug to keep pens in and perhaps a nice photo frame, though I hadn't the foggiest clue what I would put in it. A framed selfie would be asinine, and I didn't have any children or pets to boast like Nora did.

Maybe I could take a picture of the winter wonderland that was my backyard?

I would think of something.

Of course, Trip had timed another stroll through the corridor so that we would run into each other on our way to our respective classes. Mine was in the conference room directly beside my office, and his was upstairs in the theater.

"You almost survived your first week teaching," he congratulated me good-naturedly. He had meant to sound casual and off-handed, but I could tell he had gone over his cadence, at least mentally, once or twice.

"Almost."

He strode ahead of me and turned, as I paused at the conference room door in polite anticipation that he would have more to say. Walking backwards, he continued with our light conversation.

"I'm going to hit up the casino for a little atmosphere after class. Celebrate the completion of three classes. You should come."

"I'll think about it," I said and his eyes lit up.

As he cracked a grin, turning back around and heading off, I ducked into the conference room where a few of my students had gathered at the far end of the table, some sitting on it, others standing nearby.

All of them were listening to Scotty de Barra tell a wild tale of football glory.

I had only had two classes with them so far, but I felt like I knew them well, and they certainly knew each other since they attended the same high school—Liberty High.

Scotty had made it known that he was a JV superstar, and at only sixteen years of age—apparently that made it even more impressive.

I had learned, because he had forced me to, that he was the quarterback on the junior varsity football team and the captain of the soccer team. He held the fastest sprinting times on the track team, but the coach—a hothead who thought Scotty was spoiled—wouldn't make him captain.

Another student, Rachel Hathaway, had dryly pointed out that Track & Field had no 'captains', but Scotty felt that was no excuse.

He was also a champion swimmer and was certain that one way or the other he would make it to the Olympics—he was also an excellent skier, but Liberty High didn't have an organized team, which was something he was currently working on changing.

His girlfriend, Valerie, strongly agreed about his Olympic potential and draped herself all over Scotty every chance she got.

I had half a mind to separate them for the duration of my course, since Valerie's lips seemed magnetized to Scotty's cheek and Lord only knew where her hands were roaming under the table, but I was holding off.

It was a 'wait and see' situation.

Plus, I wanted them to like me.

Interestingly, though Valerie had convinced Scotty to join my creative writing program, he had already proved himself to be far more talented at fiction than her.

His first story, which was tucked in my filing folder along with eleven others from my students, had been raw and daring, sexually charged, and well-paced. It wasn't especially well-written, however. His creative and often inaccurate use of grammar had tripped me up as I had read it last night, but I remained impressed.

Whereas the majority of my students' stories bled together in my memory, some sadly having been forgettable, Scotty's stood out in my mind.

He might have agreed to attend my class because his demanding sports schedule wouldn't kick up until March, but I had a sneaking suspicion he would discover an authentic interest in fiction writing, one that would go beyond his girlfriend's ass-grabbing incentives.

"We're going to make Nationals this year," Scotty boasted as though the story he had just told about saving the big game had been leading up to that very fact.

He flipped a football in the air, punctuating his point, and grinned at Valerie, as the rest of the students poured into the conference room.

I stood at the head of the conference table, my back to the dry-erase board, and greeted the kids as they found their seats around the table.

Pleased with himself to a cocky extent, Scotty leaned back in his chair, lifting three legs off the ground to demonstrate his exceptional balance, and asked me, "Hessinger, did you like my story?"

"I did," I allowed with a reserved smile that I wasn't about to afford him for very long.

"Did you like mine?" Rachel asked, her big eyes widening for my approval.

"Of course."

"What about mine?" Valerie had to know.

It was contagious, so I addressed the class as a whole.

"I was impressed with all of your short stories. I noted my personal comments on each one, which I'll pass back to you in a bit."

As I sat down, I asked, "Who here feels that they would like to elaborate their short story and turn it into a longer work of fiction?"

"Do we have to?" Gloria Wilder asked worriedly. She was all glasses and trepidation, had been since Monday.

"No, you don't have to. I was just curious. Show of hands?"

About half of the students around the table raised their hands, but not many of them seemed confident about it.

Timothy Freedman, a lanky fourteen-year-old who favored turtlenecks and corduroy pants, was wavering, lifting and lowering his hand as he glanced around the table.

A perky, gum-chewing fifteen-year-old named Margie Conway had taken to tearing a sheet of paper to add a little white noise to the situation for reasons I couldn't begin to understand.

Her best friend, Kelsey Samuels, poked her and Margie produced a stick of gum, which Kelsey promptly folded into her gothic-black mouth. She then proceeded with some light origami, turning the gum wrapper into what appeared to be a little swan.

All this while I struggled to address the class and describe how I would like to spend the month of February—I had to keep those Output Goals and Assessment Tools in mind—and excite them with the possibility of drafting a novella for their final project presentation in early May.

Scotty's hand shot up and he announced, "Track starts in March."

"I know, Scotty."

"Just sayin'."

"You mentioned. Several times."

"I mean," he sang out, filling his sculpted chest and enjoying that he had my attention, "I'm not saying I won't be *here*. I'm just *saying*."

"You'll be here," Valerie giggled, brushing up beside him before whispering something inappropriate in his ear.

Rachel rolled her dark eyes and frowned at me.

"I know I'll be here," Scotty agreed, a bit irritated with his girlfriend. "That's what I'm saying. But Coach is going to expect me at practice," he told me, as his brows lifted to his hairline.

I supposed he had meant it as a challenge so I assured him, "We'll work something out."

I steered the class in the treacherous direction of reading a few of their stories out loud.

Naturally, as a born champion, Scotty volunteered himself when the bulk of students looked intimidated and bashful.

I wished someone else had been eager, but I was also interested in hearing the jock read his work, an author using his own voice for punctuation and cadence.

I allowed it, slid his story to him, keeping the rest under lock and key in my folder, sat back, and crossed my arms.

For some unforeseeable reason, he grinned at me once he had gotten to his feet.

Then he insisted, "This *isn't* about Valerie."

"Yeah, right," Luca Martinez groaned, and Rachel rolled her eyes for the third or perhaps fourth time.

Before beginning, he asked me, "Can I say the dirty words?"

"Oh, Christ!" Rachel blurted out. She hung her head for an exasperated beat then, snapping her gaze up to meet mine, declared, "I'm going next."

"Sure," I said, sensing I might have to wrangle their focus back to Scotty and his dirty story.

Scotty asked innocently, "Yes to the dirty words, or yes to Rachel?"

"To both," I told him. "Yes to both. Please begin."

I felt like I needed a drink and we were barely twenty minutes into the class.

After clearing his throat, Scotty began reading.

As he did, the punch of his testosterone-filled tone smoothed out and became deep and gentle. His words flowed seamlessly. Sentences poured out of him.

He punctuated certain paragraphs, pausing to let the story thus far wash over us before proceeding at a clip that helped the momentum of the driving action swell.

Yes, there were dirty words and his protagonist had a boner for pretty much the entire five-hundred-word story, but not even Rachel rolled her eyes.

The students were engaged, and by the time Scotty slapped his paper onto the table, coming back into his cocky, grinning persona, the class applauded without my encouragement.

"What did you like about it?" I posed to the entire class. "What worked? Luca, let's start with you and go around the table."

As we began to discuss the strengths and then weaknesses of Scotty's story, I tried and failed not to think about Ian, the kid he used to be and the man that life had turned him into; my high school sweetheart who had become my greatest oppressor by the time I had turned thirty.

It had been a very dark era, those long years with him.

I couldn't even think of high school fondly because of it.

I refused to be nostalgic towards a period that had ultimately led to the breaking of my spirit.

In school, Ian had been pure and clever and funny. He'd courted me the way most boys did. Got handsy with me one night in the back of his car after that. A public gentleman. A private pervert.

Scotty didn't remind me of Ian. They were nothing alike. Scotty was a bright-eyed jock and Ian had been dark and brooding.

But it was starting to dawn on me that teaching a group of teenagers might call to mind the person I used to be before life had crashed in sideways and leveled me into someone I no longer recognized.

Whether that would be good or bad for me, I didn't know.

❄

"IT WAS A VOCAL exercise, Carol!"

That was Trip.

His voice echoed from what I assumed was the vacant exhibit space beyond our offices.

I had slung my purse over my shoulder, a thick filing folder of fresh stories inside, and was preparing to head out, but the rising argument between Trip and Carol drew me in the wrong direction down the corridor.

"It sounded like they were murdering each other up there!" Carol accused, as I came to the open doorway.

At the back of the vacant exhibit space near the Exit door, Trip was sucking a cigarette.

"Put that out!"

"Are we fighting about the vocal exercise or are we fighting about my smoking?"

"Trip," she warned.

He dragged on the cigarette until it was a stump and then snuffed it out against the wall, which seemed to incite Carol even further.

It took her a moment to regain control of herself.

"I would appreciate it if you could keep the volume down," Carol went on in an unemotional tone, having tempered her anger.

"It's *acting*," he informed her as though that should explain it all.

"And I would appreciate it, Trip, if you would come to me for approval about your scene study selections."

"What?" he blurted, aghast.

As I turned from the door, Carol confronted him fully.

"Your students were screaming bloody murder, and when I came upstairs I saw that scene, Trip. It was much too aggressive."

"It's called *conflict*, Carol," he insisted. "It's the foundation of well-written dramatic dialogue."

"It was much too aggressive," she repeated, this time using a deeper, more serious tone.

Trip laughed at her concern, but I was already skirting through the corridor.

The Director of Arts & Humanities, Mitch Kavleski, was coming through, heading straight for the heated argument.

I offered him a smile, which he barely acknowledged.

"'Night, Mr. Kavleski."

"Goodnight, Leeanne," he said politely, though his expression was pure displeasure.

I told myself it wasn't about me, but it was a struggle.

I knew Mitch wasn't looking forward to refereeing an argument between Carol and Trip, yet I couldn't help but feel like I had somehow contributed to his sour mood.

I had been plagued with this my whole life, taking on blame that didn't belong to me, thinking I was the cause of someone else's anger, foolishly trying to correct it. A futile effort that only tangled me up in guilty feelings that did no good.

I challenged myself to shake the paranoid worry away so that by the time I climbed the stairs, crossed the lobby, and stepped out into the freezing, dark night, I would be free of it.

My effort faltered, nearly working, but not fully.

I bundled up then started through the icy parking lot.

I liked to park my car at the very back of the lot, any lot that I used—the parking lot at ShopRite, Walgreens, the Dollar Store, wherever.

I loved walking no matter what the weather, but most of all, I loved seeing my car sitting all alone, far away from the bulk of vehicles that tended to cram closely in front of a store's entrance.

Didn't people understand how beautiful space was?

But this time, as I made my way, boots wading through slush, I was overcome with dread.

It roiled through my stomach then burned my chest.

I felt watched, quickened my pace, and fumbled with my keys. My mittens were too thick and lessened my dexterity.

When I finally pressed the key-fob, unlocking my car, Trip called out:

"How 'bout the casino?"

"Trip?"

"After the chat I had with Carol, I definitely need a drink."

As he jogged over, I advocated for the woman who had hired me.

"So, no one got murdered in the theater today?"

"Oh, come on, we weren't that loud."

"You brought my class to a screeching halt," I told him.

"Then I definitely owe you a drink."

It was tempting, but I was eager to dig into the new stories I had collected.

"I think I'm going to pass."

"It's Friday night," he reminded me, leaning back dramatically as if I had pained him to the extent that his heart had been pierced.

I gave him the laugh he wanted for his performance, but that was all I was willing to give him.

"Really?" he asked.

I winced apologetically and maintained, "Really. I'm beat. Goodnight."

He watched as I climbed in behind the wheel and fixed my seatbelt across my lap.

As I reversed to pull my car out, he stood with his hands in his pockets, all bundled up and crestfallen.

I shifted into Drive, gave him a little companionable wave in the rearview mirror, then drove off, as a warm rush of relief washed over me.

My personal time was my own. Nothing felt better than dodging an invitation to be social.

❄

AS I DROVE HOME from the Performing Arts Center, Trip weighed heavily on my mind.

There were ten miles between me and my rented house.

The roads were streaked with snowdrift, which made their windy bends treacherous. It was unbelievably dark out. I had never been swallowed in that kind of darkness, black all around me, the headlights of my puttering car barely penetrating thirty feet ahead, and I was distracted.

I missed the turn for Rt. 52 somewhere between thinking about <u>The Goldfinch</u> and worrying about Trip's subtle advances.

Being the worrywart that I was, I had begun plotting excuses I could use to decline his invitations, which I intuitively feared wouldn't stop. It occurred to me that there might not be a better excuse than the truth. I needed as much time to myself as possible in order to write my prize-winning novel, but I anticipated Trip would suggest that every skilled author needed experiences, relationships, or at least a drink every once in a while. So, I decided that reason might not hold up.

I could use my tumultuous past, doting out anecdotal crumbs about Ian and the emotional, physical, and spiritual abuse I had suffered, but I didn't want to open myself up.

I had a feeling that Trip would know how to manipulate a vulnerable woman. I needed to remain impenetrable.

I began envisioning the chilly demeanor I could try exercising around him. A cold shoulder at the watercooler. Hot, argumentative phone calls, my cell phone pressed to my ear with no one on the other end of the line, whenever I walked to and from my office. I could potentially avoid him that way.

But I wasn't an actor like Trip. I doubted I could pull it off. He would see right through the performance.

It occurred to me that a fictitious boyfriend might do the trick. That was about when I realized Rt. 52 had gotten away from me.

I didn't recognize the hill up ahead. Snow started fluttering down. I flipped the windshield wipers on, blasted the vents to help clear the condensation that was spreading across the glass, and cracked my window, but didn't turn back.

Maybe I could hang a Do Not Disturb sign on the outer doorknob of my office?

That would be off-putting to Carol and the rest of the T.A.s who I was coming to like quite a bit, especially Cassie. Crotchety old women tended to like me and I often returned the sentiment.

I soon came to an intersection and squeezed the brakes, idling at the four-way stop and trying to decipher the street sign that was partially iced over.

Swan Lake Road.

I knew that road!

I took a chance, turning left, and kept my eyes peeled for indications I had gone in either the correct or wrong direction.

It was impossible to tell, and I had oncoming traffic to contend with.

One thing I had learned about Sullivan County was that the residents didn't feel obligated to lower their high beams for oncoming traffic.

I navigated a tight bend in the road at the bottom of another hill I had just traveled without spinning out into a skid, as a truck coming in the opposite direction nearly blinded me.

Once it passed, I let out a rocky breath, blinked my vision clear, and discovered another sign—Walnut Mountain Road.

Walnut Mountain?

Could there be a *mountain* a mere two or three miles from my rented house?

I made another left, coming onto the road, which had been encrusted with impacted snow, though the town had sprinkled a decorative line of dirt along the center.

I gripped the wheel tightly and kept to a crawl, understanding that this was a residential road. The cabins along it were few and far between, and much larger than those around my little house.

At the end of the road I came to a shallow parking area in front of an icy sign for the park.

I rolled right up to the sign so that my headlights illuminated it. I couldn't believe my eyes as I read:

Town of Liberty
Walnut Mountain Park
Where Nature Nurtures the Soul

A third miracle!

I was certain of it!

There was a *mountain* right in my little neck of the woods, practically in my backyard!

As cold and dark as it was, I had to see it.

I bundled up and climbed out of my car, having killed the headlights, and pulled the key from the ignition.

The air was like dry ice stinging my lungs.

I felt invigorated as I came to a break in the wooden fence.

Holding the snowy railing of the fence for balance—I was walking on what felt like a sheet of ice lightly dusted with snowdrift—I stared out into the darkness, studying the hilly terrain that opened up at the foot of the stout, little mountain that would be mine.

All mine.

This would be my place.

I could feel it.

Carefully, inching out over the slippery snowdrift, I ventured into the park. The snow became deep as I waded farther and farther. It clung to my jeans and slipped down into my boots, melting against my ankles, but I didn't mind.

The parking area fell away into darkness behind me.

I looked up at the twinkling dome sky, the constellation of flawless stars overhead, and smiled, lifting my arms and twirling.

This was my new life!

I was going to make all my dreams come true here!

I could feel it!

I was going to show the world who I was!

The intimacy of my book—the next great American novel—would be my voice! Nature *would* nurture my soul! I would grow here, blossom into the person I had always been destined to become!

I fell in love with the sky that night, twirling and marveling at the stars.

And I drank in the crisp air, the serenity of this wild, wonderful place, and what I imagined Liberty would become for me.

Home!

But when I started through the deep snow, heading back to my parked car, I saw a man standing at the wooden fence in silhouette, staring at me.

"Thought you might like company," said Trip.

I was filled with a very dark feeling.

SHERIFF JUDY KAVLESKI

Thursday, January 4, 2018

THE FORENSIC UNIT had arrived from Monticello, the nearest city, though it could barely be described as such. Other than the casino and a Walmart, Monticello didn't have much more to offer than Liberty. Admittedly, its population was at least ten times that of my town, and they had an experienced forensics unit I needed.

The unit was comprised of two crime scene technicians, one holding higher rank than the other, and a blood spatter analyst.

They struck me as grim, efficient men.

The blood spatter analyst was making me nauseous. With gloved hands, he crouched near the body and began slowly peeling Leeanne's sweater up her abdomen until the gaping stab wound was exposed.

I had taken a number of photographs of Leeanne with my camera.

I stood over her, lifting my camera to my face, and snapped off a series of close-up shots of the fatal wound.

The aftermath of death was fast business, I was discovering. Nature didn't waste time.

The stab wound had congealed with black blood, the edges of Leeanne's cut skin curling in like bacon in a frying pan.

Her stomach had sunken, skin pale and thin as rice paper, revealing a spider's web of blue, hardened veins.

I could see her ribs, but death hadn't done that. She had grown emaciated. I had never suspected she was so frail beneath her bulky sweaters and summer outfits.

It gave me pause.

My deputy, Curt, was looking on as the crime scene technicians angled around the body, combing it for hairs and fibers that the killer could've left behind.

They had collected the murder weapon, as well, offering to run it for prints at the lab they often used.

I felt a slight twinge that this thing was getting away from me, but Curt had insisted we could use all the help we could get.

I couldn't argue.

I knew that fingerprints were unlikely. Tracing the hunting knife back to its buyer would be impossible. Knives weren't firearms, after all. And even if the lab in Monticello was able to pull a print or even a partial, unless Leeanne's killer was in the system, it wouldn't do any of us much good.

Mitch had called several times about lunch. Did I want to meet him at the house? I didn't have the stomach to pick up or return his calls. He had texted me, but I had ignored him despite the increasing urgency in his messages.

I was putting off telling him about Leeanne. He knew her from the Performing Arts Center where they both worked.

Mitch was a curt, unemotional man, but this would cripple him. I would tell him over dinner, and I hoped that Trip Turner wouldn't set the town on fire with the news of Leeanne Hessinger's murder in the meantime.

Mitch was only checking in about the baby, doing his husbandly duty, and I knew the baby was fine, kicking as always and forcing me to eat. He could wait.

"Can anyone tell me an approximate time of death?" I asked the technicians.

The blood spatter analyst, a middle-aged man with long, gray hair pulled back in a low ponytail who smelled of patchouli and had been suppressing something that resembled a grin ever since he had set foot in the entryway, rose to his feet but didn't address my question.

Instead, he continued to eye Leeanne and the fatal wound he had crassly exposed.

Another wave of nausea suddenly came over me. It was the patchouli he had marinated himself in, not the wound, that had turned my stomach.

The senior technician answered me, "Early this morning. Maybe around seven or eight."

Curt frowned, a quivering grimace coming over him from where he stood near the coat rack, and added, "Officer Ludlow said the kettle was red-hot and empty on the burner when he arrived. He turned the stove off."

Leeanne had gotten up early, I surmised, put a kettle on for tea, but had been interrupted.

"I would say," the blood spatter analyst began, "she knew her killer or at least trusted the person."

I agreed. There was no sign of forced entry. Leeanne had willingly opened the door, but the attack had quickly followed. She hadn't invited her killer into the house or hadn't had a chance to.

The analyst went on to describe the story that the body and blood told as he moved swiftly through the entryway and foyer.

"She opens the front door, steps back when she realizes who it is. She didn't turn her back to the killer to return to the kitchen, but given the location and position of the body, she backed up by at least five paces."

"A reaction to having seen the knife in her attacker's hand," I supplied. "She was trying to claim some space."

"The killer lunges," he went on, demonstrating the movements and momentum that might have been used, "and neatly thrusts the blade into her sternum with an upward motion, like this."

As he pantomimed the blow, I asked, "Can you tell if her attacker was taller than her? Shorter?"

"I'm not comfortable making that kind of determination," he responded, as he eyed Leeanne with an intrigued tilt of the head.

"Would've had to have been much stronger and faster than her," Curt suggested.

"There are no defensive wounds on her hands," the analyst allowed, implying that her killer had at least been fast. "This was clean. No signs of a struggle."

"Premeditated," I concluded.

I drew in a deep breath, absorbing the magnitude of it, and glanced at my deputy.

"When it's a crime of passion," the analyst went on to speculate, "I generally find multiple stab wounds and more cast off patterns. Her attacker came in to do a job and accomplished it swiftly and perhaps unemotionally. They just wanted her dead."

I took his speculation with a grain of salt and stepped around the body, entering the kitchen.

I stooped, eyeing the mug on the counter, the dry tea bag inside—Earl Grey—then instructed Curt to bag and tag everything in sight for the lab, as the forensic unit fell back into their work.

Taking a slow lap through the kitchen, I came to the humming refrigerator where a sad calendar hung from a magnet. It was one of those complimentary calendars that businesses doled out—small and faded.

Sam's Auto Body Shop. The car trouble Trip had mentioned came to mind. January's picture was an unimpressive shot of the sign for Walnut Mountain Park.

I was familiar with the mountain and its natural, burly beauty. The photographer hadn't captured it. Yet hand written in black ballpoint pen across the upper edge were the words, 'Remember the miracle!'

The grid of days below was mostly blank, but spanning through the first three days of the New Year was a horizontal arrow. Above it Leeanne had written in the same ballpoint color, 'FAST'.

It gave me pause.

Immediately after those marked days, she had written, 'Start novel, 3k words a day! You have everything you need! This is your year!'

I sensed more than saw Curt nearing. "Let's get this into evidence," I instructed. "I'll see if she has others."

A wall separated the kitchen from the living room.

There was nothing in the living room, not a single piece of furniture, though gauzy, red curtains draped the windows.

With gloved hands, I opened a closet where a stack of folded towels sat. A printer was below them.

I nearly broke down in tears, but pushed onward, coming into the small bedroom.

A surge of sorrow filled my chest, and I was thankful Curt hadn't followed me.

On the floor was a stack of sleeping bags, a thin woolen blanket over them, their edges tucked in neat and tidy, a little standing lamp next to the wall. A pink pillow indicating the head of the makeshift bed.

I wouldn't have lost it had I not seen a village of Christmas cards on the windowsill. They were from her students at Bethel Woods. She had kept every one.

I knew as soon as I pinched one of them open—'Can't wait to read the novel!' signed Luca Martinez—that I had made a huge mistake. Returning it to the windowsill, I completely broke down.

This woman had so little.

I silently wept, bracing the windowsill with gloved hands.

Who were you, Leeanne Hessinger?

All I knew about her was that she had worked as a Teaching Artist at Bethel Woods and she owned virtually nothing. It was her hope, her big dreams, the optimism in those exclamation points—*this is your year!*—that tore my heart right open.

She hadn't deserved what she had gotten.

I willed myself to pull it together and gain some semblance of control over my emotions. It was my hormones, the baby, I wouldn't have collapsed with a swell of sadness otherwise. I was a strong, analytical, discerning woman. I had to snap out of it.

I returned to the little bed.

Beneath the pink pillow was a hard, black object. A laptop computer. For some reason, knowing that she had one made me feel better.

I carried it back out into the kitchen where Curt was going through the cabinets and drawers, having slid Leeanne's refrigerator calendar into an evidence bag. I asked him to bag and tag the laptop as well.

The sounds of heavy tires crunching over snow drew me outside. An ambulance was pulling up. Even the ambulance looked solemn in the wake of my mood. They were here for the body.

I collected Curt and instructed him to handle things. The forensic unit was wrapping up, the blood spatter analyst gripping his kit—a canvas satchel I hadn't noticed him crack open. He conversed with the senior technician.

I thanked them and returned outside, coming to the edge of the snowy front yard.

There was another larger house through the snow-covered trees where I understood Leeanne's landlord lived.

I couldn't bear to watch Leeanne's body being rolled out on a gurney so I started through the snow, heading straight for the landlord's.

I found the snowy, two-story house charming. Garden gnomes lined the walk, their cheerful heads poking up through the snow. Christmas lights were strung over the portico, sparkling white, and there was a wreath on the door.

The car in the driveway told me someone was home, but I still waited for a bit after knocking three separate, patient times.

From the corner of my eye, I caught a glimpse of the gurney rolling out of Leeanne's house. They'd covered her with a white sheet. It was still too much for me.

"Yes?"

I stared into the crinkly, aged face and soulful eyes of the man who had answered the door. His white hair was thin and wispy, his sweater festive. His home smelled like a wood stove and cinnamon.

Finding my voice wasn't easy.

"I'm Sheriff Judy Kavleski. Do you own that house over there?"

He peeked his head out, looking in the direction I was pointing, then noticed the plastic glove on my hand. I should've pulled them off before so I did that now.

Registering the commotion, he said, "Yes, what's going on?"

"Your name, Sir?" I pulled a moleskin notepad from my winter coat and used my large belly as a table on which to write.

"George Miller." His eyes were on my notepad and he leaned in, being sure I hadn't flubbed the spelling. "Did something happen to Leeanne?"

"I'm afraid so," I told him, and he looked pained and urgent all at once. "She was killed early this morning," I informed him, omitting the details of the attack. "Did you happen to see anything? Anyone come up the walk? Any vehicles?"

"Killed?" he breathed as the weight of the news slammed into him. I gave him a moment to make sense out of what he had just learned. Stammering, he shook his head. "I've been inside all morning. Is she okay?"

He was in shock. Confused. Brain scrambling.

"I'm sorry, George. Leeanne is dead."

"Dead," he breathed, the idea taking hold as an anguished grimace came over him. "Is there anything I can do?" Before I could remind him of the questions I had just asked, he came to grips with what was going on. "Dead? My God. Dead? What happened?"

"Unfortunately, I can't give you much information. I was hoping you had some information for me, in fact. I don't know much about Leeanne, and she seemed to live a simple life. Is there anything you can tell me?"

"I have her rental agreement," he offered, then thought better of it. "Leeanne hadn't written down any emergency contacts, I recall. Oh, but she has a cousin. Marcus, I believe his name is."

"A cousin Marcus?" I repeated, jotting the name on my notepad.

He nodded. "I'm not sure of his last name."

"Any other family?" I asked.

I was inclined to get the information from Bethel Woods and all the hiring paperwork Leeanne would have had to have filled out, but if she hadn't given her landlord an emergency contact, I doubted she would've noted any such names and contact information on her H.R. forms.

"Not that I'm aware of."

"And you didn't see anything this morning?" I questioned.

"No," he said regretfully. "With all the storms, I haven't ventured out much."

"You didn't hear anything? A car earlier this morning?"

"I'm sorry," he said, and I believed him. He looked pained that Leeanne had died. "She's from Albany," he offered as soon as it came to mind, his big eyes a mix of hope and remorse.

"That helps," I thanked him.

I handed him my business card and asked him to give me a call on my cell if he thought of anything, remembered anything, anything at all, then started waddling down the snowy walk, the weight of the baby feeling heavier than ever.

THE AFTERNOON BROUGHT with it a torrent of calls, lines ringing off the hook throughout the station. We barely had the manpower to address it, but I wasn't about to lend a hand.

I closed my office door to muffle the sounds and eased onto my chair, having rounded to the business side of my organized desk.

It was a little over five years ago that I had made Sheriff, my predecessor having suffered a heart attack that Curt was convinced had been the result of his steak and cigars lifestyle.

At that time Curt had been a low-rung police officer who mostly worked the front desk taking civilian complaints when they came through the door.

I had been ill prepared, but had worked at the station long enough to trust that I would neither get swamped with a staggering caseload nor launched, headlong and panicked, into investigating a serious, hard crime.

Now that I was left to ponder the few details about Leeanne Hessinger that I had gathered, however, I almost wished that hadn't been the case. I was inexperienced and my pregnancy was complicating matters.

Leeanne's encouragement sprang to mind—'*This is your year!*'

Perhaps it would be, not for her, but for myself if I could tackle this thing and come out on top.

I was having serious doubts, though.

The only other impacting incident that had occurred in Liberty to quake the bedrock of this town hadn't even been an official crime, technically.

The previous Sheriff, a brusque lion of a man named Larry Gilford, had gone to his grave stumped.

Pamela de Barra, a wife and mother, had gone missing in the spring of 2011.

I had just been made chief deputy, but Larry was still calling me 'Peanut', a nickname I had come to like though I had fought it like hell when he first started using the endearment. Peanuts had been, and would likely always be, my favorite snack to pop and munch throughout the day.

According to Pamela's husband, a contractor by the name of Ron who constructed houses throughout the county, Pamela had up and disappeared one morning, leaving her then ten-year-old son, Scotty with no way of getting to school. Scotty hadn't told us much, just that he had heard the sound of the front door opening and closing.

Pamela de Barra was the only open case I had inherited from Larry.

When, in the late summer of last year, she returned as mysteriously as she had vanished, I received full credit for having solved the missing persons case. I hadn't done a damn thing.

Brushing off the guilt that I might be some kind of charlatan playing Sheriff without the aptitude to keep this town safe, I started looking for any information I could find on Leeanne, her previous address in Albany, any next of kin, including her cousin Marcus.

I made productive use of our DMV resources, pulling up an old driver's license that listed a house on Russell Road and jotted the address down.

I would likely have to make the trip up north, a two-hour drive, should I discover her next of kin. A telephone call to inform a loved one of Leeanne's murder would be unforgivable. Some news had to be delivered in person.

Three hours, two egg salad sandwiches, one crying jag, and a handful of peanuts later, I had established that Leeanne had moved to Liberty on January 2nd 2017 from 155 Russell Road in Albany where she had shared a house with her husband, Ian Hessinger, and her mother, Melinda, a widower who had raised Leeanne on her own from the time the girl was seven.

Leeanne had worked as a salesclerk at Walgreens downtown, had graduated high school but had never attended college. She had never even left her childhood home.

The house was in Melinda Grunke's name.

The cousin was impossible to track down. I hunted for both a 'Marcus Grunke' and 'Marcus Lancaster'—Lancaster was Melinda's maiden name—but neither searches turned up anyone related to Leeanne, though there was one Mark Grunke in Schenectady, New York, a nearby city, but he was eighty-nine years old and African-American.

I would have to proceed by first informing then questioning Ian Hessinger as though he might have made the drive down south to Liberty.

At the very least, I knew there was a story. A woman wouldn't just up and leave her husband, bringing nothing with her to rent a little house in a town unknown to her unless something had happened.

Pamela de Barra came to mind.

I rested my hand over my large belly and thanked God I had never run away from Mitch.

It wouldn't matter what happened between us. I would never leave, and I would never let him go.

There were some things in this world you had to fight for.

My desk phone rang, blaring with an internal call. "Yeah?"

"Medical Examiner's on Line Four," Curt told me. I straightened up on my chair, meeting his gaze through the window—the venetian blinds were open—that separated my office from his desk. "And some lady from the paper called for you—"

"You can tell her we're not in a position to alert the media just yet," I told him.

"She wanted to know if it was the same Leeanne Hessinger who had applied for a copywriter position at their paper," he clarified.

"How the heck would we know?"

"That's what I told her," Curt agreed.

I groaned, "Tell anyone who calls from the press to sit tight and leave it at that."

"Yes, Ma'am," he said.

I depressed the plunger and hit the button for Line Four.

"This is Sheriff Kavleski."

"Hi Sheriff, this is Walt from the Sullivan County Coroner's office."

"Hi Walt," I said grimly.

"Calling to let you know we're still working on the body of Leeanne Hessinger. I'll have a report for you in a day or two."

"The sooner the better," I hustled him.

"I'll call you as soon as I can."

I thanked him and returned the phone to its cradle.

It was dark out, but not late. The clock on my computer read 7:16pm.

I owed Mitch a phone call and I wasn't sure I could stand to look at my computer screen any longer, so I gathered my coat and purse, closed my office door, and stopped at Curt's desk on my way out.

"M.E.'s going to get back to us hopefully tomorrow. Did you eat?"

"Not yet," he said, looking bleary-eyed and depleted. He ran a calloused hand down his face, massaged his eyelids, then insisted, "I think we ought to stay on Trip Turner."

"I think we ought to as well."

"We didn't collect his clothes," he pointed out.

"He didn't have a drop of blood on him," I countered. "His hands were clean."

"Not in my book," he grumbled. He folded his arms, but it must not have felt right, because he pushed the thick sleeves of his woolen sweater up and tried again. "I was thinking about tire prints."

"In the snow?"

Curt shook his head as though he was upset with himself for considering such a thing too late.

"The cruiser pulled right up. I parked in the driveway, as well. Of course, Trip had already parked and if he did it, well…"

"We wouldn't be able to prove his tire tracks were evidence of his guilt," I supplied. "It's worth a look though," I encouraged.

"Yeah?"

"Tomorrow when you have the light, go check it out," I said.

"Crap, and there was the ambulance…"

"Even so," I told him. "It might lead to something. Best we can hope is that there's another set of tire tracks that don't belong to any of our vehicles."

When he locked eyes with me, I could see a world of anguish in his long face.

I gave his shoulder a compassionate squeeze and assured him, "This is only the beginning. Get some rest. I'm not sure there's much more we can do tonight."

"I'll try," he agreed in a small voice before glancing at my large belly. "How're you holding up?"

"Barely, Curt. Just barely."

MY HUSBAND, MITCH, and I lived in a contemporary Chalet house with vaulted ceilings, a wrapping deck and large picture windows that overlooked Swan Lake.

To me, our home had always felt like a cabin since it had rounded, log siding and wood stoves in nearly every room, but I knew that was a modest understatement.

Our home was a magnificent house, stately and secluded at the end of our long, private drive.

Mitch had helped design it and had lent a hand in its construction not long before he met me.

There was art on the walls and handsome accents. Even though this had been my home for nearly fifteen years, I had felt from the start and to this day that I was living in Mitch's house. I had married him and had settled in quickly, yet it always felt like my husband's, as regal and classy as Mitch himself.

Recently, I had been catching myself staring at him as though he was a stranger.

Mitch was handsome and polished. He had always been reserved. Strong, silent power. A shark's presence. But he had become more and more withdrawn over the past four months or so. He wouldn't let me in emotionally.

I wasn't prepared to confront him or complain. I hadn't been quite myself either thanks to the pregnancy that had begun to completely dictate my moods and needs.

Strangely, though I sensed Mitch had been pulling away from me, he was very much present and available for the baby, making me sandwiches, bringing me juice, catering to my every pregnancy-related whim and desire. He once drove to ShopRite during the first snowstorm we'd had last December to buy me pickles when I had burst into uncontrollable tears, realizing I had wolfed down the last one.

He had an intuitive knack for sensing when I might like a bath or a snack or a nap and didn't hesitate to provide whatever he anticipated I would need.

But whenever I would ask him what he was thinking or feeling, he would only grumble an appeasing reply then duck into his study to work or read or otherwise avoid me.

This was our first pregnancy. I was thirty-seven, Mitch was ten years my senior. We both knew everything would change once the baby was born.

I had been having my own emotional ups and downs and they weren't always hormone driven. My hours at the station would change. My personal time wouldn't be my own anymore. Life as I knew it would cease to exist. I figured Mitch, in his own tight-lipped, reserved way, had been grappling with the same concerns about his own life.

I found Mitch in the baby's room when I got home. Having hung my winter coat and wriggled out of my snow boots, I had climbed the stairs, following the sharp scent of paint, and discovered my husband wearing a smock and rolling yellow paint on the wall.

"Yellow?"

Setting the paint roller against the wall, he explained, "A gender-neutral color." He neared me at once, placed his hand on my belly, and kissed the baby. "Just because you're a boy doesn't mean our lives have to be nothing but blue."

"I thought we would talk about this."

"You don't like yellow?"

"I like yellow," I assured him.

He didn't look convinced. "It's just a background color. I'm going to stencil giraffes and elephants and tigers, a monkey or two probably over here," he told me, indicating the various walls where the animals would go. "The crib finally arrived."

There was a shipping box propped against the corner of the room.

"I'm going to assemble it this weekend," he said, smiling brightly at me.

I mustered an ounce of enthusiasm for him.

"You didn't return any of my calls," he mentioned, taking hold of the paint roller. "I was going to swing by the station with more egg salad sandwiches."

I had never eaten an egg salad sandwich in my life. It was only now, by our unborn son's demand, that I had been scarfing them down, sometimes six a day.

"Sorry about that."

"Are you hungry?" he asked. When I didn't answer—I was mentally composing how I would summarize my harrowing day—he did a bit of a double-take then asked, "What's wrong?"

He hadn't heard. "Have you been home all day?"

"For the most part," he allowed. "Judy, is something wrong?"

My mouth tasted bitter and dry, Leeanne's empty apartment surging to the forefront of my mind, the thin stack of sleeping bags she had made a bed out of, those Christmas cards…

"Maybe I should eat something," I agreed. My stomach was turning sour.

In the kitchen, Mitch and I maneuvered between the refrigerator, stove, and countertops, sprawling out as we made spaghetti and meatballs, the baby's second favorite.

Every time I tried to open a jar or lift the water-filled pot or select a chopping knife from its wooden block, Mitch reached to take over the task, but I maintained, "I can do it" and "I've got it" and "Please, Mitch, this isn't a strain for me," and he would stare at me, a subtle combination of insult and astonishment just beneath the surface of his expression.

He knew I didn't like being coddled.

We migrated into the dining room, me carrying our plates of spaghetti and Mitch scowling that I hadn't let him. He brought our water glasses and a long-stem wine glass of Merlot for himself, and we sat.

I spent the silence of our meal devising how to tell Mitch the ugly truth of what had become of his newest T.A.

"Leeanne Hessinger," I began, "who works at Bethel Woods…"

Mitch stared at me expectantly and lowered his fork when it took me a long moment to form the words of what I needed to tell him.

"What about Leeanne?" he prodded with great interest.

Emotion welled up and broke the surface, blindsiding me from out of nowhere. Planting my elbows on the table, I pressed my fingertips against my eyelids—hard—and willed the tears to stop spilling down my cheeks.

Mitch didn't get up. He didn't comfort me. Didn't say a word, as I scraped myself together, determined to make coherent sense.

"She's dead," I blurted, then sucked in a deep, fortifying breath and, as steadily as I could manage, repeated, "she's dead. She was killed. That was my day. Scrambling, frantically, to figure out how I'm supposed to…" My voice clipped off. "I'm overwhelmed."

Proceeding with great caution, my husband finally neared me. He placed his hands on my quavering shoulders as I fought to suppress my sobbing, sucking in lungful after lungful of air that seemed devoid of oxygen.

"You'll get through this," he quietly assured me. "You're strong."

I was hoping he would use the terms 'we' and 'us'.

He didn't…

…and then he drew away and retired into his study.

SHERIFF JUDY KAVLESKI
Friday, January 5, 2018

PEOPLE WHO WATCH crime shows on TV or read mystery novels, addicted to fast-paced plotlines, think that investigations unfold at a clip, the next clue just around the corner, some whip-smart, plucky detective acting on intuitive hunches that play out favorably, with twists and turns, in scene after scene, or chapter after chapter.

In real life, criminals rarely leave much of themselves behind. Crime scenes aren't covered in DNA. Evidence isn't crawling out of the woodwork. Piecing together the story of what happened is painstaking work. There isn't one story at play. An investigator must compile all of the stories, from a full cast of characters, and read between the lines. It's a full tapestry of lies and half-truths that could either hurt or help a case. Evidence can feel like muddy waters. Some motives elude, others don't make sense. If you can manage to trap a solid one at all, rarely does a suspect take responsibility for it.

I had known this.

But nothing could have prepared me for the profound question mark that was the ultimate result of the coroner's report.

I had looked it over. Again and again. The single sheet of paper that told me nothing more than my two eyes had when I had stared down at the body of Leeanne Hessinger myself.

She had been stabbed in the sternum.

Thanks, Walt.

The forensic reports weren't much better, preliminary though they were.

I had been informed that it would take the lab in Monticello at least a week to return with their results on the hunting knife, and that was 'fast tracking' the weapon, I was told. Apparently, they had been backed up for months. On the phone, I had begged them to tell me if there was even a fingerprint on it—I didn't want to wait around, holding my breath for nothing—but they couldn't say. No one had looked at it and wouldn't have a chance to anytime soon.

I felt sick…

…which was why I had driven out to the Sullivan County Coroner's office on the second day of the investigation, in the afternoon.

Armed with two egg salad sandwiches in each pocket of my winter coat and a bag of salted peanuts in my purse—the baby didn't like nuts, but I was determined to assert my preferences, this was still my body after all—I slid myself down from my pickup truck and started through the slushy parking lot, as a blazing sky of white haze set the whole of Monticello aglow.

Arriving unannounced and without warning as I had, I ended up waiting forty-five minutes to get into the morgue to question Walt, which wasn't entirely surprising.

I used the ladies' room several times, ate all four of my sandwiches, and wondered more than once if this was going to turn out to be a colossal waste of time.

"Sheriff Kavleski?"

That from Walt.

I recognized his congenial voice from our phone call.

I hoisted myself from the plastic chair I had been warming, and shook the elderly man's cold hand. I had expected someone younger, but Walt's eyes were bright and his gait sprightly despite his old age. I pegged him as seventy.

"How long have you been working at the Coroner's office?" I asked as he led me through a heavy set of double-doors into the morgue.

"Quite a while now," he said good-naturedly. "You were probably in diapers when I got hired."

"I bet," I smiled. "I wanted to ask you—"

"I have good news," he interrupted.

"Oh?"

"I found a hair."

I stared at him. "A hair?"

"It happens. The crime techs don't always catch everything," he allowed. "I have it for you. I understand you're using a lab right here in Monticello?" he asked, as he offered me a closed plastic evidence bag containing the hair. It was long and brown. "I can send it over if you like."

My stomach lurched.

I knew it was mine.

"No, no," I declined. "I can send it."

I had been standing over the body, waddling back and forth through the crime scene. I already felt like a fraud, completely under qualified and in over my head. The absolute last thing I needed was for the most promising piece of evidence to come back as a match for the bumbling idiot who was supposed to be at the helm of this investigation.

I tucked the evidence bag into my purse, bashful and cheeks flushing hot, and prayed that the tightening feeling in my chest that was now constricting my breathing wasn't a heart attack in the works.

"I had a chance to go over the report you faxed," I began. "Thank you for being so timely with it."

"Not a problem," he smiled.

"I was hoping that perhaps you had more information, even if somewhat speculative, to tell me that you might not have been comfortable with putting on the official coroner's report."

"Such as?"

"Considering the wound, did anything about the trajectory of the stabbing indicate the height of the attacker? It's just that the technicians weren't comfortable saying, and I really haven't much to go on."

"The blade struck her at an upward angle," he offered. It was precisely what the blood splatter analyst had described. "But other than that, I'm really not able to say. You see, if the attacker fell with her, spilled to the floor, they could've been much shorter. Hessinger was tall at five-nine. But I don't know that falling together, before or as the knife plunged in, was what happened."

Sympathy compelled him to wince an apologetic smile at me.

"I see." I was at a loss for what to ask him, out of my element and overwhelmed. But, growing increasingly curious about Leeanne, even more so than the investigation likely required—I had become intrigued more by her life than her death—I questioned, "Can you tell me… Was she unhealthy? Her body weight, I mean."

"It didn't get her killed," he said.

But I still wondered. She struck me as a peculiar woman. I wanted to know every last thing I could find out about Leeanne Hessinger.

And I wanted to know every last thing I could find out about Trip Turner, as well. He was starting to weigh heavily on my mind.

IT NEVER CEASED to amaze me that my husband, Mitch, commanded the Bethel Woods Performing Arts Center, the lone pillar of arts and culture in a county full of hicks.

I loved 'hicks.' I was born a hick and still felt like one, probably looked like one these days thanks to the pregnancy and my complete lack of interest in keeping myself trim and tidy. I would get back on that once the baby was born. I would eat healthy and jog. I had heard breastfeeding burned an unbelievable amount of calories. My mother had assured me the baby weight would melt right off. But I had been enjoying not fretting over my figure for once, no matter that I was starting to resemble a whale. Or, more appropriately, a bloated, waddling, sandwich-eating hick.

Before Mitch had swooped in and taken control of the P.A.C., Bethel Woods had been considered a place to go for summer concerts. It had always had excellent band programming, staying true to its Woodstock Music Festival roots. Mostly country music. Big names like Willy Nelson, Keith Urban, and even Carrie Underwood had graced the outdoor arena stage, as well as lesser known bluegrass and honky-tonk bands, all of which I happened to like.

The museum inside had existed since its construction. But it had been under Mitch's directive that the institution had dug deep, gotten creative, and served the local community year-round.

He had instilled continuing education programs, all focused on the arts, of course. He had single-handedly initiated a grant writing department, garnering funds to expand, for which he had done most of the heavy lifting, staying late to scour NYFA, drafting and submitting proposals to every appropriate organization he could find.

Building from there, he had soon launched the Teaching Artists initiative. At first it had been an effort to provide the adults who had taken the continuing education courses an opportunity to use the skills they had acquired, but the program brilliantly killed two birds with one stone.

Suddenly, the kids around Liberty and the surrounding towns had afterschool programs with a focus on the arts classes that their local high schools had cut.

Thanks to the grants Mitch had secured, parents didn't have to tighten their belts just so that their child could explore their interest in painting or photography or music. Most of the kids could enroll for free if not on a sliding scale basis.

Mitch had become loved throughout Liberty and all of Sullivan County for his innovative dedication to Bethel Woods. He had turned a non-profit into an empire. It had been a feat, one which I secretly fell in love with from afar before I had mustered the gumption to frequent the Performing Arts Center and begin courting him in my own, politely assertive way.

When he had ducked into his study last night, leaving me to sink or swim in my overwhelming emotions, I hadn't followed him or demanded support.

Mitch was a pragmatic man and I was aware that he thought he had married a pragmatic woman.

Tears had no place in pragmatism.

As I had requested, having eased us into a cool, level-headed conversation earlier that morning before I had left our home, Mitch had gathered all of the Teaching Artists in the vacant exhibit space on the lower level of the Performing Arts Center to relay the horrifying news that one of their own had been killed.

I was standing against the wall, listening to him address the group and watching their expressions collectively widen and twist and sink at the shocking tragedy.

Who among them had gotten dangerously close to Leeanne?

Trip Turner looked a strange mix of ill, furious, and handsome, towering over his female counterparts, as Mitch solemnly conveyed a few kind words about the woman they had lost.

I might not have found him suspicious if he hadn't been sliding his eyes over to peek at me as if interested in confirming that I was watching his performance.

In front of him were the rest of the T.A.s. Mary Roberts, who I understood to be the photography teacher, was crying so much her black eye makeup was streaking down her cheeks.

Cassie Davies, the oldest, most experienced Teaching Artist, held her arm protectively around Mary and also Nora Graham, who ran the sculpture program.

Nora looked like she was in utter shock, her mouth hanging open, her arms wrapped around her stomach, holding herself together perhaps. I sensed tears would follow, but in a greatly delayed reaction. Her husband had quite a mess coming his way.

Cassie rivaled Trip in terms of fury. Anger had swelled into her teeth-gritting expression. She would like to strangle the bastard who had done this to Leeanne with her own bare hands was what her eyes told me, though she kept them locked on Mitch, as she tempered her unsteady breathing.

Mitch concluded his speech. "I'd like for us all to take a moment of silence now for Leeanne."

I lowered my head, but kept my eyes on Trip. He didn't lower his head or close his eyes. His thumb was between his teeth. Gnawing, as he stared vacantly straight ahead.

What did he know?

"Judy?" Mitch turned to me, giving me the floor.

I joined my husband though he soon stepped off to the wayside beside Carol Patterson, but not before collecting the winter coat I had draped over my arm along with my purse. Didn't want me exerting even that much strain, I supposed. Wouldn't be good for the baby.

"I'm sorry for your loss," I began. "This comes as quite a shock for all of us. I'm Sheriff Judy Kavleski," I added belatedly. I wasn't used to this type of thing.

"Leeanne was found dead in her house yesterday morning. I'm not in a position to relay any details, but it was undoubtedly a homicide. I understand that yesterday was your first day back at Bethel Woods. Many of you might not have seen Leeanne since December. I would still like to speak with each of you, and I apologize in advance for how hard that might be. It's hard for me, too. Any details you can provide will be helpful, no matter how small or insignificant you might believe them to be."

I glanced at Mitch, gave him a nod, and he took over, excusing the T.A.s after clarifying that I would come to their offices, one by one.

I would've liked to see a glimmer of sympathy or encouragement from my husband, but he didn't give me either.

Starting with Carol Patterson, I began interviewing the Teaching Artists department.

Carol had fond, but not useful, things to say about Leeanne.

In her opinion, Leeanne had kept to herself, and Nora, Cassie, and Mary resonated that impression when I spoke to each of them next.

The last any of them had seen Leeanne was at the Christmas party here at the Performing Arts

Center, and if recollection served me, that was the last time I had seen Leeanne Hessinger alive, myself, since I had attended the party with Mitch.

Nevertheless, I pressed each of them for their observations about that evening—did Leeanne bring a date or friend, did she argue with anyone, were there any characters that stood out in relation to her, anything suspicious or funny?

I was met with blank stares and shaking heads, general bewilderment from each of them—with Leeanne, what you see is what you get.

I doubted that.

Knocking on Trip's closed office door, I couldn't deny I was surprised he had come in to work. I would've thought he would ask for the day, if not the entirety of next week, off. Needing recovery time would be understandable after seeing your coworker dead. Mitch would have granted him that.

"Come in," I heard him call out from deep inside of his office.

I entered, closed the door behind me, and eased onto one of the chairs in front of his desk.

Trip smelled of hot whiskey and cigarettes, even from four and a half feet away.

Finding the statement I had written up for him earlier that morning, I handed the paper to him.

His brows immediately furrowed.

"Would you mind reading that over? If it looks accurate, you can go ahead and sign it."

I studied him as he skimmed the statement. He hesitated to put pen to page.

What was he thinking? What fears had cropped up in his fast-working mind? Would I be met with another brilliant performance?

As he scrawled his loose signature across the bottom, he mentioned, "This is fine."

"Good," I said before folding the statement and returning it to my purse. Next, I opened the moleskin notepad I had been carrying around with me, rested it on the table of my round belly, and asked, "Let's talk about Leeanne. You said you went to her house to pick her up."

"Yes, she was having car trouble again."

"You didn't wake up there?" I questioned.

He snorted a disgusted laugh and challenged, "Am I a suspect, Sheriff?"

"No," I lied.

He was my prime and only suspect, and he likely had more information about the days leading up to Leeanne's murder than anyone, an adversary of mine who happened to hold all of the secrets.

I would have to walk a tightrope if I wanted the truth.

"Oftentimes, people who are completely innocent get scared in the face of talking to the police," I explained. "They omit things, thinking that telling the whole truth will somehow incriminate them. I just want the whole truth, Trip."

"I didn't sleep over at Leeanne's house," he insisted, then snorted out another, softer laugh. He raked his fingers through his dark hair and mentioned, "I would've *loved* to sleep over her house."

"Oh?"

"Never mind."

"I'm sure you can understand why I need your full cooperation," I told him, but it sounded too formal, even to my own ears, so I took another stab at it, this time trying to appeal to him. "I need your help. I have a big question mark spanning through the days leading up to Leeanne's murder. From an investigative standpoint, I have to work backwards, starting with the last person who saw Leeanne, dead or alive. That's you."

He loosened up a bit and allowed, "I understand, Sheriff."

"Prior to yesterday morning when you went to the house, when did you last see or hear from Leeanne?"

I pressed the tip of my pen to my notepad, poised.

"I last *saw* her at the Christmas party," he answered. "I last *heard* from her the day before New Year's."

I jotted 'December 31st 2017' down under Trip's name on my notepad, asking, "She called you?"

"Yes. Her car had broken down. According to the shop, she wouldn't be able to get it in time for our first day back at Bethel Woods. She needed a ride."

"Why did she call you?"

"I had given her rides before," he said matter-of-factly.

"But why *you*?"

"My car is reliable."

"You were friends?" I pressed.

"When she needed something," he allowed.

"What other kinds of things did she need from you?"

"Hey, look, Sheriff," he deflected, pushing away from his desk and leaning back in his chair, a distrusting smile thinly veiling his exasperation. "I really didn't have a personal relationship with Leeanne. We weren't friends. We didn't hang out. I didn't sleep with her. I just gave her rides. That's all. I'm a nice guy."

"So, she called you on the last day of the year," I recapped, focusing on the ghostly timeline. "Do you remember what time?"

"In the evening. I'm not sure the exact time."

I made notes but wasn't satisfied.

"So, you saw her at the Christmas party, then didn't hear from her or see her again until she called you on December 31st?"

He nodded.

"Then on January 4th you went to her house to pick her up and found her dead?"

"Yes."

"When she called you, can you remember the content of the conversation?" I dug.

"Ah," he groaned, rubbed his eyes, and screwed his face up some in his effort to recall. He laughed. "It wasn't anything dramatic or juicy, Sheriff. Just like, 'hey, I don't have my car, can you give me a ride?' Nothing crazy."

Nothing crazy, indeed. But it did sound awfully casual, like the type of phone conversation I would have with Mitch. No preamble. No chatting. No buttering him up before asking for a favor…because we shared a life together. Intimately.

Trip was starting to look put off, and I needed him to open up so I shifted gears.

"When I was in her house yesterday—by the way, have you been inside her place?"

"The entryway," he allowed. "The foyer. Once I went into the kitchen when I had knocked on the door and she wasn't ready yet, she invited me in."

"Were you aware of the conditions she was living in?"

"Conditions? What conditions?" he asked, fully interested.

Recalling the layout of her rented house, there wasn't much of a view of the living room from the kitchen. Maybe he didn't know.

"She didn't have much. She didn't even have furniture."

His light eyes widened as though that was news to him so I moved on. "I found a calendar of hers on the refrigerator. She had made a note to 'fast' for three days, January first through the third."

It wasn't a question, which might have been why he didn't answer.

I was about to clarify the point and refine it into an actual question when there came a knock on the door.

"What is it?" he yelled, irritated.

Carol peeked her head into the office.

"Printer's acting up," she winced through an apologetic smile.

I had a feeling that Trip wouldn't have been so eager to rush to Carol's aid had I not been digging into him.

"It's always something around here," he complained, as he hopped up to tend to the stubborn printer. "Excuse me."

There was a single photo frame propped on his desk next to his laptop computer and a dehydrated cactus. I thought those things were hard to kill, but perhaps nipping booze at work took precedence over splashing water over his lone plant. The soil was bone dry.

I turned the framed photo around to face me.

The photo was of Trip and Leeanne, his arm was around her, a winterscape behind them, Trip was beaming a smile, but Leeanne looked forlorn. Trapped, perhaps, in an embrace she hadn't wanted. In the background was the sign for Walnut Mountain Park.

He returned to the office and froze when he caught me with the framed photo in my hand.

He turned pale before my very eyes.

Caught in a lie.

"I thought you said you didn't have a personal relationship with Leeanne. What's this all about?"

TRIP TURNER

Saturday, February 25, 2017

FOLLOWING LEEANNE TO Walnut Mountain Park the Friday evening after my first week of classes at Bethel Woods had been more than just a mistake that I couldn't undo or take back.

It had been a disaster of astronomical proportions.

In the impulsive, hormone-induced, idiotic blink of an eye, not only had I crossed a serious line, careening myself into the territory of 'creepy,' but I had also carelessly turned myself into a full-blown, clutch-your-rape-whistle and fight-like-hell stalker.

It had been dark that night at the park, but even through the falling snow and distance between us, I had been able to make out the look of sheer terror on Leeanne's face when she saw me standing there watching her. Her elated grin had drooped, horror rising up, the fluidity of her willowy body—the glee and whimsy she had been twirling with—hardening, stiffening, tensing up as she had frozen, petrified at the impending attack she naturally assumed would take place.

Suddenly I had gone from the comically endearing coworker to a leering stranger lurking in a park.

I could've blamed the fortifying shot of whiskey I had knocked back in my car as the culprit that had compelled me to go out on a limb and follow her, taking a wild chance and embracing romance like every protagonist I had ever envied in all the plays I had read and movies I had watched.

Fiction could be deceiving.

I had meant for the gesture to be victorious and triumphant, a story we would tell our grandchildren—the wintry night we ran towards each other through the snow, twinkling stars overhead, and embraced in a Hollywood kiss, our magnetism overcoming us, true love winning against all odds—but I had been out of my lonely, booze-addled mind.

Even worse than my having followed and scared the living daylights out of her, was her reaction, not the initial terror that had washed over her at seeing me standing there, watching her, but the response that had followed.

She had acted friendly and unalarmed. She had remained calm. She had fixed a smile on her face that oozed with trepidation. And she had obliged me by accepting my drink offer.

She had surrendered as though it were a survival strategy in a hostage situation—obey kindly or else be harmed by the crazy man—and it ended up being the darkest drink I had ever partaken in.

To say that I felt like a monster as we had awkwardly sipped our beers in the dingy, unromantic corner of McCabe's on Main Street, a seedy bar I would've never taken her to had I not been so thrown off guard myself, would've been the understatement of the century.

I had babbled on and on, hoping that if I filled the air between us with enough conversation I could smooth out the jagged tension between us.

Gracious and polite, though she had been right to be wary of me, Leeanne had tried to act amicably, but I had known my attempt to restore my dignity was only failing miserably.

By the time we parted ways that night, I had felt I should resign my position at Bethel Woods and move to a foreign country, but even going to a great length such as that wouldn't have saved me from the haunting guilt that soon crept into the fabric of everything I did, said, and thought from that moment onward.

I had made myself dangerous to Leeanne and I knew nothing could correct it…

…and it was nobody's fault but my own.

At work I kept my distance and my eyes down. I was careful not to accidentally invade her personal space at the printer or watercooler. During staff meetings I neither sat across from her nor beside her, choosing instead to buffer myself with at least one T.A. between us so that she wouldn't fear I had calculated a clear line of vision from which to spy her.

However, whenever she voiced a concern to Carol, I seconded the notion. I supported or defended her every suggestion during our staff meetings. When the printer acted up, I swiftly came to her aid without conversation or complaint. I became committed to rebuilding my image in her eyes and was prepared to be patient as I waited in quiet hope that she would forgive me.

I couldn't say that my efforts were working with her, but at least I felt as though I was redeeming my crushed sense of self. The most important relationship that one had was with one's self, after all, and I definitely didn't like despising myself.

In a bizarre twist of fate, Leeanne began gradually warming up to me. She initiated eye contact here and there as if testing the waters. Angled her smiles my way when Nora assaulted her with a family photo. Commiserated with me around the watercooler after Carol had destroyed all of us in a staff meeting, our uniform failure to abide by the Input Goals we had promised in our proposals, her ammunition.

As the weeks wore on, Leeanne soon started peeking her head into my office, a crisp Progress Report in her slender hand. Would I look it over?

I gave her reports far more attention than I had ever given my own, suggesting better wording that would satisfy Carol's administrative judgment.

This evolved into a new routine, Leeanne emailing me her reports, us sitting down together in my office to craft bulletproof verbiage which I typed into all the fields.

The emails continued, but with more personality coming from Leeanne. She would throw in a humorous complaint about Cassie's hard nosed tyranny over her class here, a witty remark about Mary's refusal to dress in age-appropriate outfits there. The quip comments kept coming into my inbox and before long, Leeanne and I were emailing back and forth throughout the day, having conversations that both entertained and relieved me.

I found her enchanting and funny and spirited, and felt a whimsical sense of gratitude and elation that I had worked my way in, to some degree. I was getting to know a side of Leeanne that no one else at Bethel Woods saw. A peek into her particular brand of unique beauty, and though I was itching to invite her out for a platonic drink or friendly movie, I wouldn't dare cross that line ever again.

Our private emails were giving me everything I needed.

My dark friend piped down. Loneliness was receding. I felt connected to someone, content at home, and eager to head into work each morning.

Sure, I fantasized about her when sleep eluded me as it tended to do most nights. I wondered about what our secret emails might lead to. I reveled in imagining our budding relationship, strongly hoping it would blossom into what I had been craving since the New Year—a woman in my life, someone to laugh with, to wake up with, to create with—but I didn't act on any of this. The world I had developed for us in my head was enough and I would be damned if I'd push my luck a second time.

As carefully as we guarded our secret emails, those daylong conversations that revolved around workplace gossip and segued into our hobbies and anecdotes therein, Nora eventually took notice of our inside jokes, our giggle-fests in the breakroom, and my fierce support of Leeanne's ideas on improving the administrative burdens we had all come to dread. Mary caught on as well, overhearing on several occasions when Leeanne entered my office to draft up yet another Progress Report.

Before long, the whole office was referring to Leeanne as my 'work wife', and I as her 'work husband.' The teasing didn't bother me and though it brought a sheepish blush to Leeanne's cheeks, I couldn't say it ruffled her feathers much.

I liked the association. I liked being regarded in an intimate connection to Leeanne even though it was a joke. Fictitious. Roles we had come to play between the hours of nine and four-thirty. It might have been make-believe, but it still filled me with sparkling pride.

I stopped drinking at home. I craved fewer and fewer smoke breaks. I had better concentration with my students, and felt less frustrated by them and more inspired.

I began to feel—very, very deep down, deeper than I thought was ever a part of me—that Leeanne was my wife. I knew it was crazy and probably pathetic, I would have never admitted it to anyone, and I kept comically stoic as the teasing became part of our rhythm at Bethel Woods, but allowing myself to feel as though Leeanne was my wife and I her husband showed me what love must feel like.

Then one day she sent me an email responding to the long thread we had been involved in all afternoon about her various hiking excursions. My heart punched hard in my chest, drinking in what she had written. I had to read it several times to make sure I hadn't misunderstood the invitation.

'I'm going to Walnut Mountain Park this Saturday for a hike,' it read. 'Care to join me?'

Springing to action, every cell in my body tingling I was so poised, I quickly replied:

'What time?'

The very next day, I met her in the snowy parking lot of the park, Walnut Mountain glimmering in the distance, snow-capped yet thawing in the sunlight.

I had put way too much thought into how I should dress, so to compensate and possibly sabotage myself I wore a pair of faded jeans, muted sweater, my beat-up hiking boots, and of course a parka that I didn't need to zip, forgoing my hat, scarf, and gloves since it seemed the weather had finally decided to turn in my favor.

Leeanne greeted me with a big smile that accentuated the seductive powers of both her wide mouth and dark eyes—a quality I doubted she was aware she innately possessed—and I knew I had come full circle when she poked fun at me, gently breathing, "I won't let you catch me off guard this time."

I was inclined to avoid presumption. She couldn't be referring to the biggest mistake of my life, could she? But I knew she was when she twirled her way through the break in the fence, raising her arms fancifully like she had that night and reminding me:

"You're quite scary in the dark."

"If it's any consolation, I'm still mortified," I admitted honestly.

She lowered her arms and her smile as well as her guard, and looked at me.

It felt like a very long moment. Leeanne searching my eyes. Me, peering down inside of her, the light behind her eyes bright and inviting. The world around us, disappearing.

I saw something in her during that sustained moment, something I had never seen before. It was more than vulnerability, which I had always recognized in her. From where I was standing, gazing down into the deep pools of her dark eyes as I dropped the jovial mask I usually wore so that she would be able to see the real me as well, I caught a brief sight of the woman she truly was.

Strong.

Determined…

…and also broken.

She wasn't lonely like myself.

She was healing. Slowly, maybe even futilely, she was fighting to survive like a bird with broken wings trying to fly.

I could see that her heart was soaring, but would that be enough to lift her up?

It was during that instant that I fell in love with Leeanne Hessinger, but I knew, right then and there, that she was in no position to love me in return and never would be.

Whether she could see it within me that I had just fallen for her, I couldn't decide, as we started strolling through the snow towards the hiking trail.

As we ascended the western side of Walnut Mountain, we talked about Bethel Woods, our shared apprehension of all things 'hippy,' the city she had moved from—Albany—as well as other delicious topics such as my dismal dating efforts and faltering acting aspirations.

I learned she was gearing up to write a novel but felt that she needed to 'live a lot of life' in order to feel ready to proceed. She was certain she could accomplish as much in a matter of months now that she was in Liberty, and cram in enough experiences to influence her story. She wanted it to be sensational and I strongly advocated that if she could find a way to pour herself, that radiant spirit of hers, into her novel it would be.

She confided in me her periodic fasting routines that she was convinced cleared her head and cleansed her soul.

Internally, I questioned her motives, but didn't pry, and I remained engaged when she went on to explain the health benefits of autophagy and a ketogenic lifestyle, both of which fasting promoted according to her and some guy named Dr. Fung who had an established YouTube presence.

I felt an incredible urge to hold and protect her, as we reached Lookout Point, all of Liberty tiny and adorable below. The need to provide for her and give her the life she wanted overwhelmed me, but I kept it bottled in. What else could I do, but be her friend?

When we reached the base of the mountain, having looped around the eastern side during our descent—fluffy snowflakes dancing down all around us as we stomped through deep, crusted snow—I caught some passersby, ready with my iPhone in hand, and asked the friendlier of the two if she wouldn't mind taking our photo.

It was Leeanne's idea to come around to the front of the large, wooden sign for the park. There we stood, me with my arm proudly wrapped around Leeanne, Leeanne smiling up at me, stealing a shared moment of excitement that we were about to capture and memorialize our adventure. But when the girl who had agreed to take our photo lifted my cell phone to her face and sang, "Say cheese!" I felt Leeanne stiffen rigidly under my arm.

I thanked the girl, retrieved my phone, and looked at the photo.

Staring up at me from the screen was not the Leeanne I had gotten to know over the last three hours of our hike.

I turned to her and saw the same forlorn expression on her face.

She looked petrified, as she stared at the parking area.

A man was standing next to the fence.

"Who's that?" I asked her.

It took her a very long time to say, "That's the reason I left Albany."

SHERIFF JUDY KAVLESKI

Saturday, January 6, 2018

I HADN'T BELIEVED a word Trip had told me about his hike with Leeanne at Walnut Mountain, which he had claimed had been the first and last time he had ever socialized with the dead woman outside of driving her to and from the Performing Arts Center when she didn't have her car.

Seemed too neat and tidy.

Unlikely.

One isolated outing?

I wasn't buying it, and the look in Leeanne's eyes in that framed photo haunted me. I couldn't get it out of my head all night, even as I helped Mitch stencil brown giraffes in the baby's room.

By the next morning, it was really eating me. The romantic undertones of his story. The private grin that had tugged at his boyish mouth as he had told it. The way his light eyes had misted over and a swell of emotion had risen up when he had characterized the bond he had formed with Leeanne as platonic.

Then why had she looked like that in the photo? Trapped. Fearful. Pretending. Why would he want her looking at him like that, framed and imprisoned under gleaming glass, all day every day? As a reminder of the power he had over her, I surmised, that's why he kept that disturbing photo on his desk.

There had to be a hell of a lot more to it than what he had mentioned. According to Trip, a stranger had taken their picture, then they had climbed into their respective cars and that was that. A perfect outing shared, but never again duplicated?

I knew when I had been lied to, and I didn't much appreciate it.

At the station, Curt was still in a despairing funk over the tire tracks. The weather hadn't been working in his favor and he had come to find a substantial dusting of fresh snow covering the driveway of Leeanne's rented house the morning he went back.

Commending him on the idea and complimenting his smart police work had done little to alleviate his mood. In Curt's world, there weren't any 'A's for effort, and I respected it.

He had been struggling with our IT guy all morning in one of the interview rooms, Leeanne's laptop on the table, trying to crack the code of her password.

I didn't want to have to call a forensic computer technician from Monticello, but it was starting to look like I might have to, even at the risk of them taking over.

In terms of jurisdiction, I rested assured that they couldn't and wouldn't. They had more than enough of their own cases, certainly. But I was on the precipice of embarrassment. One more nudge and I would fall clean off the edge.

I had been letting Trip Turner simmer in our second interview room, while I worked on some leftovers I had brought in for lunch.

Marinated meatballs.

I placed a quick phone call to my ob-gyn about my next visit—Nance wanted to see me one last time before my delivery.

I had been adamant about having a natural birth and we had been negotiating what felt like heated debates because of it, her opinion being that my age made me an ideal candidate for a timely c-section.

I had vehemently refused, but she maintained that I ought to prepare myself for the likelihood that I might not have a choice. Our conversation was cordial this time and as I returned my desk phone to its cradle, I considered whether or not it would be advantageous to let Trip worry himself a bit longer into an honest mood in that interview room.

This would not be an easy hand to play. My cards were bad, and if I wanted to win, I would have to bluff my way through until the bitter end. I would be waiting to hear back about the hunting knife for God only knew how long, and I hadn't much hope that any DNA would turn up from under Leeanne's fingernails or otherwise on her person. But Trip didn't know that.

With a DNA swab kit in hand, I swung by Interview Room One where Curt was angling over our IT guy.

"Any luck?"

"Not hardly," Curt grumbled.

"I'm going to take another run at Turner," I informed him and closed the door to do just that.

As I entered the second interview room, Trip lifted his face as if the weight of the world had slammed into him. His hair was cowlicked, his eyes glassy. Arms folded, his posture was slumped. This was not how he had planned to spend his Saturday.

I didn't apologize. Didn't say anything as I eased onto the chair across from him and set the DNA kit on the table.

"What's that?"

"It's a DNA kit," I told him frankly. "I would like to swab your cheek."

"To clear me?"

"Wouldn't you like to be cleared?"

He sat up, bringing his elbows to the table and it was then that I realized he was hungover.

"I don't know what the hell to do here, Sheriff. I didn't kill Leeanne, and sorry if this offends you, but I don't trust any of you. How do I know you haven't found, I don't know, some ancient eyelash I left in the entryway from any of the times I waited for Leeanne just inside the door? If you have my DNA, you can connect dots that aren't supposed to be connected."

It stung, but I assured him, "Our forensic scientists are better than that."

"I doubt it," he countered. "All I know is that I'm here and I didn't do it so I have to assume your judgment is off."

I leaned back, calmly and coolly, and reminded him, "You told me you didn't socialize with Leeanne and that you didn't have a personal relationship with her. Yet, you have a framed photo of the two of you at the park. You can see why I'm a little hung up on you."

"I can— Look, I can explain that—"

"Please."

Everything about his broadening expression was meant to appeal to me.

"I was friends with Leeanne. It centered on work—Wait now, hang on," he blurted as I was about to object.

"We did hangout outside of Bethel Woods," he admitted. "But I had nothing and I mean nothing to do with her murder. I know how it looks, Sheriff. Believe me. I'm able to have an outside perspective of myself, and I know it doesn't look good that I was there, that I called it in when I found her. I saw how all of you guys were looking at me that morning and I see how you're looking at me now. That's why I didn't tell you I had a relationship with Leeanne—"

"A relationship—?"

"Friendship," he corrected, getting frustrated. "I didn't want to make it worse. Make things look worse for me. But everything I told you, everything in the statement I signed, is the truth."

I wasn't about to sugarcoat it for his benefit. He looked red-faced and pained, which was where I wanted him. "By lying to me, Trip, you did make things worse."

"Well, damn," he laughed. "What do you want me to do about it?"

"I would like for you to tell me the truth."

"I did."

"The whole truth?"

He wavered, pressed his mouth into a firm line, and stared at me, considering his next move.

"Did you tell me the whole truth, Trip?" I pressed, determined he would collapse like a house of cards.

"I'm not taking a DNA test," he asserted. "There's no point in explaining to you…" he trailed off, crippled by the wall he knew he was about to hit.

"Explaining what to me?"

He was shutting down, shaking his head at the surrealism he currently found himself trapped in. He stared at the wall where a window should've been.

"She saw some guy," he said. "That day in the park. That's why she looked so serious in the photo. It wasn't just some guy," he revised, angling his light eyes in my direction. "It was Ian Hessinger. Her husband. You should talk to him."

I was planning on it, but I challenged, "Why?"

"She was terrified of him. That's why she left Albany. She was afraid her husband was going to kill her."

After a defeated beat, he said, "Hell, give me the damn test. I want this thing over with."

LEEANNE HESSINGER

Monday, February 27, 2017

CONCENTRATION WAS VIRTUALLY impossible to maintain. I felt threatened.

Ian's sudden insurgence into my new life, this beautiful and wild place I had been calling home because that's what it felt like—*finally, I lived in a town that was all mine!*—would change everything.

It already had.

Seeing him standing there in the snowy parking area of Walnut Mountain Park had rocked me. My world was bleeding dull colors, gray and dreary. Liberty had been invaded and I had every reason to fear I would be next.

How did he find me?

I was supposed to be listening to Scotty de Barra read his latest short story. His words washed over me but didn't stick. He was sitting on one of the chairs across from my desk, his backpack and sports bag lumped high in a floppy heap in the other, my office door closed behind him. A private meeting to accommodate his soon-to-be vigorous Track & Field practice schedule.

I had fixed my gaze unseeingly—I was fighting the urge to sink into a mile-long stare—on the comical coffee mug I had barely been able to afford. Sleek, black ceramic. 'Live Dangerous & Write About It' branded across its front. Carol had taken issue with it, of course, so to appease her I had turned it to face me. It was filled with pens and pencils. I selected one now, needing something physical to anchor me back into my body.

I had scrimped and saved and bought a photo frame as well, but had been too lazy to remove the glossy, black and white commercial print of the happy couple it had come with.

Baby steps.

I reasoned that in the interim, I could mention that the woman in the photo was an old friend from elementary school if anyone questioned why I hadn't slipped a personal picture inside. *She had finally made something of her modeling career. I had been blown away when I came across the frame in Walmart, had to buy it, Theresa had always had big dreams.* Luckily, it hadn't yet come to that.

My Bethel Woods paychecks were excruciating. Making ends meet required rationing food. I had stepped up my fasting routine, but it didn't feel healthy. It felt forced and strained my mental capacity, though I had managed to build a Word document of ideas for my novel in my downtime.

Smart tidbits.

Moving revelations.

Latching onto prize-winning themes and metaphors.

Every great work of literary fiction was chalk full of symbolism. It seemed like a decent place to start. But nagging at me was the next bill I had to pay, or rent around the corner.

When I had been with Ian for all of those dispirited years, I hadn't had to manage my finances. Having competently handled that area of our lives wasn't an exemplary enough feat to make me miss him, but it was making me think twice. Breaking out my calculator before every trip to ShopRite wasn't a chore I was especially fond of.

The answer to my financial stress had also been gnawing at me. There was a Walgreens across from the ShopRite in the heart of town. But I refused to compromise my off-time. I knew I would never write my novel if I was exhausting myself stocking shelves part-time.

If I had to eat less, I would. If I had to get conservative with the use of my car, reserve gas, perhaps bike instead when the weather let up, I would do it. If I had to keep the lights off and use candles instead, so be it.

I was prepared to fiercely defend the narrow slivers of personal time that my weekly routine provided. Anything to draft the book I had been dreaming about for so long.

Scotty flipped another page aside, sucked in a deep breath, and continued to smoothly read out loud, but the content of his story barely touched me. A senior varsity champ was his protagonist, the character bogged in sexual desires for a bookish girl who would stain his otherwise impeccable reputation. I had been able to grasp that much, thank God.

I absently jotted a responding thought on my notepad then another so I would be prepared with some semblance of the feedback he deserved.

I found his voice soothing and hypnotic.

Scotty had a strong, unruly presence, and it was a welcomed break to see him calm and subdued, having drifted deeply into his own imagination. His use of grammar was no longer overtly confusing, which I took full credit for. He was improving, narratively speaking, even after only a mere month, and part of me envied him for it. He hadn't crippled himself with grand desires to make certain his work was excellent. Judgment hadn't discouraged him, that quiet, critical voice that writers tended to struggle with, doubts streaming like white noise in the mental background of every sentence we aimed to string together.

Perhaps his affection for sports had taught him to try, try again, keep trying, the only failure was quitting, never quit.

I wondered how long it had taken him to write the seven pages he was now in the midst of sharing with me. Had he wrestled for hours? Or had it flowed out of him easily, his fingers clacking over his keyboard?

I couldn't help but think of Ian. The memories of him kept tapping down against the surface of my mind like a toe on a pond. Rippling outward. Gently disturbing my serenity.

The only thing Ian hadn't quit was drinking…

…and guilting me into working long hours while he nursed his beers and anger at home.

When I had met him in high school, my mother had already bent and twisted me, had already rung the self-esteem out of me until I had become bone dry.

As a little, goofy-toothed girl, I had wanted to be precious and loved and cherished, and somewhere between being a gangly tomboy and a developing young woman I had decided a boyfriend could do just that.

Ian had slid right in, filling the space I had created in my heart for such a character, and my mother had liked him as well. Her largest concern had been that I would screw it up.

Looking back, I wondered if they had conspired against me, but I knew it was a paranoid notion.

I had always been someone who intuited the wants and needs of others, and would provide to keep everyone around me content, even at the expense of my own happiness.

Marrying had pleased my mother and satisfied Ian.

I had promised myself I would give that mentality up, because that's what it amounted to—a personality trait I had fallen into unconsciously, a choice, an addiction of sorts. But it was rooted in self-preservation. It wasn't easy being a woman.

I couldn't deny, however, that the void in my heart or psyche or soul was still there, a dark yearning to be valued.

But I was wise enough at this point in my life to understand that a man wouldn't relieve that tug on my soul.

"Hessinger?"

"Hmm?" I perked up, tightening my grip on my pen.

"I asked you if you thought Dylan was too perfect?" Scotty said as he pulled his chair right up against the front of my desk and set his seven-page story down.

Planting his elbows on the desk, he clasped his large hands together. They covered my notepad, the loose thoughts I had scrawled.

"I thought a lot about what you said, how characters needed flaws, how it gives them texture. The Achilles heel that threatens to sabotage their dream."

He had paid attention to that?

"When I came up with the idea, I thought Dylan's flaw could be that he's secretly in love with Sarah. She's not his type and doesn't fit his image, you know? Liking her is a risk. But see, I wrote it so that he's the star quarterback and he never made any mistakes in the game. Maybe he should? Like, maybe liking the wrong girl isn't a flaw. Oh!" he blurted, an epiphany having slammed into him.

"Maybe he can realize that! Like, what he thought was a flaw isn't a flaw. Oh!" he burst, lurching further towards me across the desk. "Maybe he can realize that loving Sarah isn't a flaw, and the realization is so huge for him that he's distracted and blows the big game! But he doesn't care, because knowing that he loves the right girl is more important than winning! Like he really has won, for himself, just not in terms of football!"

He scrambled for my pen, stole my notepad, and began frantically writing.

"I think—"

"Ut, ut, ut!" he silenced me. He couldn't let himself get distracted, his idea was too good.

When he finally finished, having flipped the notepad to use a second page—all the space his fantastic revelation had required—he slumped back into his chair victoriously, raked all ten fingers through his sandy-blond hair, and let out a sigh, exhilarated.

I couldn't help but smile at his elation.

He impressed me despite my commitment to remain wary of him, and watching him discover his talent and perhaps love of writing was inspiring.

"It sounds like you know exactly where to take this story for your revision," I concluded.

He was so young and determined, and I unexpectedly felt a twinge of connection to him, though I sincerely hoped we weren't on the same level.

"Do you like to draw from your own life?"

He had a think on that, taking the question as a challenge I hadn't intended.

"You're right," he decided. "I should go outside of my comfort zone."

"I'm not suggesting that," I amended, and his light eyes rounded, intrigued.

He returned his arms to my desk, giving me his full and undivided attention.

"You know a lot about sports, and writing what you know is a tried and true adage," I allowed. "But is playing sports the deepest, darkest part of you?"

A fascinated grin came over him, his interest piqued.

"You want to see the deepest, darkest part of me?"

The way he was looking at me, the glimmer behind his eyes, and how he lifted his chest, straightening his spine as he leaned farther onto my desk gave me pause, but I found the words to explain, "I think that when writers find a way to share their hidden truths in their work, it makes for the most compelling stories."

He had been prepared to rise to the challenge, as was Scotty's nature to tackle any obstacle that stood between him and greatness, but his conviction faltered. His erect posture slouched ever so slightly, and a glint of uncertainty came over him.

"You would be taking a risk," I encouraged and he seemed to agree.

"I don't think I could pull it off," he determined, but I could tell he was still in the throes of considering his own aptitude for succeeding.

"Perhaps it's something to keep in mind. Something to work towards. I'm inclined to push you, Scotty."

He grinned. "I like being pushed."

I busied myself, tearing his hand-written notes from my notepad along the delicate perforation, and slid them over.

As he folded them with the utmost care, found his backpack, and secured them along with his seven-page story into the front pouch, he mentioned, "I worked it out with Coach that on my Bethel Woods days I'll get to practice at five-thirty. It's the best I can do. He's going to have me running laps at lunch to make up for it."

"So, I'll have you from four-thirty until—"

"About five-fifteen," he supplied, twisting his face some at the approximation. "Shouldn't take me longer than ten or twelve minutes to get back to the school. Two or three to change my clothes."

"I can work with that if you can keep up with your writing."

"I definitely can," he boasted. "It's easy for me to get here right after school, too," he offered and my eyebrows shot up to my hairline. "Make the forty-five minutes up that way. I like this one-on-one stuff."

This was our first one-on-one and it had come completely unannounced, Scotty having appeared in my office without warning. He had barreled in, uninvited and without knocking, and had sat right down as if he owned the place, never minding that I was in the complicated throes of structuring our final presentation day agenda, a task that Carol had demanded the T.A.s turn in astonishingly early.

I wasn't sure I wanted my every Monday, Wednesday, and Friday to be Scotty-saturated, especially considering all the administrative work I had been juggling, but if the kid's expression was any indication, he wasn't asking.

"I'll save you a seat," he informed me as he slung his backpack and sports bag over his muscular shoulder and started for the conference room. "But you'll owe me."

He flashed me a grin after throwing the door open.

"Just kidding. Hustle up, Hessinger!"

❋

CASSIE STEPPED AWAY from the watercooler so that I could fill my controversial mug with hot water. I figured I would need a strong cup of Earl

Grey both to ward off the chill of the conference room and jolt me out of the Ian-induced stress storm that had been rolling in.

Trip had seen to it that I had gotten home safely that afternoon and he had been a doll not to pry much, but I could feel that my husband was still in town.

The air that had once felt crisp and refreshing now seemed toxic and suffocating everywhere I went. I hoped he would leave town, but knew he likely wouldn't. Confrontation was scratching at the door.

"Scotty's monopolized you," Trip said good-naturedly as I steeped my tea bag and mustered the energy to get to class on time.

As he filled his water bottle, I mentioned my most athletic student's track practice schedule in an off-handed explanation.

"I've been dying to get my hands on him."

"Scotty?" I asked.

"Jocks avoid thespianing like the plague."

"'Thespianing' isn't a word, Trip," I smiled, lingering around him.

Trip had become something of a friend and though I still felt a pinch of wariness that he might seep into my personal life, take root in my alone time, and distract me, I had come to look forward to our entertaining emails and the future hikes I hoped to squeeze in with him.

"New words are invented every day," he insisted with an air of humor before musing, "Scotty's quite a character. I would love to get him into an acting class. I have piles of scenes I haven't been able to make use of because I don't have a brawny bonehead type to pull them off."

"I'm sure he would be flattered to hear you say that," I dryly teased.

Little did Trip know, Scotty was far from a 'bonehead,' brawny as he might appear.

Cassie's eyes swelled as if haunted and she confided, "Scotty de Barra's the reason I went into menopause."

"Jesus," Trip muttered, taking a horrified beat.

Cassie supplied, "Taught him third grade art. It ruined me."

Trip locked eyes with me and I felt the giggles rising up, so I started through the breakroom, Trip at my heels, and made my way up the corridor to the conference room, my steaming mug of tea in hand.

"Hey, everything okay? About… you know, the other day?" Trip asked.

Ian.

Everything was not okay, but I kept that to myself, offered him an easy yet admittedly reserved smile, and breathed, "I'm fine."

"Sure?"

"Have a good class, Trip," I told him and slipped into the conference room where Scotty had claimed the seat next to the one I always sat on, his arm draped protectively around my chair, the bulk of my students were nestled around the table as well, punctual and ready to get started.

Scotty had been migrating closer and closer to my seat with each passing class, and as I greeted my students and settled into my spot, he took his sweet time withdrawing his hand.

Valerie did not look pleased.

"No need to start with my story," he announced to his classmates with a big, smug grin. "Hessinger already coached me on it, one-on-one," he bragged, which seemed to incite his girlfriend and a few others around the table.

"Starting next week," I informed them. "Scotty will be ducking out at five-fifteen, but he won't," I pointedly warned, "disrupt us as he leaves."

"No, Ma'am," he agreed.

Valerie was desperate to wrangle his affection. She was attempting to coil herself around him, but he wasn't taking the bait. Insulted, she gave him a pissed shove and, turning serious in response, he promptly admonished her:

"Pay attention. Go ahead, Hessinger. They're listening."

"Thanks," I said flatly and, feeling somewhat disturbed that I had acquired a 'teacher's pet' that I had never asked for and didn't want, I had them crack open their notebooks and free-write their stream-of-consciousness responses to the question, 'how will I survive?' to begin our class.

It was meant to be an abstract, open-ended, prompt they could sink their imaginative teeth into to jumpstart the inspired flow of their creative ideas...

...but it was also a question I had been asking myself ever since my heart had sunk at the threatening sight of seeing Ian planted in a world I had hoped would be mine and mine alone.

How would I survive?

I didn't know.

❄

AFTER CLASS, TRIP was considerate, keeping his head down and to himself, as he crossed the slushy parking lot.

It had been raining more than snowing recently, though winter remained stubborn about melting away.

I gave him a wave, stepping off the walkway into a puddle that surprised me, as he swung his car out and puttered off into the night.

At the far end of the lot was my parked car, but it wasn't the only one there.

Two spaces away, a Jeep sat idling, exhaust billowing out from the tailpipe, the cabin light on within. No one ever parked back here and I would've been alarmed if I had recognized the vehicle as belonging to my husband.

I hated that I still thought of Ian as that—my husband.

If I had a dollar to my name, I would divorce him, but as of yet, it remained a long-term goal.

As I neared my car, I realized Scotty was inside the idling Jeep. He didn't notice me. He was too busy furiously writing something down and it made me smile. When inspiration struck, it had to be captured, and the jock was in the hot throes of doing just that.

"Leeanne!" Ian barked.

That voice. Cutting through me. I flinched. Blood freezing in my veins. My mouth went dry and my heartrate kicked up, pounding at a deafening rate.

I didn't have to turn around to know who was advancing on me through the slush and snow, but I did anyway, forcing myself to hold my head high and willing my tone to sound firm and strong and formidable with conviction.

I sounded like none of those things as I thinly breathed in a raw, quivering tone, "Go back to Albany."

"I'm not going anywhere," Ian informed me.

He looked larger than I remembered. Ian had a towering presence, his shoulders broad, hands rough, eyes deep-set and alert.

Ever-brooding in a violent mood I had once believed was always my fault, Ian stalked towards me, closing the safe gap between us.

"Not without my wife," he added, making certain his warning wouldn't be misunderstood.

I turned for the door handle, panicked to jump in my car, but he grabbed my wrist.

"What do you think you're doing here?" he demanded. "You think I wouldn't find you?"

"Let me go," I asserted but my voice sounded wind over reeds.

In terrible timing that instantly mortified me, Scotty sprang out of his Jeep, his cell phone in hand, and got right up in Ian's face.

"This guy bothering you?"

Ian found the kid funny and laughed, "Run along."

I didn't twist my wrist or try to break free of Ian, but instead submitted and tried to smooth over our marital confrontation so that my student wouldn't be alarmed.

"No, I think I'll call the police instead," Scotty bravely threatened.

Whether or not he was bluffing and only pantomiming pressing 9-1-1 on his cell, he had gotten his point across, and Ian, snorting out another laugh as though inconveniencing him would only make matters worse for me in the long run, released my arm and backed away.

"I'm not leaving town without you," Ian warned, completely ignoring Scotty who was now doing his best to stand in front of me so that my husband couldn't have another go at me. "I'll stay in my crappy motel all week if I have to. You're coming back to Albany."

"That guy's lucky," Scotty told me after we had stood in tense silence watching Ian climb into his pickup truck and tear out of the parking lot with all the anger I was sure he would like to crack over my head instead. "I could've really hurt him. I made the wrestling team, you know?"

For some strange, unexplainable reason, the next thing I knew I had burst out laughing…

…but tears were spilling down my cheeks, as well.

SHERIFF JUDY KAVLESKI

Sunday, January 7, 2018

THE TWO-HOUR DRIVE up north to Albany came as welcomed relief.

The phones hadn't stopped ringing off the hook at the station, the local newspaper and TV stations having pecked the smallest kernel of information—that Leeanne Hessinger had been murdered—and inflated it with speculations and spins that defied both logic and accuracy.

Leeanne had been on the run, they had collectively decided. She might have been drug-addled, they had guessed, or criminal, or—the media consistently implied—somehow deserving of her harrowing fate.

This was how the town chose to make sense of the tragedy.

Painting Leeanne as a suspicious character who might have had shady dealings in whatever hellhole she had crawled out of helped them sleep at night.

She hadn't made statewide or national news, and I knew she wouldn't. She wasn't a celebrity or a teenager or a saint. Her life and death didn't demand more attention than Liberty had to offer, but it was still making my investigation a waking nightmare.

Our local paper had managed to artfully twist my 'no comment' response into five-hundred-words of front-page drivel, insinuating—outlandishly—that Leeanne had been moonlighting as a prostitute at the new casino in Monticello.

Where in the holy Christ they had gotten that impression, I didn't have a damn clue.

Worsening matters, the article had been printed with an unflattering photo of myself taking a piggish bite out of a sandwich with the caption: *'Sheriff Kavleski takes a bite out of crime.'*

I had known the residents of Liberty were inclined to gossip without regard for how their adult game of 'telephone' tended to spiral out of control, monstering into wild fiction that didn't even remotely resemble the truth. But seeing it in print, seeing with my own two astonished eyes that even the newspaper and television reports were indulging in the same game soured my stomach and caused my brain to burn.

My deputy had been itching to set the myriad stories straight but I had insisted he sit tight.

A press conference would be held when the time was right.

Until I had substantial information or until I actually needed the public's help, our investigation would remain under confidential wraps. Period. The press could wait.

The only reason I didn't want to leave Liberty on this particular morning had to do with Mitch.

I had hoped to help finish painting the baby's room with him, stencil more jungle animals on the walls, assemble the crib with him or perhaps read the instructions out loud, as he wrestled with the radical quantity of odds and ends we had found in the shipping box the night before.

Mitch had assured me he could handle it by himself. He would have the baby's room fully finished by the time I got home from Albany, he had promised, after which he had reminded me that we still needed to load up a delivery-day bag, everything we would need at the hospital to get us both through what we uniformly anticipated would be a very long labor.

He wanted this baby out of me even more than I did.

Having taken Rt 52 clear on through to the Hudson, my route connected to I-87 northbound. The roads were treacherous to navigate despite the salt and dirt. Highway patrol cars crawled along the shoulder, looking out for vehicles that might've flown off the icy road.

Eventually, I found 155 Russell Road tucked in a residential neighborhood.

The area didn't quite strike me as a 'keeping up with the Jones' type' suburban landscape, but it came close. Modest houses and manicured, snow-covered lawns. Expertly shoveled walks, each home having outdone the last with its Christmas decorations.

To me, it felt cramped, houses practically on top of one another, only a breath of space between each one. The type of place where the residents didn't have to wait for rumors to learn about each other's business. They could easily hear the drama first-hand, coming directly from next door.

I had never liked cities, and the suburbs outside of them rarely charmed me.

The house in question was a stout two-stories. Brick siding. Five icy steps leading up to a porticoed front door. The driveway led straight into a one-car garage that was nestled within the left side of the brick home.

No cars in the drive, but snow had been cleared from in front of the garage door, promising that someone was home, parked inside.

It looked ordinary, not the kind of place I could see Leeanne living in, but then again, I could've never guessed that she would be holed up, getting by without furniture or possessions in the quaint one-story she had been renting.

I felt eyes on me as I hoisted myself up the slippery steps.

Coming to the door where I found an old-fashioned knocker, I pressed the doorbell instead. Purse clamped under my bulky arm, DNA test kits inside. I was ready to present my Sheriff's badge since I wasn't equipped with a single warrant, but something told me these people wouldn't be so easy to intimidate as Trip Turner.

The ghost of Leeanne Hessinger opened the door, and it took me a startled clip to shake it off.

Those dark eyes. The wide, dramatic mouth—though this much-older woman's eyes were pale by comparison—was nearly identical to my victim. Her figure, as well. Tall and slender—frail as a sparrow. Though her blackish hair, white and gray, was streaked.

"Can I help you?" Melinda Grunke greeted me.

"I'm Sheriff Judy Kavleski from over in Sullivan County. Is this the home of Leeanne Hessinger?"

"Leeanne's not home right now."

It gave me pause.

"Melinda Grunke, I presume?"

"I'm Melinda, yes," she confirmed. There wasn't even the slightest flicker of concern at my arrival. "I'm Leeanne's mother. What can I do for you?"

I was saved from having to deliver the extreme blow of informing her that her daughter had been killed when a huge man filled the doorway, coming up behind Melinda.

He appeared to be in his early 40s with chiseled features and intense eyes. Looked more like a brick wall than the siding of the house he lived in. Had to be Ian, her husband.

"Who's this?" he asked Melinda, and I introduced myself, presenting my badge, which neither of them seemed especially impressed with.

"You're here about Leeanne?" the mother asked me.

Bitter wind lapped at me sideways.

"Would it be possible to talk inside?"

Melinda looked up at Ian as if the house wasn't in her name. Would he permit the Sheriff in, or hold his ground?

Rather than respond, he urged his mother-in-law aside and widened the doorway for me.

"You're making me nervous, Sheriff," he told me, his voice booming but good-natured.

I followed Melinda into a little living room, feeling sheepish about the snow and slush I had tracked in, and eased onto the armchair she indicated with Ian's assistance.

When it had registered how far along I was, he had taken hold of my upper arm, his hand so large it had wrapped the bulk of my winter coat easily.

Neither commented on my pregnancy, but Melinda looked remorseful about it as she took up on the couch. I wondered what that was all about as I waited for Ian to join her.

"What did Leeanne do?" Ian barked, and I nearly flinched as his hard voice cut through me.

I had mentally rehearsed this during the two-hour drive so I stuck to the script I had devised without allowing either of them to derail me.

"This past Thursday morning, Leeanne was found dead in the house she was renting down in Liberty, New York."

I gave them a moment to recover. Melinda looked stunned and Ian clenched his prominent jaw as if a bad taste had seeped into his mouth.

"She was killed," I went on and the older woman's bony hand fluttered up to cover her mouth. She angled her widening eyes up at Ian, who remained stoic. A brick wall, indeed. "I'm very sorry for your loss."

"Killed?" Melinda asked, but she hadn't directed the question to me. She was staring, white-faced and shaken, at her son-in-law. "Killed, Ian?"

Why was she asking him?

I found it suspicious.

I answered anyway. "It was, without question, a homicide. I've taken on the investigation. This type of thing doesn't happen often or at all down in Liberty so I'm proceeding with the utmost care," I assured them, as I pulled my moleskin notepad from my purse, found a pen, and got ready. "I would like to ask you both some questions, if you don't mind."

At that point, Melinda completely broke down. Choked-sounding sobs burst out of her, both hands to her mouth.

Ian was, to my trained eye, phenomenally unemotional, but the light behind his intense stare seemed to darken as though he would like to kill the messenger.

I apologized again, softly this time, allowing my mood to shift with theirs.

This was a solemn, grave matter, but I had my eye on Ian.

Trip could be a lot of things—performative, sneaky, narcissistic—but that didn't mean he didn't have a point in terms of Ian Hessinger.

There was something not quite right about the man.

"I understand that Leeanne moved to Liberty just after the New Year, last year," I began, as I studied Melinda who had quieted down some. She had acted as though Leeanne was out at the grocery store when I had mentioned her daughter's name at the door. What had she been trying to hide? "I'm in the midst of questioning her coworkers to piece together her final days. Did you hear from Leeanne recently?"

"No," stated Ian.

Unsteadily, Melinda supplied, "She vanished one day. We didn't know what happened."

"Did you file a Missing Persons report?"

Melinda looked to Ian for guidance and he told me, "No."

"Why is that?" I questioned, being as sure as I could to come across sympathetic or at the very least neutral.

After a brief hesitation, he admitted, "She had a breakdown after she lost the baby. She needed space. Time and space. We gave it to her."

Thrown, I asked them, "She had a baby?"

"No," he corrected me, and it was as if the wind had been knocked right out of him. His entire demeanor drooped. He put his arm around Melinda, but whether it was to comfort her or vice versa, I couldn't decide. "She was about two or three months pregnant. She had a miscarriage."

"It destroyed her," Melinda insisted, but Ian didn't seem to agree.

I thought he might voice his perspective but all he said was, "That's why she left."

"It was a nervous breakdown," Melinda hotly insisted to him.

But Ian disagreed. "She never wanted that baby." Disgusted, he reminded his mother-in-law, "She refused to eat right. If she had eaten correctly and hadn't been sneaking all of those fasts…"

He looked sickened.

"Leeanne never wanted to be a mother," he told me. "She was too self-centered. Wouldn't act her age. Wouldn't act like a woman or a wife most of the time."

He glanced at Melinda fondly and I got the distinct impression that he felt she embodied everything he had hoped to find in a wife.

It was odd.

"When she took off," he went on, "I let her go. I didn't care to see her face after that."

"You let her go?" I questioned.

"Like 'good riddance'," he confirmed, nodding his head.

"So, you never made the trip down to Liberty to talk to her?" I dug.

Ian angled those intense eyes of his at me and it felt like a glare. "No."

Melinda insisted, "We didn't even know where she had run off to." She looked innocent and bewildered as she searched my face. "Ian's been out of work—"

"She doesn't need to know that," he snapped.

"You wouldn't have driven all around tarnation to find Leeanne. Gas is expensive," she reminded him apologetically before boasting to me. "He's a contractor."

Aiming to seem impressed so that they would keep talking, I replied, "Oh?"

Melinda was instantly proud, patting his knee, "Ever since high school. Ian worked his way all the way up to the supervisor position." I thought Ian might shut her down, but he liked the accolades. "Leeanne was ungrateful," she hissed as though her own daughter had cut off her nose to spite her face, disrespecting Melinda's years of hard work having raised her. "She wanted to live in a fantasy land. She didn't like to work, you know, and when Ian hurt his back and went on disability—"

"Mom," he barked, not especially appreciative that his mother-in-law was airing his personal business.

But Melinda's point was too important to be silenced.

"His checks aren't much. Leeanne resented the fact that she had to work a bit more. She refused to hold up her end of the deal!"

The deal?

"Being a wife is a job," she informed me. "It's hard work. It isn't always fair weather, and Leeanne never accepted that. She kept trying to wriggle out of her role, and it was unacceptable. Smartest thing she ever did was snatch this one up in high school," she told me, giving Ian's thigh another pat.

"You guys were high school sweethearts?"

Surprisingly, Ian warmed up, his dour expression lifting into something that almost resembled a nostalgic smile.

"You could say that," he allowed. "Leeanne used to be..." he trailed off as though an enchanting memory had suddenly gripped him.

"Used to be..."

The word eluded him again then he captured it. "Perfect."

He glanced at Melinda, making sure the compliment landed squarely on her shoulders.

"She didn't want to grow up," he complained to me. "Thought she could write some book. Be some kind of hot shot. She has no education, you know? We had bills piling up and taxes to pay, but Leeanne had her head in the clouds. When she had to work a few more hours a week, she really hated it. I thought the baby would knock some sense into her. Christ, never in a million years did I think she would kill it."

"Ian," Melinda warned.

"That's what she did!" he cracked. "She starved that fetus right the hell out of her body." He snorted out a laugh I hadn't seen coming and maintained, "All those big-name authors have degrees. That's how they get book deals. Leeanne didn't have a damn prayer, and she refused to accept what life had handed her. Ungrateful is right. She could've been a mother. How in the hell was that not good enough for her?"

"And you never went down to Liberty?" I pushed, yanking him back on track.

"No, never. Not once. I told you. 'Good riddance' was how I felt about it."

"I see."

I scrawled something unrelated onto my notepad, giving them the impression that I believed him, that this statement of theirs was valid.

"I have to ask, did you hear from her? Did she call or…?"

Melinda pressed her mouth into a worrisome line and shook her head as Ian darkly told me, "No."

Sorting wheat from chaff—I had to weigh what Trip had told me against what Ian was claiming—I glanced over my notes, buying time.

Trip had insisted that Ian Hessinger had shown up at Walnut Mountain Park the day of his hike with Leeanne.

However, in my eyes Trip had also established himself as a liar. Had he lied about seeing Leeanne's husband at the park that day? Had he fabricated her fear of him? Had it been pure fiction that Trip's impression of the marriage she had abandoned had been abusive in some way? 'She thought he was going to kill her' was how he had put it, but had she actually never indicated any such abuse?

Perhaps Leeanne had offhandedly mentioned a husband and Trip, with his back against the wall, had come up with the rest in order to throw me off his scent.

Of course, it was also possible that Ian had in fact gone down to Liberty, but his effort to either confront or retrieve his wife hadn't resulted in her murder nearly a year later.

Or had Ian resented his wife so much for having miscarried their unborn child that he had tracked her down?

As I proceeded to collect their whereabouts on the morning in question—conveniently Melinda and Ian were each other's alibi so I pressed them for any grocery stores or gas stations receipts they might've gone to in the early hours of that day that would place them both in Albany—I kept my eye on Ian, scrutinizing his every quirk of the brow and tug of the mouth.

Was it plausible that he could have murdered Leeanne Hessinger?

"One last thing before I go," I said, pulling the DNA kits from my purse. "I would like to swab each of your cheeks, if you wouldn't mind."

Ian stared dead at me and said, "Not on your life."

LEEANNE HESSINGER

Monday, March 6, 2017

IAN WASN'T GOING to let up or leave town.

It was obvious.

He had tracked me down at Walnut Mountain. He had found out where I worked and had ambushed me there.

I knew Ian. He wasn't about to give up. He wasn't going to leave Liberty without me. It had been more than a week since I had caught him spying on me at the park.

I was desperate to put an end to this.

I had missed my hike with Trip that we had scheduled via emails. I had been afraid to go anywhere or do anything all weekend for fear that Ian would find me, follow me back to my rented house, and do what he always did.

I didn't want him to know where I lived. He already knew too much, and the walls were closing in because of it.

The absolute last thing I wanted to have to do was sit down with him and convince him to *let* me go, but I couldn't see any other options.

In order to be free, I would have to beg my husband to walk away.

He had agreed to meet me at the New Munson Diner off of Main Street when I had called his motel room that morning, explaining that I was willing to talk.

At the top of my lunch break, I drove from Bethel Woods, my bones chilled to brittle glass, into the heart of town where the historic diner sat, blue and cheerful, on a hill overlooking the length of the street.

I had become bogged in crippling doubt by the time I parked in the slushy lot.

Ian wasn't going to let me leave him. He was cunning and manipulative, expert at guilting me into doing and being whatever and whoever he wanted.

I had been obsessing over the various ways this could play out, envisioning every tactic he might use and the responses I could return. Mental chess. In every scenario, he forced a checkmate against me.

I truly believed and feared his power over me. I kept forgetting my own free will—that I possessed such a thing—as I neared the diner and stepped inside from the warming afternoon.

I felt at war with myself, one side of my mind insisting Ian had no control over me, and the other quickly reminding me of every past instance that disproved the notion. An elephant need only be chained for a little while, then remove the chains, and it won't think to run away. It's learned. It's been trained.

My husband had trained me.

I found Ian stewing in one of the booths with animosity rolling off of his mountainous shoulders. His glaring eyes fixed hard on me.

I was glad he'd agreed to meet me in a public place, but couldn't say I was relieved. I felt like a child who was about to be punished, severely, for having committed the egregious error of disobeying her parents. I was in a world of trouble, but I also had a brand-new life to fight for.

I was prepared to do battle.

"Ian," I coolly greeted him, as I sat on vinyl across from him.

He stared at me for a long moment as if debating what in the hell he was going to do about me, but I didn't shy away from holding his angered gaze, though my heart was racing and my hands felt limp.

Finally, "Your debit card statements come to the house, you know."

He wanted me to feel stupid.

"If you wanted to run away, you should've picked a big city. Damn near everyone in this town knows exactly who you are." He snorted a laugh and dumped sugar into his watery coffee. Stirred it as he sized me up. "You got some fancy job over at the museum?"

"It's a performing arts center," I informed him. "I teach creative writing."

"How did you pull that off?"

"I'm a teaching artist. I have students." I leveled with him at the risk of inciting an argument, "I'm not leaving my program. I signed a contract."

"Oh, yeah?" He was keeping a lid on it, but I sensed rage percolating just under the surface of his tense demeanor. "When is your contract up?"

I knew I was being weak. Using the Bethel Woods contract as a reason I had to be in Liberty, as if my hands were tied and there was nothing I could do. That tactic didn't address the real issue, but I already felt locked in so I answered, "May."

Exercising patience as though he was willing to work with me, he mulled that over some. "You teach until May. Then what?"

"They have summer programs."

"Summer programs," he echoed, wrapping his head around the implication. He didn't like the taste of his coffee so he pushed it aside. "What the hell are you doing, Leeanne?" he confronted me.

The way his eyes searched mine caused a flare of regret to burst in my chest.

He hadn't seen it coming, my vanishing act, my up and leaving him without warning. He was confused and hurt and humiliated, and for a flickering moment I could see within him the kid I had fallen in teenage love with all those years ago.

"I'm sorry," I breathed.

"Is this about the baby?"

"In part," I allowed.

"What do you want, Leeanne?" he challenged. "You want to forget about me? Forget about your mother, and what we're going through?"

"No," I wavered, pained for him.

"It was our loss, too, you know," he pushed as he leveled his gaze over me, coming more fully into his towering height. "You didn't lose anything, did you?"

When I, overcome with shame, said nothing, he accused, "No, it was no skin off your nose, was it?"

Leaning in, I pleaded, "I want to create something, Ian. Something amazing, and it isn't a baby."

"Why can't you snap out of it?" he hissed across the table. "Why can't you be normal? Where's the girl I married? I've got your damn mother up north trying to fill shoes you barely fit into yourself. Do you understand what you've left me with? Where's the white picket fence we talked about, huh? Where's the happy ending? The dog and the kid and the barbeque summers? Isn't that what we wanted when we were young? We can still have it, Leeanne. But not if you up and quit on me."

"No. No, Ian," I repeated, finding my voice. "We can't."

He eased back against the vinyl booth, studying my conviction, as our waitress swooped in, righted my mug, and filled it with coffee.

"Get you anything?" she asked, all business.

"Few more minutes?" I replied, and she padded off, busy as a bee making the rounds.

"I know I've been laid up for longer than we all thought," he admitted, referring to the ceiling that had collapsed on him. "I know the checks are nothing and it put too much on you. But 'for better or worse'," he reminded me. "That's what we promised each other. 'For better or worse'."

I was tempted to point out that the 'worse' aspect of our vows was never meant to include his fist connecting with my jaw while my mother pretended nothing violent was taking place in the next room as she dried the dishes. But Ian had been gradually softening as he voiced his own pleas and I didn't want to push my thin luck.

"I'm sorry," I told him again, surprised by my own sincerity.

He studied me for a long moment. I had never seen him defeated, but that's how he looked and I felt a surge of hope rise up in my chest because of it, though I tempered my elation.

"May, it is," he negotiated. "I'll be back for you in May when your contract is up."

"Ian—"

"I'm not asking, Leeanne," he warned as he plucked one of the laminated menus from the condiment stand.

I had won the battle. I considered it a victory, as Ian began perusing the lunchtime options.

"You're going to eat," he stated, "and I'm not going to let you push your food around your plate, either. You're not leaving until you finish every bite."

I took the other menu and looked it over.

I didn't know it then, but I had slid into immediate denial about the expiration date on my freedom…

…and what would become of me when Ian returned in May.

The war was looming…

❋

WHEN I RETURNED to Bethel Woods after a quiet, unappetizing meal with Ian, I avoided Trip and the rest of the T.A.s and hid out in my office with the door shut.

Trip made a few attempts to bridge our connection that hadn't been solid since Ian had come to town. I found one email from him in my inbox, asking simply if I wanted to get lunch. He must have sent it just after I had started off for the diner.

The second check-in email came in after I had been struggling—for what felt like hours but in actuality had barely been twenty minutes—to concentrate on my Lesson Plan for that evening's class. Trip wanted to know if I would like to go hiking this weekend.

I was tempted to respond right away. I could use a little conversational back and forth as a welcomed distraction from the ugly mix of emotions that Ian had left me with, but I held off from replying until I had plowed through the bulk of Carol's emails of memos and FYIs, one of which had been a scathing witch-hunt to track down the culprit who hadn't cleaned a spaghetti explosion from the microwave—*I'm not the maid, people!'*

Nearly everyone in the office had chimed in, declaring innocence and alibis. Nora had only eaten a salad and Cassie had never used a microwave in her life. Carol had pushed her investigation, building upon the thread with her every reply, until she had narrowed her list of suspects down to Trip and me.

I quickly typed, 'Wasn't me. I had lunch at the diner,' and hit send, replying to all, after which I composed a separate, private email to my work husband:

'Spaghetti explosion? Better dispose of all evidence before you're caught red-handed!'

I had nearly toggled back to the Lesson Plan I had been revising when Trip's replying email popped up in my inbox.

'As the recently cast star of Killer Joe, I can get away with murder!'

In an instant, I forgot all the grief of Ian having slammed into my new life. I couldn't be happier for Trip so I fired off a responding email:

'Congratulations! You'll be Joe Cooper? I'm thrilled!'

He replied, 'Yes, the lead, Cooper! Thanks! It took Mitch's muscle to get the P.A.C. to do Tracy Letts. This has been years in the making!'

I reminded him next, 'But seriously, though. Carol is on the warpath. Best that you tend to that microwave.'

To which he replied, 'Yes, dear.'

The afternoon got away from me after that, and 3:45pm came early.

I had managed to refine my Lesson Plan and print it out without the copy machine protesting too badly when Scotty de Barra barged into my closed office.

I had forgotten it was Monday, our first private tutoring day that he had suggested and that I hadn't formally agreed to, if recollection served me.

"Give me a second," I told him, as I wrapped up composing a responding email to Mitch Kavleski, the Director of Arts & Humanities, who usually never emailed the Teaching Artists.

Generally, everything that Mitch needed us to know was filtered through Carol, but this time he had sent a group email to all of us directly, only CC'ing the intermediary.

Scotty was unusually subdued as he plopped onto the chair across from my desk. He didn't so much set his backpack and sports bag down as *whip* them with a frustrated thwack. Dramatic. Something was obviously eating him, but I gave Mitch's email my full attention.

Mitch was soliciting volunteers who might like to draft verbiage for him, condensing their respective program into no more than seven hundred words, for an arts grant he was in the midst of submitting.

My first impression was that this type of thing was Carol's domain, and I felt a twinge of remorse for the embarrassment I assumed was coming over her at this moment. Then I wondered if her job was in jeopardy, so I sent Trip another sidebar email, questioning that very possibility.

Scotty sighed loudly.

"Sorry," I said, as I reread my email to Mitch agreeing to send him my draft by the end of the week as he had specified.

There were no typos or grammatical errors so after double checking my 'tone'—everything sounded harsh and angry when in email form, something I had come to learn could cause interoffice tension and start fights—I hit send, shifted in my chair, and saw that Scotty's eyes were pink and glassy.

Had he been crying?

It felt like a slippery slope, but I found myself asking, "Is everything okay?"

He groaned. "Today sucked," and wiped his nose.

He crammed his knuckles into his eyelids next, ran both hands down his face, then plowed all ten fingers through his sandy-blond hair.

When finally, his arms fell heavily to the arms of his chair, he looked frayed and undone.

"Coach had me running an insane amount of laps outside—" he paused for emphasis, staring wide-eyed and tortured at me— "all lunch period. My sneakers were soaked, drenched—" he amended loudly— "with ice water. Took an hour to get the feeling back in my feet. I was late for Fifth period and hadn't eaten. Of course, Mrs. Wolcott gave me a demerit for scarfing a bagel in class. Juggling Track with our writing workshop is going to be harder than I thought."

Our writing workshop?

"Scotty, if it's too much for you—"

"I'm not dropping out, Hessinger. Coach can suck it."

I feigned a delighted smile.

"I'll toughen up. Get used to it. It's only three days a week. I'll be able to handle it."

It sounded like he was trying harder to convince himself than me.

"Valerie's on my case because she thinks I won't have time for her."

He groaned again, letting his head fall back, mouth gaping and chest heaving.

He lifted upright and continued venting, "Why isn't it enough that I have Second and Third period with her, as well as this writing class here at Bethel Woods three days a week?"

He genuinely expected a response so I said, "I have no idea."

"I think she gave Adam a hand-job, but I can't prove it," he added, having a good long chew on that one as if stumped. "You know, to get back at me for being so busy."

I didn't know what to say, so I diplomatically offered, "That doesn't sound like Valerie."

"I know," he said as he narrowed his eyes, pondering the genius of it all. "That's why she probably thinks she'll get away with it."

I wasn't entirely interested in discussing his girlfriend's propensity to dole out hand-jobs in retaliation against Scotty's demanding sports and academic schedule so I gently steered the conversation in a direction that would be relevant.

"Sounds like you might have a story there."

Highly skeptical, he slowly agreed, "Maybe." He fell silent for a beat then a second wind of complaint hit him. "I got no sleep last night. Today probably wouldn't have been so miserable if I had. Man, I got to get back to Track right after class, too. Never ending day. God."

He was staring at me and I didn't know what to say.

Undeterred by my ineptitude to relate—to the contrary, I could relate to his plight, but it didn't seem appropriate to bond with him on a personal level—he openly explained, "I thought a lot about what you said last Friday, about putting the deepest, darkest parts of myself into my stories." He unzipped his backpack and pulled out what appeared to be some kind of typed outline, and regarded it with affection.

"This is why I couldn't sleep. I was up all night working on it. It's about my mom."

"Oh?" my voice hitched up, high-toned, as he offered me the outline.

I felt a bit lost looking it over.

"She's gone."

My eyes snapped up and locked on him.

"Not dead or anything. Or, I guess we don't know. She just vanished one day when I was a kid. We don't really talk about it, me and my dad. I just sort of, you know, dealt with it on my own. No one at school asks me about her anymore. It's like she never existed." Scotty looked at me for a long moment before he concluded, "That's the deepest, darkest part of me. I'm not sure it'll pan out as a book, but I would like to try writing it for my final project, you know, for the presentation in May. Will you help me?"

SCOTTY DE BARRA

Wednesday, March 22, 2017

MY INFATUATION WITH Leeanne was going to get one of us killed.

I was more than halfway through my sophomore year of high school, a junior varsity champ, killing it in English lit and calculus, and nailing the fastest sprinting times in Track & Field now that the snow had melted and the team could practice on the outdoor track.

The hottest girl at Liberty High was my girlfriend.

The senior quarterback of the varsity football team had taken a shine to me.

And I was finally getting along with my dad to the extent that his grunted greetings had evolved into actual conversation.

I had everything going for me, including passing grades from Mrs. Rosenberg's retarded 'women's studies' class that shouldn't even exist.

Mr. Rosenberg had a serious gambling problem and apparently, when I had scored the winning touchdown in last season's championship game, one which he had bet the farm on, *literally*, Mrs. Rosenberg had felt so indebted to me that, to this day, she continued to give me Cs and sometimes C+s even though I deserved to flunk.

I knew I should stick to doing what I did best. Sports, and pouring every last shred of focus I had into trying to have sex with Valerie.

I didn't have time for an extra-curricular course at Bethel Woods. I knew it. My dad knew it. Even my girlfriend knew it, though she was the sole reason why I had enrolled in the fiction writing workshop in the first place.

Valerie had *ways*.

I had been on the precipice of losing my virginity for longer than the guys in the locker room would ever let me live down. And even though I knew Valerie had no immediate plans to make good on the carrot she had been dangling in front of my face… Well, I kept falling for it.

Her tactics generally included brushing her lips against my ear, as her warm hand rubbed across my jeans. She tasted like strawberries and liked to press her boobs against me no matter how many eyes looked on… And those were her *public* incentives.

Privately, she had gotten far more creative in order to entice me into signing up for the Bethel Woods class.

I was still a bit bitter that despite all that I had only ever touched the undercurve of her boob once in my Jeep. I had felt her up between the legs on another occasion, but quite frankly, she had been leading the charge that time, and she had gotten more pleasure out of it than I had.

And then there were the seven times—I had been keeping a tally—when she had jerked me off in the basement of her step-dad's house, but it had felt all wrong, both physically and sexually.

Valerie hadn't exactly been gentle, and because of her bored stare and gum-popping—she had treated the situation like a plumber snaking a clogged drain—I had learned to finish quickly to stop the discomfort.

I was catching on to the likelihood that Valerie was getting more out of this relationship than I was. Dating the JV captain, namely me, had boosted her reputation around Liberty High. But she wasn't actually getting to know me in the process, not that I was about to complain.

When she had pressed her pillowy body up against me, detailing the dirty poems she would like to write about me for Bethel Woods—*Wouldn't you like to hear me read them to you, out loud, in class?'*—I had fallen for it, hook, line, and sinker like everything else she had suggested.

I had known I wouldn't really have time to participate in a three-days-a-week class. For God's sake, that's a huge commitment! Plus, I was already struggling to stay on top of a million responsibilities I had previously agreed to.

The plan was—not that Valerie knew this, sometimes a boyfriend had to lie and agree to stuff to make his girl happy only to then secretly plot his exit strategy from said promise—I would show up to a class or two, instigate a big fight with the teacher, and let the teacher do all the heavy lifting and kick me out.

It would've been failproof.

I could've vented to Valerie about how unfair the situation was, but—shrugging as if my hands were tied—what could I do? I would then be able to maintain my packed sports schedule without the additional burden of Bethel Woods. Valerie wouldn't be able to blame me, and sooner or later, things would go back to normal, and I would eventually get laid.

Of course, I had devised this genius, almost diabolical plan before I had met Leeanne Hessinger.

I didn't know why, couldn't pinpoint the exact reason or explain what had come over me when I had first seen her greet the class, but I guess you could say I had wanted to stick around…

…and, it was no secret, I had to be the best at everything.

Within five minutes during our first class, I had known I wasn't going anywhere.

You could call it a 'dark knowing,' the feeling in my gut that told me one of us would end up dead.

Maybe it was guilt or shame or a twisted thrill I couldn't back down from, but something deep in my soul told me that this would not end well.

I ignored it.

And there I was, nearly a month deep into incorporating Bethel Woods into the insanity that was my life. I felt like I was drowning in schoolwork.

I knew I was being stubborn and only hurting myself by not dropping out of the creative writing workshop. But it didn't take me long to accept the probability that I was, in fact, infatuated with the willowy, dark-haired teacher that seemed to breathe magic into everything she talked about or commented on.

What was worse—and I wasn't sure there were worse things than getting blindsided by a schoolyard crush on someone who would never reciprocate or even see me in that particular light—was the unshakable fact that I actually liked writing. It might have been easier to walk away had I sucked at it or dreaded my time in front of my laptop.

Reality proved to be the stone-cold opposite.

I preferred to draft short stories over working out calculus problems. I applied my best brain power towards constructing my outlines, typing into the wee hours of the night and letting my homework fall to the wayside, only to scramble the next morning, pulling together drivel and shoddy efforts that—I prayed—would satisfy my crotchety, impossible teachers.

Leeanne was at the forefront of my mind when I composed stories for our class—*would she like this, would she find this part funny, would this move her?*—and I soon realized that I hadn't been writing for myself.

I was writing for her. To please her, to entertain her, and perhaps to make her like me.

Would she?

I had never backed down from a challenge.

When the JV coach had eyed me sidelong and doubtful before tryouts my freshman year, I had played hard and proved him wrong. When my Track coach had snickered as I had thumbs-upped him, indicating he could raise my hurdles higher, I had punched the balls of my feet into astro-turf, sailed over each hurdle, and let him eat it.

I knew, with every fiber of my being, that I would one day make it to the Olympics. Call it intuition or insanity. Call it hubris or arrogance. I *knew*. That day was coming. It was on the horizon. I could see it. Gold medals!

And just as I could see my Olympic future—I had a hunch it would be ski jumping related, but that was beside the point—I could see just as clearly that I would be a star in Leeanne's eyes.

Special.

Cherished.

Valued.

Maybe even loved.

I realized I wanted her to love me like that, because that was exactly how I felt about her.

…whether it would get one of us killed or not.

"Scotty!" my dad's voice boomed up through the floorboards as I banged out the sentence I was holding in my mind, getting every word of it down. "Dinner!"

"Hang on!" I yelled over my shoulder.

I had left my bedroom door open and the stairs were just beyond it, Dad at the foot of them, more or less, where the kitchen sat.

Leeanne had challenged me to dive into drafting the story about my vanished mother that I had outlined.

It wasn't lost on me that this dark part of myself had greatly interested her. I was struggling to carve out the last time I had seen my mother into a compelling fictional scene, but I had been ten years old at the time and though the raw feeling of something having been very, very wrong that morning had been so clear I felt I could touch it still to this day, the actual sequence of events had been eluding me.

In the de Barra household, men didn't talk of such things.

Feelings and loss and grief and confusion that left a person vulnerable and deflated were not discussed.

Dad and I weren't emotional, or so his every grunt and sigh and curt greeting were meant to be a reminder to me of that fact. Up until this day I had abided by his subtle directives, obeying his unspoken law never to poke at the wound that had refused to heal for nearly a decade.

It had been out of fear and a gnawing twinge of empathy that I had never dared ask him about Mom.

Oftentimes, it seemed like Dad was holding on by a thread, diligently hauling off to the construction company where he worked as a foreman building houses around the county.

Cheering for me at whatever sports game I happened to be leading towards victory was the best I could hope for from him after hours. That had been our lives since Mom disappeared.

If I wanted him to know I loved him, I played harder and made damn sure I won the game.

If he wanted me to know the same, he drank less and made eye contact. Occasionally, he would jab my shoulder good-naturedly and shoot me a proud grin, but it never lasted.

Tonight, I was feeling brave…

…and Leeanne's admiration was the touchdown line I was barreling towards.

"Hey, I wanted to ask you," I delicately ventured, as I piled spaghetti onto a plate in front of the stove, Dad settling down in front of the living room TV, a plate on his lap, Kansas City versus Minneapolis chattering as March Madness unfolded at a crawl before him. He was glued to it, but not entertained. Avoiding me. "I'm working on a story for that Bethel Woods program that Val roped me into."

"Yeah, how's she doing?" he asked, completely distracted by a bad call from the ref.

"Good," I said as I stood in the living room.

There was a wall between us. Had been since Mom up and vanished, but looking back, I couldn't say that my dad had ever been all that available to me. I wasn't about to judge what he was up against, what he had been up against since Mom disappeared.

But the older I got, the clearer my vision became when I looked at him. Ron wasn't a man that met life head on, and I was coming to find, conversely, that that's exactly who I was. It wasn't easy discovering that you might not be cut from the same cloth as your old man.

"For the class," I edged in, eyeing my dad so I could remain cautious about testing the waters.

Dad wasn't one to fly off the handle. Instead, he would shut down, and the result could be that he would lock himself away in his bedroom and avoid me for weeks. I would rather not instigate another rift.

"I'm trying to write a story about Mom."

He stiffened but didn't look at me.

"Maybe you can tell me about that day when she disappeared? How did it feel for you? What did the police do? I need the whole story."

I knew I had made a grave mistake when I saw how he set his fork down on his plate.

He turned to me, looked me in the eyes, and said, "She's gone. There isn't a damn thing more to the story than that."

When he fixed his gaze on the basketball game on TV, I knew that whatever ground I had earned with my father, whatever small semblance of peace we had achieved silently and without argument over the months and years, had been, in the blink of an eye, destroyed.

Because of me.

Because of Leeanne.

Because of my obsession with and my tenacity to be the best.

When I sat down at my laptop minutes later, having closed and locked my bedroom door to shut my father—and the world—out, I began composing a story, not the one about my mother I had been ambitious about, but a work of fiction written specifically for Leeanne.

I had never written a love letter in my life, but that's what it felt like.

Pure love pouring from my heart onto the page…

…or it might have been infatuation.

Either way, it felt dangerous.

I kept going.

LEEANNE HESSINGER

Tuesday, April 4, 2017

TRIP PROWLED THE stage. Aggressive. Gaze angling up through his eyebrows. Bent script in hand. A pencil was tucked behind his ear.

He advanced on his co-star, and when she skirted around a stack of black, theatrical boxes meant to represent the table that the scenic department was still working on providing, he slammed his hands down, ready to throw the table aside in order to get to her.

I had only read Killer Joe. Had never seen it in production. But I could still tell that Trip Turner, the charming, boyish goofball I had become close with over the months, was bringing his own unique flare to the character of 'Joe Cooper.'

Trip was playing the hitman against the grain and wowing the Chicago-based director who had flown in late last month. The animated director seemed to live and breathe every word of Tracy Lett's dark comedy with gusto, as he wildly gesticulated from the aisle like an orchestral conductor, reminding his players of the blocking they had collaboratively devised across the stage.

This was the first theatrical rehearsal I had ever attended. It was intimate and captivating, two actors on stage muscling through the scene. Peeking at their lines brought brief lulls but they charged onward, maintaining the established intensity and compelling one another through the driving actions of their characters' diametrically opposed objectives.

Trip had invited me before we each set off for our respective classes.

It was going to be a late one for him. Class until 6pm. Rehearsal on the main stage until eleven. He usually felt wired after leaving the theater, so we had tentative plans to grab a drink at McCabe's afterwards, a stinky little bar that seemed always on the brink of collapse. It had become our place, an inside joke of sorts. We didn't belong in McCabe's. It was a real *drinkers' bar* where dreams went to drown themselves in booze and die. For some reason, the awful decorum and pungent smell gave us a bad case of the giggles whenever we set foot in the place.

I had nestled myself in the front of the theater to the far left so that Trip would feel my presence and know I was watching. Armed with my winter coat to ward off the blasting AC, and a knit hat on my head, I gave him my enthralled attention and offered him two, enthusiastic thumbs up whenever he slid his light eyes in my direction after the big-name director had stopped the scene to give an onslaught of notes.

"Tuna casserole!" Trip boomed, spreading his arms and beaming his flawlessly boyish grin at the actress playing Dottie, who—in my opinion—naturally embodied the trailer trash queen she had been cast to play. "May I serve?"

"How are you gonna kill my mama?" the actress returned, impressively balancing heat and apprehension in her performance.

They had moved on to another scene, one that seemed to require less explosive energy since Trip and his co-star appeared to be slowing down, even to my untrained eye. It was fast approaching ten and the director would have to pace all of them if he wanted to squeeze every last drop of juice out of their final rehearsal hour.

"That's not appropriate dinner conversation, Dottie," Trip flirtatiously countered, as he closed the gap between them onstage.

I had been fighting the urge to reread the latest letter from my secret admirer. It was the third I had received over the course of the past two weeks. Each had been deposited in my teacher's cubby in the break room downstairs, gingerly sandwiched between two novels I kept there—<u>The Secret History</u> and <u>Paint It Black</u>—both of which lived under a mountain of loose papers.

The anonymous love letter author had been certain to leave each folded letter poking out conspicuously so it wouldn't be overlooked and had even tidied up some, organizing the loose papers into a tight stack.

When I had discovered the first, it had filled me with a warm rush of excitement. My name was handwritten in block letters across the back. Its three-quarter fold perfectly aligned as if 'anonymous' had taken great care to conceal the racy contents. I had known immediately that it was a secret, private matter, and I had rushed into my office and closed the door before reading it.

Looking back, I would have to say that the bulk of the thrill had to do with what the situation reminded me of.

High school.

Notes wedged between locker slats. Secret messages. Teenaged thrills.

Yet, during my four years at Albany High, I had never actually received any such surprise.

Maybe it was the fact that I had never had the pleasure when I was a teen that made the experience of reading this unexpected gift so magical to me as an adult.

The first love letter that I had read within the confines of my locked office could only be described as a cross between a love letter and prose fiction. A single page. No more than four hundred words, it had been about me.

The author hadn't used my name, but had painted the woman in his story as a fragile, fearless loner, someone with blackish hair and big dreams who longed to be touched, not for gratification but for connection. She was an island. Isolated. Treacherous waters surrounding her, though the author had meant for those particular characterizations to be symbolic and metaphorical.

The story concluded in a cliffhanger of sorts, the woman unable to sleep, cool sheets covering her nudity, tossing and turning and touching herself as she yearned for a greater life than the one she had.

I had found it both moving and endearingly clumsy.

But most of all, I found it dangerous.

It had *Scotty* written all over it.

Though he might have written 'anonymous' across the bottom in the same blocky hand as he had used with my name, the telltale dangling participles and signature overuse of the phrase 'some kind of'—both of which had been peppered throughout and matched just about every story he had turned in for my workshop—had given him away. But not more so than the look in his eye that he had come to regard me with in class, sitting always to my immediate left, from that moment forward.

I hadn't pulled him aside to address or otherwise confront him about the love letter. I remained neutral—cool and reserved—as if I had never suspected Scotty or any of my students of having given it to me.

Perhaps that had been a mistake.

Adult responsibility began nagging at me to have a talk with him. Nip this thing in the bud. Remind him that I was old enough to be his mother.

Yet, though I knew it was wrong, I liked the letter.

I liked feeling flattered, and there was something about the purity and innocence that Scotty had brought to the delicate sexuality of his prose that both warmed and intrigued me. I wanted to see where he would take this fictitious story about my secret life…

…and a week later, I had discovered a second installment of exactly that in my cubby.

Similar to the first anonymous letter, the second detailed a restless world of longing, this time from the poetic perspective of a seasoned Olympian—a ski jumper to be precise—who had crammed so much ambition into his life that there wasn't a breath of space for love.

He, too, tossed and turned in bed, and when he touched himself beneath his own cool sheets, the writing became highly graphic, sexualizing and also emotionalizing the private act.

My cheeks had reddened reading it, my skin breaking out in a flushed sweat, as a chill of goosebumps had tingled across my arms.

I had darkly mixed feelings knowing that Scotty de Barra, my most demanding student, had succeeded in arousing me with his erotic prose.

I tried not to think about the undeniable probability that he had 'written what he knew,' that this masculine protagonist and his self-pleasure in the dead of one restless night was meant to convey how Scotty felt and what Scotty was apt to do with himself when the same sleeplessness took hold.

I didn't like the association and was uncomfortable with the peek he had aimed to give me at his own yearning.

Did he want me envisioning him in the throes of such a lustful act?

Whether he did or didn't, whether piquing my interest—arousing me—had been an innocent, accidental result or a calculated one, one thing was for certain. My mind was now wandering in Scotty's direction and my thoughts were hardly pure.

I slumped deeper into my seat in the fourth row of the theater, as Trip and his co-star breezed through, drilling lines on stage, the director marking his script with what I imagined were brilliant revelations he would soon convey to his cast.

Pulling the third, page-long letter from my purse, I winced not to make a crinkling sound, then unfolded the titillating prose onto my lap.

Though I had already read it several times and had nearly memorized every word, I couldn't stop myself from skimming through it one last time. I had resolved to burn or otherwise dispose of the love letters, fearing that if one of the T.A.s or God forbid Carol came across them, the dots would be easily connected linking Scotty to me, and I would be fired or worse.

It was as though I was chasing the sharp adrenaline bump that had sparkled through me the first time I had read it. An addict angling to recreate the initial high she had once felt.

Scotty had brought his two lonely-hearts together in this third letter, merging the dark-haired beauty with her Olympian in the hungry throes of X-rated passion. The prose was racy and honest. Dirty and sexy. Guilt inducing.

"Hey!"

I nearly had a heart attack, scrambling to hide the page away, as Trip kneeled on the seat in front of me, looking down at me with those fiery light eyes of his, smiley and winded in his exhilaration.

"What do you think?" he asked breathlessly as the director offered quiet suggestions to Trip's co-star at the foot of the stage.

"I'm blown away. I can't wait to see the show opening night with all the lighting and music cues and a full stage set," I beamed. "Really, Trip. I had no idea you were so talented."

He gave me a comical frown at my unintentionally backhanded compliment.

"Still up for the bar later? I think Lila's going to come along."

That was her name—*Lila!*—the young, New York City actress who was playing Dottie opposite Trip's Joe Cooper.

I wasn't used to sharing Trip's company and felt suddenly weird about the prospect of socializing with a stranger who had obviously captured my friend's affection.

"I'm actually feeling kind of tired. I'm not sure I'll last."

"You're kidding?" he said, beefing up his reaction as if he was pained. He splashed an air of humor over it however so that I wouldn't feel bad. "McCabe's won't be the same without you."

After glancing at Lila, I assured him, "I have a feeling you'll get by."

"Maybe," he said in mock allowance before barreling off towards his director and the actress who I was fairly certain he would like to sleep with.

I wanted that for him—a woman—because I knew that deep down that's what Trip was really after…

…and I needed him to stop trying to take from me something I didn't want to give.

❄

THE SPRING RAINS we had been having had washed most of the snow away, leaving soggy grass and warmer nights, though ice stubbornly clung in sheets along the shoulders of most roads.

Daylight had been lasting longer as well, dusk holding off from pressing in until nearly six most evenings.

I had never seen Liberty in springtime, and it seemed my quiet neck of the woods was gradually perking up after months of hibernation.

I had been spotting gophers and woodchucks, had learned to be careful of squirrels and chipmunks darting across the roads whenever I drove, and had even spied a little black bear in the far distance when I had last hiked Walnut Mountain, a sighting that had, unfortunately, scared the living daylights out of me and been my sole excuse for not returning to the park that I had held in miraculous regard.

I really didn't want to get mauled by a protective mama bear, and I wasn't willing to carry a firearm to feel safe.

Trip had assured me that the lumbering bears around Liberty were shy and avoided human confrontation, but I was too intimidated to take his word for it.

It was as though I had also been coming alive, waking up from my own wintertime slumber that I had been functioning in.

I had been enjoying walks around my rented house—an area devoid of black bears, I trusted—had taken to spring cleaning my bedroom and living room, the latter of which I had come to chuckle was a roller-skating rink.

I often danced in there, in fact, in wine-drunk celebrations when I felt particularly strongly about the fresh ideas that had come to me for my novel throughout the course of the day.

I had come up with an even better, mature-sounding title—<u>This Side of Kiamesha</u>—a nod to the small, Native American town I lived north of.

I felt strongly that I was honing in on literary greatness. I was practically bursting at the seams to write my book, but knew if I kept it bottled up inside of me for just a little while longer, I would soon find myself in the organic throes of a powerful birth.

Patience was key.

As I drove home from the theater that night, having left Trip to embrace his raw character and tangle himself up in Lila's, mixing fictional and actual emotions that I knew would spill over into their intimate drink at McCabe's, I focused my tenacious creativity on characters I might develop for <u>Kiamesha</u> so that Scotty de Barra wouldn't creep back into my mind.

Bogged in a thrilling brainstorm—I had been scrawling tidbits on the notepad I kept on the passenger's seat—I negotiated the dips and bends of the road one-handedly and hoped my handwriting would be legible.

BAM.

The impact stunned me.

The deafening thud.

My head whiplashed, forehead-to-wheel. Hood collapsing like an accordion as a deer—bloody and screaming—rolled up and violently slammed into my windshield, splintering the pane.

Holding my foot on the brakes didn't help.

The steering wheel twisted and jerked from my fisted grip, tires screeching and vibrating across asphalt.

I careened sideways, that's all I knew, until my car crashed sidelong against a tree, knocking me into my door, my head bounced off the driver's side window, as the alarm triggered and started wailing.

The airbag deployed, punched me in the face in a delayed reaction that hurt more than helped.

The windshield wipers made a feeble, tapping attempt at clearing the deer carcass away.

Stars filled my tunneling vision.

I made slow, sloppy work of dislodging my seatbelt. Crawled to the passenger's side door, and spilled out into the soggy ditch.

Crawling to the icy shoulder of the road, I ordered myself to stand up, but my head was spinning.

Exhausted, it felt like my brain was rattling around in my skull, I surveyed the wreckage woozily as I sat.

Though I feared the collision had totaled my lousy car, all I could think about was the deer I had killed.

I wept, knees to chin, head trickling blood, palms pressing wet asphalt, and became vaguely aware of the pickup truck pulling off onto the shoulder ahead of me, its headlights illuminating the scene.

As a man climbed out of the truck and started towards me, backlit by blinding high beams, I struggled to my feet, dried my cheeks, and discovered I was in one piece.

I felt marginally fine, all things considered. Nothing felt broken, not even my nose where the airbag had bonked me hard in the face.

"You okay?"

"I hit a deer," I dumbly explained as if it wasn't abundantly obvious.

"Your head's bleeding," he pointed out, and I pressed my hand to my temple.

The blood felt sticky like the gash was already congealing closed, and though a pounding headache was sweeping in, I didn't want to make a big fuss about this and rush off to a hospital that I didn't have insurance for.

"I'm fine, it's just a cut."

"Alright," he said, highly skeptical as he pulled his cell phone from his jacket pocket. "Let's get a tow truck on out. See about getting you home. What's your name?" he asked as though he would need that information for the towing company. He had already dialed, his cell was pressed to his ear.

"Leeanne Hessinger."

"Sorry to meet you under these circumstances," he said. "I'm Ron."

"Nice to meet you," I murmured and watched as he proceeded to handle the situation over the phone as though he had placed calls like this a hundred times.

"Got to keep an eye out for deer," he told me after he had relayed key information to whoever was on the other end of the line. "They outnumber us, you know. 'Bout a hundred to one."

"Where were you an hour ago?" I dryly returned, implying that I could've used that information to my advantage had I known in advance.

Ron struck me in those moments as level-headed and working class to the bone. He looked about forty or forty-five. Had a strong build, and he dressed down in jeans, work boots, and a flannel shirt that his jean jacket exposed. A friendly, though rugged, face. Trustworthy eyes, an honest look about him. He didn't look like a serial rapist, or someone who would drive the streets at night in search of his next car-wrecked victim.

It was beyond me why I was thinking of this now, except that it seemed like a worthy idea to explore for Kiamesha.

As Ron returned his cell phone to his pocket and informed me, "Tow truck will be here in about twenty," a herd of deer nosed out from the woods like they owned the place, lazy-eyed and unalarmed by our presence. "What I tell you?"

The herd swelled up all around us as they gracefully crossed the road.

I couldn't believe my eyes. Such gentle creatures.

I wanted to ask for their forgiveness for having stolen the life of one of their own, or at the very least, shield their innocent eyes from the carcass, but they seemed unperturbed, as if they had come to accept that the circle of life included being accidentally killed at the hand of some stupid, distracted woman from out of town.

"Silly things," Ron commented, as we watched them leap and frolic into the field across the way. "I've hit a number of them myself. They like to stand in the middle of the road for no reason, just sniffing the air. Came around a bend one night and wham! My car insurance jumped two hundred percent, just like that."

I groaned at what this would mean for my own barely affordable car insurance. It didn't help my swelling migraine.

"You live around here?" Ron asked, getting comfortable as we stood on the misty shoulder.

"Maybe two miles away," I approximated.

"Let me get my boy out here," he suggested, finding his cell phone again. "We'll get you home one way or the other."

"Oh, that's okay," I awkwardly declined. "I'm sure the tow company will be here soon."

Ron shot me a sideways grin as though I had just fallen off the turnip truck.

"Something tells me you don't know how things work here in Sullivan County."

"That's probably true," I allowed.

"They'll gouge you for a lift but not before they make you wait around for hours, and if you call a cab, you'll have to wait for 'Joe Sleepyhead' to roll out of bed, and it'll cost you triple." Ron was already sending the call through. "My kid will have to roll out of bed, too, but at least he knows how to hustle up."

I didn't think he would let me get away with declining a second time, and arguing with him wouldn't be an option since he was already doing that with his son who had groggily answered the call. I could hear hot, teenaged complaints on the other end despite the distance I was standing from Ron.

"Old Loomis Road off 52 near the Lazy Pond," Ron told his son then he covered the mouthpiece and asked me, "You hungry?"

"What?"

That was confirmation enough so he told his son, "Bring snacks— No, how 'bout the chips. The *blue* chips… The *fancy* ones! Pop a soda in a koozie for me—Just do it!" He hung up and made light of the short fuse his son had brought out in him. "Teenagers. You have any?"

"Me? No, no kids."

"I've got the one," he summarized before filling our wait with small talk about the staggering deer population and how, in Ron's opinion, hunting season should be year-round to control it.

As he went on to list the wildlife in the immediate area and warned me to think twice before taking on any gardening projects—according to Ron, the rabbit population had gotten just as bad as the deer—I found that this simple, salt-of-the-earth man made me feel comfortable…

…and safe.

I was glad he was waiting with me, and I started looking forward to those chips.

"Hey, listen," he said softly as the headlights of an oncoming Jeep blazed up the road. "I don't mean to be forward here, but I couldn't help but notice you don't got a ring on your finger, and you seem like a nice lady. How's about you let me take you out to dinner sometime?"

The Jeep came to an idling stop just beyond Ron's truck as I realized I might very much like that. There was something about him that put me at ease, and I could see myself enjoying his company. He hadn't come on too strong, if at all.

Then Scotty de Barra climbed out of the parked Jeep and made his way towards us, a bag of chips in one hand and a can of soda in the other.

I froze.

"What, did ya shower and clean the whole house, boy?" Ron teasingly barked. "What took you so long?"

Scotty slowed his step, freezing up just as badly as I had, as he neared us. Absently, he replied, "No, just, ah, got dressed and whatever."

"Yeah, it's always the 'whatever' that holds you up," Ron admonished good-naturedly as he took the soda, wasting no time slugging it back. "Don't be rude now."

Scotty handed me the bag of chips and we both stared at each other, then, as if trapped in a Werner Herzog film that would never make sense, we began eating fancy blue chips, as Ron marveled at the night sky between gulps of his soda beside us.

IF RON HAD made me feel comfortable, sitting in the passenger's seat of Scotty's Jeep as he drove me home made me feel the opposite.

I was nervously thrilled.

I was tense from head to toe, holding my purse in my lap, Scotty's many letters to me stowed deep inside.

The silence between us felt electric. But I didn't dare break it by speaking.

"Straight?" he asked when we reached the four-way stop at the top of the hill.

"Yeah," I breathed, as I locked my gaze onto the shock of salt-faded asphalt before us where the headlights stretched out.

Ron had stayed behind after I had called my insurance company to report the accident and dealt with the tow truck driver when he had finally shown up, Ron having taken full charge of looking over the paperwork before I signed anything. He had been firm with the driver about rates and timelines, dictating on my behalf the quality of service he expected even though the driver shrugged and reminded him that he was just the tow truck guy and didn't actually do much auto body work himself.

The man who had asked me out and hadn't pressed me for an answer was out there somewhere right now following behind the tow truck to see to it that my crumpled sedan made it safely to Sam's Auto Body Shop. I had forgotten that there were 'good men' in this world...

...and I wished that the idea of a date with Ron gave me even a fraction of the thrill I felt now that I was alone with Scotty, making our way to my rented house.

Our profound lack of conversation seemed almost as risqué as the love letters themselves.

"That's my house," I barely found the voice to say. "Up ahead on the right."

Scotty angled the Jeep up the driveway and rolled to an idling stop. Shifted in the driver's seat. Looked at me with eyes that seemed to burn with the need to address the letters he had been slipping into my cubby.

"You didn't want to introduce me to your dad?" I asked so that he wouldn't go there.

"I'm half asleep," he shrugged, but I sensed there was far more to it than that.

"You don't want him knowing who I am?"

"You guys didn't figure that out before I got there?"

"I guess I got knocked in the head harder than I thought," I said as I opened my door. "Thanks."

"Wait, Leeanne," he blurted, taking hold of my arm.

He had never used my first name before.

I gave him my attention in polite anticipation of what he might feel compelled to say, though it felt risky to do so.

But he just studied me for a long moment. Then he released my arm, and said, "Sleep well," the faintest hint of a grin tugging at the corner of his mouth.

"I will," I breathed.

It wasn't until I had climbed out of Scotty's Jeep, made my way up the walk, and locked the front door of my rented house behind me that I realized I had reciprocated his suggestive remark with one of my own, matching his subtext in such a way that I knew would invite a dangerous dynamic.

This would not end well…

…and it was only just beginning.

SCOTTY DE BARRA

The Month of April 2017

ONE HUNDRED METERS stood between me and victory.

Chalk-lined lanes, mine in the middle, some punk from Monticello was to my left, my buddy Jimmy was to my right, suited up in Liberty red.

Hurdles lined the astro-turf.

Blue skies overhead.

Cool breezes.

I circled one ankle then the other, checked the laces on my tight cleats, shook out my right leg, made sure my starting block had been set correctly.

I had to win this one.

Jimmy had messed up the relay race that we had just survived. Coach had figured that Jim would mess it up, which was why Jimmy always sprinted the first leg, and I sprinted the last during relay races.

That strategy usually worked. But during the relay, Jimmy had stumbled out of the starting block, dropped the baton, and scrambled to make up for the flub.

It had been a real disgrace.

I had taken off at a sick clip as soon as I had seen Sam, another boy from our team, flying inbound, grunting and snarling and fighting like hell to finish strong even though we were dead last.

When he had slapped the baton into my palm, I kicked up my sprint like a maniac, knowing I was at a severe disadvantage—eight seconds behind the slowest team.

I had punched the balls of my feet with every battling stride, kept my knees up, and had pumped my arms like crazy, legs burning inside of two seconds. But I had ignored the pain and had managed to close the gap, driving my team from last to third place.

Third place was nothing to sneeze at, but it wasn't good enough for me, and Coach hadn't looked especially happy about it either.

He had been suffering some kind of conniption ever since, gritting his teeth and reviewing the timesheets, doing angry math to calculate where Liberty stood in all of this.

I had the home track advantage, but if I was being honest with myself, it didn't give me that much of an edge over 'Monticello'—the lean, ruthless kid who was my greatest challenger. He had a solid three inches on me. Longer legs meant a longer stride. He had been smug about his times all afternoon. Smirked at me whenever he got the chance. Knew he was my only real competition and I, his.

He was going to eat it this time. Hurdles were my jam. I was feeling confident.

I keenly sized 'Monticello' up from the corner of my eye as I positioned myself over the block, fingertips to astro-turf, cleats pitted against metal, starter pistol aimed high on the sidelines, Valerie jumping around with her pompoms and leading the cheerleaders in a chant meant to rally all the onlookers in the stands.

I could feel Leeanne's eyes on me from where she sat beside my dad, a cooler of soda and snacks next to him.

It had been weeks of fancy chips and manly favors, but I knew what their dating was really all about.

"On your marks!"

I locked my attention on the runway of hurdles stretched out before me.

"Get set!"

I lifted up into a starter's stance and Leeanne slammed into my mind.

Yeah, I was going to kill it.

BANG!

I flew, driving my arms, pounding my feet, forcing air into my lungs.

I cleared the first hurdle, sailed over the next, my contenders falling behind.

I sensed more than saw navy blue streaming up beside me—'Monticello' in his track uniform.

I fought harder, whipping over hurdle after hurdle, tearing out after I nailed my landings.

It was as though my cleats never touched the ground, but 'Monticello' was giving me a run for my money.

Coach angled over the finish line, his thick hands on his knees, he wasn't about to blink as the sprinters came rushing in.

Digging deep, I gave it all I had as I closed the gap—fast—coming upon the last hurdle.

This was for the team. This was for Coach and for my dad, and this was for me, because I *knew* my dad would commend me for being a winner. He would clap his hand on my shoulder in warm congratulations as though there hadn't been an unbridgeable rift between us ever since Mom disappeared—I would kill for those fifteen minutes of my dad showing unveiled pride, which only came after I had won—and this was for Leeanne, who I knew—*knew!*—had begun dating my dad because Ron was *my* father.

My muscles burning, my heart clamping rapidly, sweat stinging my eyes, I leapt over the final hurdle, clearing it like a champ, but before my cleat touched down onto turf, 'Monticello' spilled into my lane, and I didn't have a second to think as he fell on his face.

My toe caught on his uniform in a terrible stroke of bad luck, twisting me.

I hopped out of the tangle, the other sprinters milliseconds behind me, and fought like a beast, recovering then charging towards the finish line.

I dove, becoming airborne to steal the win.

I was pretty sure Coach swore something nasty when I hit the ground, shoulder scraping over turf that took a layer of skin off.

The gallery of onlookers in the stands rose to their feet, jumping and cheering.

Dad punched the air.

Coach jogged towards me.

Valerie did a cartwheel, flashing her panties for all eyes to see.

But it wasn't until I saw Leeanne smile at me from the stands, that beautiful, wide mouth beaming an overjoyed grin, her dark eyes lighting up—ecstatic—that I knew I had won.

❄

DAD COULDN'T GET enough of Leeanne and as far as I could tell, Leeanne couldn't get enough of me, though she pretended otherwise, keeping her guard up around me, saying very little when it was just the two of us in the living room if Dad had ducked into the bathroom or hopped on a phone call or slipped out into the garage for some tool.

At Bethel Woods, she acted shy and reserved during our private meetings. She seemed committed to saying only what was necessary, offering her thoughts and feedback about my story.

I had finally worked up the nerve to dive into writing the idea I had outlined, which Leeanne had encouraged me to turn into a novella.

The story of my vanished mother.

As April wore on, I settled into a new rhythm of life, one which happily centered on Leeanne but was constantly plagued by my father's incessant presence. Valerie hadn't been much better, but at least she had come to terms with my airtight practice schedule and had stopped complaining to me about it.

I soldiered through school, squeezing in laps and training during my lunch period on Mondays, Wednesdays, and Fridays to accommodate my creative writing class at Bethel Woods.

On those days, I drove straight from Sixth period over to Leeanne's office to meet with her privately, always resting my forearms on her desk and giving her my full, undivided attention.

Finding ways to get close to her wasn't easy, but I relished studying her expressions and moods especially after I had slipped another love story into her cubby.

I felt like I could see past her guarded veneer and detect the intrigue in me she was probably fighting.

I had never met a challenge like trying to weave my way into her heart, but I could tell that I had. It was hidden in the quirks of her mouth and those lingering glances she tried not to give me whenever we were seated around the conference table during her workshop.

I found ways to brush my thigh against hers or touch her in some way as I headed out to join the team at Liberty High for practice. Gave her a little something extra to maintain the ground I had won with her, the energy between us having connected and bonded and *fused* us together in a way that I could *feel*.

Whenever I got home from practice, Leeanne was often at the house, cooking dinner with Dad or sipping wine in the backyard as he barbequed under the floodlights.

She revealed herself—gave her true feelings away—every time she tried to put a wall up between us. She wasn't fooling anyone except for Dad, of course.

She avoided engaging me in conversation and would grow tense if Dad left us for a minute, but I took it all as evidence of her attraction to me. She was trying too hard to fight what was happening between us deep beneath the surface.

I liked testing her. I got into the habit, after returning home from practice, of wrapping a towel around my showered body and parading through the kitchen where she and Dad were chopping vegetables or watching pasta boil.

I knew what I looked like and what girls thought of me, how they responded to my muscular body. Rosy-cheeked smiles at my sculpted chest and strong arms. Giggly at the sight of my ripped abs. I was chiseled. Hard-bodied. I didn't have to flirt to suck them in, a fact that Valerie often glared at me for.

Of course, Leeanne did none of those things as I found ways to reach around her for a celery stick or grab a glass from the cabinet.

But I still caught her looking from time to time, and if Dad was distracted, Leeanne would drink in the sight of me then our eyes would touch and a thrill like I had never felt before would burn through me.

We started doing a lot of stuff together, the three of us, on the weekends after my track meets or practice, as the weather warmed up.

Hiking and fishing, both of which Leeanne greatly enjoyed though I suspected she wasn't catching any bass on purpose.

We would eat out at Mr. G's and the New Munson Diner, Dad sitting with his arm braced around the back of Leeanne's chair, me across from them and savoring the electric spark of her every glance my way.

Sometimes Valerie joined us and draped herself all over me, needy and oozing, but I discovered I could get away with staring and smiling at Leeanne even more on those occasions, indulging in our secret connection that we both kept hidden under the burden of tending to our insignificant others…

…because that's what Ron was to her—insignificant.

I could tell.

She never leaned into him. Never kissed more than his cheek. Never spent the night or invited him to her place.

The closest Leeanne allowed herself to get to me was dating my dad…

…until the weather turned consistently sunny in late April and his construction work had him off building houses throughout the county.

Soon he wasn't getting home until after nine or sometimes ten at night, leaving Leeanne in the lurch at our house, which was fantastic.

On those nights, I did my homework in the living room, stealing glances at her while she worked on her laptop.

We slapped dinner together, laughed hysterically at the gruel we had created that was supposed to be a casserole.

Once we attempted to bake a pie from scratch. It might have come out fine if we hadn't forgotten about it as we discussed my novella and my own suspicions about what had really happened to my mother.

I was convinced she had simply had enough and had walked out. My dad had never been violent or given her any reason to abandon us, but he had always been withdrawn and unwilling to raise me in any kind of direct, hands on manner.

Leeanne seemed extremely interested in that—my speculations on my mother's motives and what might have driven her away that morning—so I kept going until the smoke alarm went off.

Her dark, guarded curiosity about my mother remained, and though I ate up the opportunity to intrigue her, I also found that talking about Mom helped to mend a wound I hadn't allowed myself to acknowledge for perhaps my entire life.

Neither of us ever mentioned my love letters. Leeanne didn't bring it up and I didn't confess to having authored them, though I was dying to. I tried to instigate bringing the subject to light more and more, wishing her to 'sleep well' whenever she was heading home, a direct reference to the elaborating story I had been secretly parceling out to her in sexy installments.

Her response remained the same as it had been that night in my Jeep. 'I will' was all she ever replied, but the faint smile she had to suppress as she did started becoming more and more obvious.

That's when she began warming towards me and opening up.

She read out loud to me passages from novels that had moved her like <u>The Odd Sea</u> and <u>White Oleander</u>, wanting or needing someone to share in the joy those particular stories had given her.

She solicited my feedback about a rough outline she had been struggling with for her novel, which she had cleverly entitled, <u>The Body at Bethel Woods</u>.

She had been going back and forth on titles, she had explained, but felt strongly about this one since she was certain the story would revolve around a murder.

She livened when she talked of writing, twinkling and bursting with aspiration and I found her ambition pure and innocent and gorgeous.

The urge to pull her into me and feel her against my body and bury myself inside of her became overwhelming. I craved her, had memorized her scent and moods and hopes and dreams, and I was starting to feel like I would explode if I didn't capture her soon.

I began swooping in on her morning bicycle rides whenever I could. Her loop began at her rented house, continued down Old Loomis Road, and cut onto Rt. 52, then hooked up Loomis Village Road, which eventually connected back to her street, completing the circle at the bottom of the winding hill.

It required expert timing, but I had come to understand that Leeanne was a creature of habit.

If I started riding my bicycle on Rt. 52 at a little after 7am, I would find her puttering along 52 and could catch up and join her, having locked my sights on those long legs pumping bicycle pedals as her tires whooshed over pavement. And we would bike together for a little over a mile.

One day, I surprised her with a pair of Bose headphones that matched the ones I always wore. We stood beside our bikes, and I insisted she trust me—I was going to revolutionize her workouts—as I placed the big, Princess Leia headphones on her ears. I had already connected the Bluetooth to my iPhone and as we took off biking along the shoulder, listening to the same sick beat, Leeanne shot me a bright-eyed smile that told me this was all the motivation she had ever wanted.

I knew her like that. Could intuit her likes and preferences. Provide what she wanted. Wow her. Tease her. Make her laugh. I gave her feelings that no one else could, and I knew that she needed me.

She wanted me…

…and I wanted her, *badly*.

Dad never suspected my growing closeness with Leeanne as anything more than a mentorship. There was still a clear line separating Leeanne from me, one neither of us had been able to bring ourselves to cross. But I knew…

…as surely as April's showers would bring May's flowers, I could feel it in my bones…

…sooner or later, one of us would dare.

"SCOTTY!" LEEANNE blurted, alarmed that I had jumped into the passenger's seat of her idling car.

It was pouring and I was drenched, having sprinted up her driveway from my parked Jeep. Rain beat against the roof of the car and streamed down the windshield. A beautiful sound that I happened to know we both loved.

"Why aren't you in school?"

I had overslept and when I had caught the time on my cell phone, I had made a snap decision, knowing that if I hustled, I could catch her before work.

"I want you to have this," I told her, getting the latest love story I had been keeping folded in my pocket.

I held the letter in my hand. This felt like the biggest decision of my life and I was halfway home.

It had been building in me, the strong pull I felt towards Leeanne. I was bursting with it, coming apart at the seams, and if I stopped to think through what I was itching to do—to cross the line that we never acknowledged was keeping us apart—I might not have handed her the love story I had stayed up practically all night to write.

I offered it to her, everything inside of me was forcing us to face this secret, that I had been writing her love letters and she had been reading them, knowing full well it was *me* who had authored them. That we had been building a world of attraction upon this simple foundation. That it was time to get real about it.

She wouldn't take it so I set the folded page on her lap and we both stared at it, her handwritten name upside down, raindrops sprinkled across the paper.

She grew tense, the air thickening between us, as rain pounded down over the car.

When finally our eyes touched and locked, she looked scared. Scared like I had never seen another human being look.

"Read it," I breathed, watching her, that controlled composure she was so good at, the measured yet unsteady rise and fall of her chest, the way her pretty face clenched with apprehension that, from where I was sitting rain-drenched and heart galloping, couldn't mask the glimmer of affection I knew she felt for me. Had always felt for me since day one.

"Scotty…" she murmured warily.

"Read it," I pushed.

She hesitated then unfolded the page, but a faraway look came over her as she stared, unseeingly, down at the words I had typed.

"I knew these were coming from you," she admitted. "But…"

"I know you knew." It took me a long moment to ask, "Did you like them?"

It took her an even longer moment to breathe, "Yes."

Studying her, I whispered, "What did you like about them?"

She couldn't look at me but she said, "Everything."

I waited, hoping she would read the paragraph in her lap that I had composed for her, hoping I would get to witness a wash of arousal, unguarded, that might sweep through her in response. Hoping that we could, at long last, have what I knew we both wanted.

She pressed her mouth into a pensive line and quietly read what I had written for her, for *us*, then folded and folded and folded the page until it was small enough to ball in her hand.

She couldn't hide. I wasn't going to let her. We were going to face what had been secretly building between us since January, since she had first glided through the conference room and had tamed me with a single glance.

"Leeanne?"

"It's very good."

She almost smiled, but seemed sad.

"I want to do that with you," I boldly told her, referring to the sexual act in the story. She said nothing, as she stared at me, a strange mix of horror and yearning in her dark eyes. I dared, "Do you want to?"

She pressed her slender fingers to her mouth and her eyes widened a touch as she watched rainwater pour down the windshield.

"Do you?" I pushed, getting very scared myself. If she backed down… "You think I can't see what you're doing with my dad, what dating him is all about? You don't want him," I hotly pointed out. "You're not sleeping with him. You barely touch him, and I know you don't like it when he tries to show you affection," I confronted, voicing the facts we both knew proved I was right.

"I move slowly," she said in a small voice, defending her behavior towards my dad. "I haven't felt ready, not that it's any of your business."

"We can keep it a secret," I proposed, having consciously ignored her argument.

She knew damn well she would never sleep with my father because she knew deep down, whether she wanted to admit it to herself or not, that she had feelings for me. Strong feelings. Feelings that had compelled her to read fiction to me out loud and bike with me most every morning, things she never even tried to bond with Ron over.

Leeanne and I made sense. It might be inappropriate or taboo, but we belonged together. It was so clear to me and I knew she could see it, too.

"No one has to know."

"Scotty," she warned, tone deepening in a way I didn't like. "I want you to focus on your novella. Stop sending me these letters. I don't want them."

It took a very long time for me to climb out of her car.

I felt gutted, as I stepped into the pouring rain.

Leeanne was lying to herself…

…and I was already devising ways to seduce her.

SHERIFF JUDY KAVLESKI

Monday, January 8, 2018

FIVE DAYS INTO the investigation, that was how far along we were. Five days and I was still working the case like it was the chummy 1950s, without the help of DNA and without clues, as if questioning enough suspects would magically cause one of them to confess. It had been five crawling days and I didn't have a damn thing to sink my teeth into.

My gut told me that Leeanne's husband, Ian Hessinger, could be culpable. He had a motive. He struck me as a hothead, and I found his dynamic with his mother-in-law highly bizarre.

Refusing the cheek swab didn't exactly bode well for his innocence, but then again, the fact that he had refused wasn't exactly a smoking gun.

There was no probable cause evidence that I could use to put in for a warrant to look into his finances, see if he had pumped gas or bought a slice in town that would place him in Liberty around the time of Leeanne's murder.

But even if I had such proof, I knew the D.A. would laugh at it as circumstantial. A wet-behind-the-ears court appointed defense attorney could wriggle off that hook without breaking a sweat, even if it *could* be used in court.

I was tempted to send my deputy out, have him go around door to door to all the local businesses that had working surveillance cameras—the gas stations, the liquor store, the one antique shop in the heart of town that valued their Chippendales and rare Tiffany lamps—in order to place Ian in Liberty, but that approach would be insanely impractical and would likely yield the same laughable result.

It was also becoming harder and harder to wrap my head around a plausible timeline in terms of Ian's motive. I hadn't liked the guy, and while flying into a murderous rage in response to his wife having starved their unborn baby out of her was possible, it didn't make a lick of sense that Ian would put a hold on his emotions for nearly a year then kill her out of the blue. Unless there had been another catalyst. But I hadn't been able to sniff one out.

Nevertheless, I kept Ian Hessinger on my suspect list along with Trip Turner, who I also strongly believed was good for the murder. Maybe I would get lucky with his cheek swab later down the road. I was still in the impatient throes of waiting for the final forensic report. If a fiber soaked in DNA was found, and the stars aligned in my favor, it might match Trip's sample.

I didn't like sitting on my hands or wrestling with my insurmountable doubts.

What if I wouldn't be able to connect this murder to anyone?

What then?

Complicating matters was the local press who had taken up in the parking lot outside of the station. The wolves were scratching at the door. Hungry.

I knew they would tear me apart the first chance they got, which was why I had been coming and going through the rear of the precinct, getting in as dawn cracked the horizon and leaving close to midnight in order to avoid the aggressive cluster of reporters who—thank God—weren't so committed to their efforts that they would forsake their families for a scoop. Even wolves had principles.

Apparently, I did not.

I felt like I hadn't seen Mitch in days, and gnawing at me was the sense that he hadn't even noticed my prolonged absence.

Was my marriage in trouble?

Curt wasn't at his desk when I got in, but his coat was draped over the back of his chair and his computer was on.

After hanging my winter coat in my office and setting my purse on my chair, I quelled my kicking baby with a soothing tap to my enormous belly—I didn't have the appetite to choke down another egg salad sandwich—and waddled my way through the station, figuring my deputy was holed up in the same interview room where he had been struggling for days to hack into Leeanne's laptop.

"Sheriff!" he livened, jumping to his feet, as I filled the doorway.

Curt had been bogged in a squall of irreconcilable moods ranging from determination and horror to remorse and fury ever since Thursday morning. A wrecking ball of emotions had been steadily degrading his faith that we would catch Leeanne's killer.

But he looked exuberant as he ushered me into the interview room, the pendulum swing of his spirits having brought him back full circle into the strength of his determined character.

"Got a lead," he urgently told me.

Not only had my deputy succeeded at getting past the dead woman's tricky password, he had managed to print and pile what appeared to be the entire contents of her computer onto the table.

"Take a gander at this."

I was skimming the many Post-Its Curt had slapped onto each pile to organize the categories—'freewriting,' 'students work,' 'outline notes,' and 'diet'—when he thrusted a printed calorie log under my nose.

"Look," he pointed out, tapping his finger over the list of food Leeanne had eaten on May 4th of last year.

"Dinner with Ron," I read out loud.

"Mr. G's with Ron and Scotty," Curt enthused. "Pasta with Scotty," he went on, going down the dates and flipping the page. Beside each meal, Leeanne had approximated the calories, keeping a tally and totaling the day's calorie count. "It goes on and on, clear through December."

"Right up until her three day fast?" I asked, recalling the arrow she had drawn through the first few days of the New Year on her refrigerator calendar.

"You bet!"

It still left a big, fat hole during the days leading up to her murder, but my deputy was right. It was a lead. 'Ron and Scotty' could only refer to the de Barras.

"And look," he went on, shoving another stack of papers at me. "Scotty de Barra was one of her students. Leeanne was involved with Ron and teaching Scotty. There's a story there, Sheriff, one that might have ended very badly for Leeanne."

I couldn't agree more.

"Good work, Curt."

The discovery had him all lit up. He was jumping around the table, plucking this sheet and that, gathering the puzzle pieces to a picture that could very well crack this thing wide open.

"I read through a number of Scotty's class stories," he explained, "matched them against some book Leeanne was working on."

"Slow down. Let's not dive off the deep end—"

"But Sheriff—"

"Fiction will get us nowhere. Let's not get distracted."

I eyed the calorie logs, the meals Leeanne had eaten with the de Barras.

"I can work with this, question Ron, see what shakes out. This is good, Curt," I assured him when it seemed the wind had been knocked out of his sails. "Keep going," I suggested. "But look for facts, not the fiction Leeanne might have created around it."

"Yes, Ma'am," he agreed, straightening his spine.

"I'll pay Ron a visit. Curt," I said, connecting fully with him. "You did good."

Conviction filled his voice as he promised, "We're going to get him. Whoever killed her. We'll catch him."

"We will," I said before starting through the station for my coat.

※

I ARRIVED AT THE de Barra's house at a little after seven that morning.

Parked in the driveway was a pickup truck and a Jeep.

Promising.

I pulled my truck behind the Jeep and carefully slid out from the driver's seat into falling snow. Made my way to the door, boots crunching through four inches of fresh snow, winter in full swing without a prayer of letting up.

I rang the bell.

Eyed the string of Christmas lights around the windows. There were dead bulbs peppered in with glowing red and green ones which seemed to lend a downtrodden tug on the de Barras effort to be festive, or maybe my own mood was coloring the impression. Dreary thoughts adding to a dreary atmosphere.

I was coming to find that I admired Leeanne. I didn't identify with her. Didn't feel the need to walk a mile in her shoes. But I respected her.

Leeanne had been flawed yet courageous, and I couldn't shake the feeling that her high hopes to make a fresh start in Liberty, one where she would be free from her controlling husband and critical mother, had ultimately gotten her killed.

Death had not been a fair price to pay for her freedom.

Mitch came to mind and my stomach lurched.

Maybe I should've choked down another sandwich.

I rang the bell again.

Ron finally answered the door, instantly thrown. "Sheriff?"

"Mr. de Barra, do you have a few minutes?"

His confusion at my arrival soon hardened into what could only be described as apprehension.

"What's this about?" he hazarded to ask.

I noticed he was keeping the door as closed as possible.

"I'm sure by now you've heard about Leeanne Hessinger?"

"Just a second," he said. "One second."

He closed the door and reappeared a moment later wearing his coat and boots, and stepped outside to accommodate the conversation away from his family.

"I *did* hear about Leeanne," he said in a solemn voice as he led me down the walk. "We're torn up about it."

"So, you were involved with Leeanne?"

From inside the house, Scotty pressed his nose against the window, spying out at our huddled chat, his light eyes as round as saucers, mouth twisting, and looking raw with remorse. Jagged emotion threatening to crack his teenaged composure.

"We dated for a period," he allowed, unaware of his son's curiosity, "but that was a while ago. She was killed?"

When Scotty moved away from the window, I asked, "When exactly did the relationship end?"

Ron clenched his jaw in grim recollection. "Around autumn."

"Did you guys remain in touch?"

He grimaced, had a cautious think on that, then told me, "Not outside of Bethel Woods. My boy had a class with her. Did one in the spring of last year, but couldn't work it in come autumn because of football."

"When did you last see or hear from Leeanne?" I ventured.

This was a cursory interview and I didn't want to lean into him too forcefully. If anything, I was aiming to compile information. If what he told me turned out to be lies, I could then circle back, use his lies as leverage, confront him, and pressure the whole truth out of him.

"Had to have been sometime in September, Sheriff. I might have seen Leeanne around town, but other than saying 'hi' or giving her a nod I couldn't say we spent any time catching up."

"What about Scotty?" I edged further into the question. "Did he keep in touch with her?"

"Not at all," he insisted. He folded his arms and concern crashed over him. Guarded. "My boy had nothing to do with that woman after he completed his class over at the Performing Arts Center."

He seemed adamant if not pointedly confrontational.

It gave me a serious pause.

"I would like to speak with him briefly, if it's all the same to you."

Ron hesitated, frowned, and glanced warily back at the house. It was obvious he didn't want that to happen, but after debating it a moment he agreed.

"He's got school," he explained as we trekked through the snow, coming to the front door. "I'll get him."

He slipped inside and when he emerged a minute later, Scotty looked as sick and crestfallen as my deputy had the day we'd found Leeanne. Pale and somber, he didn't so much walk as lumber out into the snow to meet me, shoulders slouched, face long, posture deflated or defeated or…

…weighed down with guilt he couldn't handle?

"Tell the Sheriff that you haven't seen Leeanne since September," Ron instructed his son with the kind of authority that made me wonder what the boy might feel compelled to tell me if he actually had a choice in the matter. "Wasn't it around then we saw her last?"

Ill, that's how Scotty struck me—he looked ill at the news of his former teacher's murder.

Seemed like he had been wallowing in despair for days.

I felt for him as he mustered up the nerve to meet my gaze, his chin quivering all over again.

"Go on," Ron pushed.

A glimmer of defiance came over him, and he pleaded, "It shouldn't have happened, and I didn't mean for—"

"Don't take that the wrong way," Ron blurted in horrified defense. "He's been in a funk, beating himself up—"

"No, I haven't, Dad," he asserted.

"What didn't you mean to happen?" I coaxed, thrilled.

Was Scotty on the precipice of confessing?

Scotty de Barra looked me square in the eye and said, "I'm in deep trouble, aren't I?"

Ron paced away, furious but resigned, as I said to the kid, "Tell me what happened."

He swallowed hard then began.

SCOTTY DE BARRA

Monday, May 1, 2017

BREAKING THE LAW. Was that what I was doing? It honestly didn't occur to me until I was faced with precisely how difficult it was to get her window open. All I knew was that running laps would have to wait, if I made it back to school during my lunch period at all.

I had never felt adrenaline quite like this. I was *beyond* alert. Every cell in my body felt poised, humming with an exhilarating thrill. I was on a mission and could see the full scope of my plan.

Leeanne was going to love it.

After debating where to park—instinct told me that leaving my Jeep in the driveway would be too risky—I had pulled around behind her rented house, bouncing over soggy grass, and had tucked my Jeep out of sight.

The scent of lilacs had filled the cab, masking the smells of my gym bag, old sneakers, and part of a bagel I suspected had rolled under one of the seats. I had yet to find it, but teenage wisdom told me that nature would eventually take its course and disintegrate the moldy remnants.

The front door of her little rented house was locked.

Surprisingly.

Who locked their doors and windows in Liberty? I hadn't anticipated any obstacles other than potentially being caught, though a thin line of trees was blocking the closest house from view, so I had to think on my feet. Improvise.

Having doubled back to the rear, I neared one of the windows. Peered in. Examined the pane. Tested it. I could have given up then, but I had never quit anything in my life. Challenges didn't deter me, but rather inspired my innate zest to overcome them.

That was about when I started working on the window. Single-mindedly. My vision tunneled. It took a tire iron, twenty-three minutes, and a hell of a lot of elbow grease, but I pried the glass pane off of the sill, bending then popping the lock by sheer force of my determination, and climbed in through gauzy curtains, spilling across—more than landing on—wooden floors.

The room was empty.

Completely.

There was nothing there, but I could tell it was the living room. I walked into the kitchen where there were slightly more signs of life, getting the lay of the land until I found her bedroom.

It gave me a serious pause.

Her bed was on the floor, but it looked too limp to be a mattress. She had made the bed. The corners were neat and tidy, the pillow was positioned squarely at the head, and a pair of slippers had been set with care at the foot.

She had left her laptop computer at an angle, but even that seemed intentional as though the exact spot where she had placed it was its home.

My first thought was that she should move in with me, but then she would probably have to sleep with my dad, the very prospect of which deeply disturbed me.

My second thought was that I hadn't brought enough lilacs.

In the span of those moments I spent walking through her remarkably vacant house, I saw a side of Leeanne Hessinger I hadn't known was there.

She was a person full of life. Her imagination was vast and unlimited. She had struck me as a very deep well, even the dark pools of her eyes seemed endless.

But she owned nothing.

Maybe she didn't want to take up space.

I felt a complicated twinge of sadness warm my chest and hoped that life hadn't taught her to shy away from leaving her mark. She didn't need to bottle up her magic, containing it secretly inside of herself, hiding it away and never allowing her quirky spirit to burst forth and overflow into her world. Was that what she was doing, living like this? Pretending she didn't exist?

I would fill it up for her, I decided. With the lilacs I had foraged in the woods behind my house. I would cover every inch of the bare floors with flowers. And turn the emptiness she had been living with into the scent of hope itself.

It took countless trips and I never once used the front door. When all was said and done, her humble bed was surrounded with bushels of those tiny, purple flowers. I lined the living room with lilacs as well, placed sprigs of them in the kitchen and bathroom, and sprinkled what I had left across the wooden floors wherever I could.

I had bought a paperback copy of Taylor Brown's <u>The River of Kings</u> at a bookstore in Monticello after practice the other day. Leeanne had mentioned it to me several times, how she had been itching to read it, but had been holding off because her car was bleeding her dry. It never ran the same after she had hit that deer.

I propped the book against her pillow and stepped back, marveling at my work. Part of me wanted to draw her a hot bubble bath and light candles around the tub, go the extra romantic mile, but I reasoned that the water would turn cold by the time she got home later tonight. Besides, I hadn't thought to bring those kinds of reinforcements.

She might have tried to push me away when I had climbed into her car that rainy morning, but her tone had betrayed the words she had used to tell me to stop writing her love stories. She couldn't hide what was in her heart. She was a cracked dam. She could burst at any moment, gushing with the powerful overflow of how she felt towards me. One more chink in her walls should do it.

I wasn't going to be sixteen forever. I had looked into the New York State laws. It wasn't great that I was her student, but it wasn't like she taught at public school. There were ways to get around it, hide the scandal, abide by the laws, and keep things legal, except of course for the breaking and entering I had just committed.

She might have been trying to deny how she felt and ignore me, but Leeanne was not going to be able to ignore this.

I knew what she wanted and I was prepared to make her see it, as well.

✳

"WHAT DO YOU THINK of <u>Albacore Man</u>?" Leeanne asked me as I breezed into her office before creative writing, my backpack and gym bag slung over my shoulder, heavy as all hell though nothing could weigh me down.

I had been floating through the afternoon in a giddy haze of heightened anticipation about what was in store for her, imagining how she would react once she discovered the flowers. I fantasized the many ways she might swoon in response, how she would yearn for me, and how she might like to thank me or possibly return the favor, giving my body the feeling I had given hers.

Without looking up from her computer, she mentioned, "It came to me last night when I couldn't sleep. Would you read a novel called <u>Albacore Man</u>? I can't decide if it sounds intriguing or pompous."

I plopped down into one of the chairs opposite her desk, flopped the bags I had brought with me onto the other, and grinned.

"Couldn't sleep, huh?"

"I know the novel is going to be about a fisherman, and it'll definitely center on a murder, though its genre will be firmly rooted in general literary fiction and not mystery," she explained, thinking out loud.

She had already drilled it deep into my brain that literary awards were never won with genre fiction, which I now understood to be lowbrow.

"I want the title to contain a hint of symbolism, but something about <u>Albacore Man</u> doesn't sit right. Or maybe that's because it doesn't roll off the tongue…"

She pondered the conundrum then asked, "What do you think?"

"'Albacore' as in 'tuna fish'?"

She groaned, sat back, and frowned.

"Alright, back to the drawing board."

"I like it."

"It sounds sophomoric when you say it like that," she complained.

"Maybe that's because I'm a sophomore?"

She frowned again, but this time her expression seemed to tap into the electricity that had become our constant subtext.

I had been fairly good about not highlighting my age, and I wished I hadn't let the error slip just then.

Leeanne was more open than she had been with me in weeks and I would like to keep her that way.

"I had some thoughts about your novella."

Switching gears, she turned from her computer and opened a manila file folder containing all of the chapters I had turned in about my vanished mother. I was proud of it so far and there was something very satisfying about seeing the thick stack of printed pages. I had maybe three chapters to go, but finishing the book was starting to feel like pulling teeth, and discussing the ending now was probably the last thing I was capable of concentrating on when all I wanted to do was reach across the desk, take hold of Leeanne's hands, and ruin the surprise I had left in her rented house.

"But first tell me how you're planning to conclude the story."

I pretended to have a think on that as I secretly wondered what it would be like to kiss her.

Would she drive recklessly through the night and jump through my bedroom window in a hot surge of passion as soon as she realized it could only have been me who had spread lilacs throughout her house?

Imagining her smashing those lips of hers over mine and tumbling with me onto my bed brought a tugging grin to my mouth, but I did a masterful job of suppressing it, and hoped she would drive carefully and wouldn't wake my dad.

"Scotty?"

Dazed, I said the first thing that popped into my head.

"Dad and I are going to have dinner with some big-time coach after practice, so you should probably go straight home after the workshop."

"And that has to do with your novella, how?"

"It doesn't," I admitted.

"The final project presentation is this Saturday," she firmly reminded me.

She probably would have exacerbated the importance of the strict deadline further to perhaps scare me into a productive brainstorm so that we could both feel confident I would be ready, but we were interrupted by a knock on the office door.

Leeanne straightened her spine in full attention, which was enough to compel me to turn around and see who had just barged in on our meeting.

"Mitch, hi," she stammered, greeting a middle-aged man who looked like he should be sucking on a pipe in front of a fireplace somewhere in snob-town instead of spoiling what little time I had with my future lover. I hoped he would leave. "Do you need something?"

"You nailed those seven hundred words," he complimented. "We got the grant."

"Fantastic!"

"I have a few others I would like to apply for, if you might be able to come up with a little verbiage?"

"Of course, my pleasure!"

I had seen Leeanne light up before, but not like this.

"I'll email you the guidelines?"

"I'll get right on it," she agreed with a huge smile.

After Mitch excused himself and eased out of the office, it took Leeanne a very long time to tear her gaze from the door.

❋

WORKSHOP FELT DIFFERENT than it usually did. There was nervous energy in the air. Only three more classes until the final project presentations.

The kids seemed jumpy and frantic, almost irritable because of it, each student clawing for Leeanne's nurturing attention as if in a blind panic.

Everyone was desperate for her directive and encouragement.

Margie Conway had crammed so much gum into her tight mouth that I worried for her safety. She looked more like a cow chewing cud than a teenage girl.

Her best friend, Kelsey Samuels, whose gothic look had always made me cringe, had draped herself around Margie with the kind of grim intensity that would better suit a candlelight vigil after a mass shooting, but it was nothing compared to how Valerie was smothering me. She was practically sitting in my lap, and no amount of icy glares rolling off of Rachel Hathaway could shame her to her side of our chairs.

Timothy Freedman and Gloria Wilder's behavior seemed normal, however, the lanky scarecrow of a boy and his pan-face female counterpart had been trembling seat-warmers of doubt and doom since day one as if it had been the night before presentation day the entire year.

The only student that wasn't even remotely concerned—besides myself—was Luca Martinez, but that was only because she had finished her novella weeks ago. I had seen her with her manuscript a few times in the hallways between classes, scooping it out of her pink backpack and affectionately stroking it. Once I had caught her sniffing the pages, which was weird.

Leeanne was pure grace and understanding. She managed their concerns with care. Whenever our eyes touched, I tried to pour back into her the same kind of support that she was selflessly giving the kids as if I wasn't a student but rather her equal. I didn't want to take anything from her. Instead, I wanted to continue to fill her up like I had her rented house.

I couldn't wait for later that night.

Just as Rachel Hathaway began walking Leeanne through the ins and outs of how she planned to wrap up her science fiction paranormal romance novella that for reasons I would probably never understand was supposed to be an allegory about the Trump administration—Rachel tended to be dizzying like that, too alienating to form interpersonal connections—I leaned towards Leeanne and whispered:

"I have to duck out and get to practice."

Being sure to brush Leeanne's jeaned thigh under the table—her eyes immediately widened at me as Rachel droned on and on—I added, "I'll be up late tonight."

She whispered back, "I don't need to know that."

Yes, she would, I thought.

It was definitely information she would need.

LEEANNE HESSINGER

The Months of May, June, and July, 2017

"YOU'VE DONE IT again, Leeanne," said Mitch as he sidled up to me.

He angled his appreciative smile down into the plastic cup of white wine he was swirling in his hand, as proud parents passed us in droves, making their way into the theater at Bethel Woods.

"Not everyone takes naturally to drafting grants, but you clearly have a knack for it."

The Director of Arts & Humanities was singing my praises?

I thanked him, then I didn't know where to look or what to do with myself. Drowning in self-consciousness—the yellow dress I had bought for the occasion felt suddenly skimpy, too thin and not long enough—I nervously gulped my own white wine and mentally scrambled for something to say.

He lingered next to me and inched in a bit closer to accommodate more parents, patrons, and locals who were piling in.

Everything about Mitch boasted aristocracy from his polished leather shoes to his blue cashmere sweater that brought out his eyes. Even his posture and the way he sipped his wine exuded the kind of pedigree I had only seen in movies. He smelled of sandalwood and spices.

I coughed up a dumb response about enjoying the grant writing experience then mentioned Carol and how inspiring she was for generally being at the helm of those things, which was my meek way of mining for information since the Teaching Artists had become collectively concerned about her job.

"You must be a prolific writer," he complimented.

"You, too," I heard myself reply stupidly, but Mitch was gracious enough to chuckle and give his wine another twirl around the cup. "Sorry, I'm anxious. Public speaking isn't my forte. I hope I don't mess up."

Trip was standing across the aisle, greeting parents and saying all the right things. He didn't have to overhear the disaster I was making of my conversation with the most important man at Bethel Woods. He knew me well enough to read my body language.

He shot me a reassuring wink.

"Working on anything at the moment?" asked Mitch.

"Um, yeah," I stuttered, getting all clogged up. I was eager to survive this small talk without tongue tripping, but couldn't see how I would pull it off. "I've been kicking a novel around in my downtime. I have volumes of notes and not a single chapter written."

"These things take time," he allowed. "I would love to read it when you have something."

"Okay!"

Did that come out loud? Trips eyebrows had shot up to his dark hairline, his eyes locking on me, a strange sympathetic smile on his face, so I had to assume as much.

"Good luck up there," Mitch offered, shifting away from me and stepping into the slow-moving parents that were congesting the aisle. He gave my arm what felt like an intimate squeeze and said, "Try not to be so nervous," before disappearing into the crowd.

I weaved through the incoming stream myself, crossing the aisle as politely as I could, and stood beside Trip.

"Wow," he teased.

"Oh, God," I cringed and rolled my eyes at myself, forcing the air out of my lungs to rid tension from my muscles.

"It was like you were shrinking. I think you lost two inches."

I straightened my spine and held my head high, but was painfully aware of my broad shoulders and the shape of my chest. My body didn't feel like it belonged to me. It was an oversized coat that wouldn't fit right.

"How's Lila?"

He furrowed his brow at my changing the subject, but didn't make me suffer any more than I already had.

"We're in full-blown fling mode, which is fantastic. But of course, the entire cast figured it out, and the director has been hard on her because of it. Jealous, I suspect."

"Rehearsals are going well?"

When he beamed a huge grin, I knew it wasn't in response to my question. His co-star and 'fling' had just swayed her bubbly way into the auditorium, exuding doe-eyed femininity and turning heads.

Trip started off to meet Lila and helped her get settled near the front of the house, and I felt a pinch of loss.

I hadn't lost him, not really, but the part of Trip that used to focus on me and used to aim to entertain me was now fully reserved for his starlet. I missed my work husband, but it was for the best.

Plus, I figured I could use these emotions I was feeling. I could pour the pinches and knots and sinking feelings that came over me from time to time whenever I thought of Trip Turner into my novel. The more I could feel, the more I could transform those emotions into fiction, the better my story would turn out.

I had been wrestling with two other tremendous emotions that I also planned to funnel into <u>Albacore Man</u>, though I was frustrated with that title. It made me sound like an eighty-year-old Scotsman who had drunk himself into grandiose revelations on his deathbed, and didn't even remotely capture the eternal youth—my fearless optimism and blind naivety—that constantly burned in my heart.

I would come up with a worthy title eventually...

<u>Wounded Dove</u>?

Too trite.

<u>Lady Flowers</u>?

Too stuffy.

Damn.

The dismal, unrelenting state of my dripping finances caused me perpetual stress, a strong emotion that also had nowhere else to go except into my novel.

I had been struggling to get by on canned beans, millet, and Doritos if I wasn't white-knuckling it through another three-day fast to save money, or holding my breath until my paycheck cleared.

My car had become a blackhole, sucking away my every last dime as though the deer species had perfected some kind of immaculate revenge from the afterlife.

<u>Immaculate Revenge</u>!

I might be able to work with that!

The other source of overwhelming emotion that had been tormenting me was Scotty de Barra.

I never thought it possible to feel tortured by fondness, but my deep affection for Scotty was intense and gut-twisting.

It haunted me.

I was crippled with shame, yet the guilt riling up inside of me didn't outweigh the rushes of euphoric excitement I felt every time he made another play for my heart. I had been promising myself his teenaged attempts at seduction were hormone induced. Once the swell had passed, he would likely feel embarrassed and recede back into his high school routine of friends, sports, and girlfriend drama. But the lilacs had tipped the scales in his favor.

The lilacs had consumed me.

Exquisitely.

When I had stepped into my rented house last Monday night and smelled the heavenly fragrance of my favorite flower, I had nearly levitated with delight. But it was bittersweet, tinged with sadness, because I knew who had done it.

A boy.

A kid too young to understand the language of his own emotions and how everything was exaggerated at that age. But though I could clearly see the trap of infatuation he had gotten himself tangled up in, I knew at that moment that he had won my heart.

I had curled up with my lilacs that night and had read the book he had left for me on my pillow, and for the rest of the week, I had looked at him, not like a teacher would her student, but as a woman who couldn't tear her eyes away from an attractive man.

It was wrong, but it was also delicious.

Scotty was special to me. Precious. I was plummeting towards a beautiful mistake, and there was nothing I could do to break the fall.

The auditorium lights flickered, and the audience fell in a hush.

I used the far aisle to find my seat next to Carol, as Mitch took to the lectern and welcomed the parents and patrons for coming.

Then, as Mitch traded places with Carol, who had further opening remarks before introducing Nora Graham and her sculptors, I felt eyes on me and found Scotty sitting three rows behind, next to his father.

There he was—those penetrating eyes, tousled hair, the red JV letterman jacket he always wore, tall and sculpted and confident as ever—discretely observing me as Ron frowned at the folded program in his calloused hands.

Scotty flashed me a guarded grin, which terrified and thrilled me, and I returned a reserved, cordial smile, all the while feeling my gaze smolder over him.

I faced forward, stiffened, and willed my racing pulse to quiet so that I wouldn't make an absolute fool of myself up there on stage when the time came.

Mary Roberts and her photography students followed Nora's presentation. There was a frantic, shuffling lull in-between presentations, Mary skirting around the stage to pull down the large prints her students had just shared as Cassie Davies rushed around, her painters clunking into Mary's photographers in a mad dash to swap out the prints and fill the easels with acrylic-on-canvas.

Towards the end of Cassie's spiel, Carol Patterson prompted me to slink out into the aisle.

As soon as Scotty saw me standing near the wall, he took charge and tapped the shoulders of Luca Martinez and Timothy Freedman. Word swiftly spread, and my students ducked out of their seats, joined me at the side of the stage, and lined up in the order we had all practiced during last Friday's class.

Scotty stood next to me and brushed the back of his warm hand against mine.

That was the last thing I remember before our group was called up.

Riddled with mind-splitting nerves, I was pretty sure I blacked out as we took the stage. Whatever I said up there was a blur to me, but apparently funny, because I got a few laughs, and the next thing I knew the audience was clapping as I stepped aside for Scotty to set his novella on the lectern, clear his throat, and begin reading.

Each of my students read a chapter from their respective novellas, one after the next, with proud applause in-between that gave away the precise locations of where their clusters of family and friends were seated.

Gloria Wilder was the last to present and as she did, Trip collected his theater students at the side of the stage, readying them for the big, dramatic finale, which would start with an acting exercise, break out into a series of monologues, and end with a spirited scene from Twelve Angry Men, an old play from 1954 that I happened to know Trip despised.

It was the only scene, however, that met his criteria for dramatic conflict and also satisfied Carol's mandate to avoid too much hostility among the students, though one of them definitely dropped an F-bomb out of sheer rebellion right away.

Trip snickered.

I couldn't help but laugh as well as I gazed out at the audience, drinking in the sight of this incredible event I was a part of. It was inspiring, and I savored knowing that there would be many more final project presentations at Bethel Woods. I had found my tribe, *my home*, and I would never look back.

But all humor drained out of me in an instant when I saw Ian standing at the back of the auditorium.

My stomach lurched then bottomed out through the floor, and my brain felt like it was swimming around in my skull, the world suddenly tilting off its axis and sucking me sideways.

He had come back for me and like an idiot I had thought he wouldn't.

As the theatrical scene unfolded onstage, Trip's players energetically blurting their lines and barreling around, I rushed up the aisle and pulled Ian into the lobby before he could make a scene.

"You were good up there. Are those your students?"

"You can't be here, Ian," I hissed.

"You said 'May' so here I am," he reminded me in earnest, but I recognized the calm before the storm when it was leering over me.

"I can't do this with you—"

"I can wait until after the party," he compromised, referencing the folded program in his hand. "We'll head back tonight."

"You think I'm going to leave with you? You think I'm going to give all this up?"

His tone deepened by an octave as he said, "We had a deal."

"We had *no* deal, Ian. I didn't agree to anything," I insisted. "You have to leave. Now." My warning didn't faze him. "I'm going to stay and you're going to leave and that has to be the end of it."

He clenched his jaw and hardened into the man I remembered.

"Where are you staying?"

Drained, I wasn't sure how much more fight I had left in me. I had been reduced to shaking my head, pressing my mouth into a quivering, frustrated line, and refusing to look up at my husband.

"Leeanne," he barked and I flinched.

I let out a rocky breath and crossed my arms.

"I want a divorce."

Ian laughed, but he sounded furious. He took a tight lap, pacing away from me then returning. The folded program was now bent in his large fist.

"That's what you want, huh?" he snorted, glaring down at me.

That's when he reached the breaking point.

He smacked his hand into the side of my head, balled my hair in his fist, and forced me through the lobby.

I tasted blood in my mouth where my teeth had clipped my tongue, as he shoved me out the door and into the gorgeous, spring afternoon that felt all wrong, blue skies and chirping birds oblivious to our domestic violence.

This was nothing new.

He would let me have it then shove me into his pickup truck.

I would hide behind my scraggly hair and cry quietly.

We had done this a hundred times and usually with an audience of concerned grocery shoppers or bar flies looking on while pretending to mind their own business.

My mother would make me a drink, probably vodka, then push a crusty casserole on me, while Ian cooled off on his recliner in front of a blaring football game, muttering insults at the TV that we would all know were meant for me.

I felt like I was stuck in some kind of time warp, like the past four months hadn't happened or mattered, like there had been a wrinkle in time that had just erased the life I had built, jumping over Liberty as though it had been some fantastic dream I should have never been stupid enough to believe would last.

Teaching and writing, curling up with lilacs and feeling adored, feeling like Walnut Mountain had risen up from the earth just for me, had all been an illusion, and I had been sucker enough to trust every breath of it.

Ian was in the hot throes of informing me how things were going to be from now on, but we had barely stepped off the curb when Scotty, and what I could only assume was the entire JV football team, tackled Ian to the ground.

I gasped and felt blood against my fingers, as I covered my gaping mouth, staring in wide-eyed horror at the sea of red letterman jackets that were swallowing Ian in an unbelievable brawl, the sight of which soon garnered one hell of a crowd, parents and patrons and locals and donors having drifted out from the auditorium into the lobby before catching wind of what they must have initially supposed was the dramatic encore to Trip's theatrical presentation.

"Boys! Boys!" Carol shouted, peeling the kids back one by one in her effort to get to the center of the fight. "Break it up!"

When Scotty marched away, roughed up and heaving, he didn't look at me.

And when Ian clamored to his feet, brushed himself off, and stared at me with rage and shocked despair in his eyes, I knew that I had finally broken free.

IT WAS RH DISEASE. That was what had killed the fetus, the baby Ian and I had thought we would have last year. I didn't find out in time. Hadn't known that my body regarded the pregnancy as an infection to be destroyed. There was a shot I could've taken if I had known. RhoGAM would have prevented my antibodies from attacking the fetus, would have stopped the autoimmune response that had ultimately resulted in my miscarriage.

I never told Ian or my mother about what the doctors had said, that I could try again and get the necessary shots to protect the pregnancy.

I had let them think what they wanted about me, that I was mentally unsound, that I had starved the baby out of my body with my obsessive fasting, that I was deficient and unfit to be a mother.

They were right about the latter and I agreed.

I had wanted to create something miraculous and spectacular, but it wasn't a baby. I *did* want to pour myself into something beautiful that contained my bursting spirit, but not a child. And when I had realized that the people in my life would never understand this burning desire that drove my every thought, hope, and aspiration, I snapped, took off, and promised myself to never look back…

…because so against my nature was having a baby that ingrained in my very DNA were the ingredients to abort it.

I accepted it and committed myself to birthing something that only I could.

But my novel was not coming along.

I felt a gray sense of satisfaction, however, after the final project presentations at Bethel Woods.

Maybe now that Ian had let go, the heavy stone I had been in denial about hiding under might roll away too, unburdening me to finally soar through drafting the story I had always felt destined to write.

Optimism for that possibility carried me out of the shower and into my bedroom where I had left The River of Kings cracked open on my pillow for inspiration.

I had exactly fifteen days to myself, a sizable respite of alone time before the summer programs would start again at the P.A.C.

Gearing up for the stretch, I had been plowing through the novel Scotty had snuck into my rented house. I had gotten in the habit of falling asleep with it in my arms, as if by some magical osmosis I might absorb Taylor Brown's genius in the night, hoard his particular brand of brilliance in my mind, and craft my own book imbued with his talent in the coming weeks.

The prospect filled me with jittery excitement as I sat cross-legged on my makeshift bed, hunched over the novel, and softly began to read out loud.

I was startled by the faint sound of a heaving grunt coming from the living room and sprang to my feet, racing out of my bedroom in time to find Scotty falling through the broken window. He landed badly on a mountain of withering lilacs.

I clutched my robe closed and pushed my towel turban so that it wouldn't slip off my head.

"What are you doing?"

He dusted himself off and little lilacs fluttered from his jeans.

"I broke up with Valerie. You aren't my teacher anymore."

I had done similar math in the shower, but only on the latter half of that equation, then Ian had slammed into my mind, turning my thoughts in the direction of how un-female I had always been.

"This isn't a good idea," I warned.

"It might be," he said as he closed the gap between us. "I'm going to kiss you now and then you can decide."

I froze.

He inched closer.

I didn't breathe.

He leaned in, moving slowly, and brushed my cheek with his thumb, memorizing my face in case this never happened again.

I couldn't say I had ever been alive before that moment.

It seemed like he was smiling at me but only with his light eyes. The rest of him looked as scared as I felt, like the thrill of what we were edging towards might stop our beating hearts.

Scotty kissed me that night, but we didn't stop there, and when we finally fell asleep, I felt content and complete and safe like I had never felt in my entire life.

❄

I LOST THOSE fifteen days of writing to Scotty.

When I biked in the morning, Scotty would swoop in and join me, his father having already taken off to White Lake, or Harris, or Livingston Manor to build houses, never the wiser of his son's whereabouts.

We would shower at my rented house after, hot water rushing over our bodies as we kissed and coiled around each other, then we would explore the lines and curves of each other's nudity on the narrow stack of sleeping bags I called a bed, warm spring air breezing through open windows and across our bare skin.

We made a habit of driving separately back to Scotty's house after reading to each other for hours and wrapping ourselves in conversations that ranged from where Scotty's mother, Pamela, might be to why I had run away from Ian to Scotty's Olympic potential and my own aspirations for greatness, which I often teased him he was distracting me from.

At his house, we would hug and joke around as we cooked dinner which, despite our nonsense, gradually got better and better.

One night, we managed to pull off braised lobster and clam chowder, our culinary skills having improved without either of us ever trying.

The second we heard Ron's pickup truck pull into the driveway, all pawing would cease, but in a lot of ways that was when the real fun began.

Stolen glances and hinted smiles became our secret language.

I even found ways to open up to Ron when it was just the two of us on his couch, explaining in a timid, fluttering voice how brutal my marriage had been. Sharing with Ron about Ian's drunken violence, the rough forced sex that I had rarely been able to stop, bought me time in terms of Ron expecting to sleep with me.

Ron didn't pressure me to spend the night, but I sensed the milestone of our future intercourse was looming.

He returned my confidence by sharing with me the nightmare that had been his own marriage, how his wife, Pamela, had disappeared, and how Scotty's novella scared him. He had only heard his son read the first chapter out loud in the auditorium at Bethel Woods that afternoon, but felt certain he wouldn't be able to stomach the rest.

As spring pushed into summer, my relationship with Ron became perhaps what it had always been.

A full-blown charade. A clever cover masking a love affair that was both wrong and illegal.

But it worked.

Ron never noticed my inappropriate advances towards his teenage son, nor did he ever suspect Scotty of having pleasured—time and again—the soft-spoken woman who he himself had been so patiently courting for months and months with virtually no reward.

What Scotty and I had was real, our connection palpable, and it was starting to feel like love. We shared a genuine sweetness, and he made me feel happy.

Often, I found myself wishing that it had been Scotty I had met in high school instead of Ian. My life could have turned out so differently if that had been the case. Just imagining it made my heart ache.

But broiling below the surface of our secret, sexual romance was a glowing ember of paranoia which threatened to spoil the happiest thing in my life. The invigorating relationship I had finally found was threatened by reality itself.

It wasn't designed to last.

Whenever there was a lull in conversation with Ron, a searing wave of anxiety would flare hot in my chest. Was he working up the nerve to confront me?

When my car required another expensive stint at Sam's Auto Body Shop and Trip picked me up for Bethel Woods, the summer programs having started, I would agonize over searching his expression and hunting for indications that he might know about me and Scotty, all the while trying to survive the blade of shame twisting through my guts. Making certain that Trip remained none the wiser to my unease was no easy feat.

I was walking on thin ice, but I couldn't stop.

Scotty made me feel cherished and valued, everything I had always wanted when I had been a lost, teenage girl, ill-equipped to esteem myself thanks to my mother's horribly oppressive version of raising children. It wasn't fair that I had met the right person at the wrong time in my life, and I wasn't willing to give him up.

No matter what.

SCOTTY DE BARRA

Thursday, August 10, 2017

MY LIFE WAS amazing, and I mean *amazing*.

I was literally on top of the world—well, not 'literally', Leeanne would have glanced at me sideways and in that breathy voice of hers corrected me, saying 'figuratively,' but you get the point!

All summer I had been jogging daily, lifting weights and swimming three days a week, and once a week I trained with an Olympic coach who had scouted me last spring.

Matthew Rappaport hailed from northern New Hampshire, but worked out of a training center in Lake Placid where he had taken kids like me and turned them into ski jumping gold, silver, and bronze medalists.

Every Thursday for the past three weeks, I had gotten up before the sun, driven the four and a half hours north to Lake Placid, NY, and had spent the day interchanging plyometrics exercises and zooming down dry shoots, while Rappaport literally critiqued how I engaged every muscle and used every breath—and when I say 'literally' this time, I'm certain I'm using that word correctly. Thanks, Leeanne.

The facility was spectacular.

I was in the company of elite ski jumpers, and Rappaport had been pushing me to consider moving nearby so that he could coach me at least three days a week.

He felt confident that if I could commit—seriously commit—to working with him, even if it meant moving and homeschooling, I would be ready for the 2022 Olympic Team. Tryouts would be months before the games.

I couldn't believe that Rappaport saw such potential in me that he was envisioning my future five years in advance.

I had never thought too far beyond the next sports season, myself, but I had always hoped to one day make it to the Winter Olympics. It wasn't just a dream anymore. This could actually happen!

I was ecstatic about my future and enthralled with Leeanne. It was more than love. She was the only air I wanted to breathe. I thought of her constantly and spent almost all of my free time with her, and whenever I plunged my body inside of hers, feeling the hot sheath of her sex clamped around mine as I held her head and searched her dark eyes, I felt like our spirits were merging.

Our connection was powerful. Fated. I once caught a glimmer of my own soul inside of her when she gazed deeply at me during one of our many afternoon trysts. What we had was otherworldly, as magical and mysterious as Leeanne herself.

Standing in front of a Keith Haring painting that was almost as large as the white wall it was mounted on, I spied Leeanne.

She was chatting with that important-looking guy who had interrupted one of our last meetings back in May. Mitch something. He was the Director of Bethel Woods, but his fancy title escaped me.

Dad and I had missed the opening night performance of Killer Joe, a play that Leeanne had raved about. It had gotten such great reviews that the theater had decided to extend its run, hence my waiting around in the exhibit space on the lower level. I was early and knowing Dad, he would probably be late.

I had yet to tell Leeanne about my Olympic coach's confidence in me. My dad was in the dark, as well. I was still unsure about what I wanted to do. Uprooting my entire life, and Dad's, on the gamble of my making the US Team would be a big conversation. For the time being, I loved how things were and I wanted to hold on to that for as long as possible.

Maybe Leeanne could come with me? She could homeschool me. Dad could stay in Liberty and hopefully never find out about us until I was in my twenties and engaged to Leeanne. I happened to know that Leeanne, deep down, felt perpetually nervous about her husband, Ian, since he had ambushed her on more than one occasion. If she moved to Lake Placid with me, Ian would have no idea where she was, and I wouldn't have to jump him again. It was a thought.

"Hey," she breathed, joining me in front of the giant Haring.

She kept scanning the exhibit space, smiling out in a welcoming manner and being sure not to give me too much attention. I was used to this, her veiled affection.

"Where's your dad?"

"Hopefully on his way."

It was challenging, navigating our public dynamic. Trying not to stare. Resisting the urge to touch her.

I glanced around the exhibit space, giving her strategy a whirl. I didn't recognize anyone except for Carol Patterson, but she seemed occupied in what looked like a concerned conversation with Mitch. She didn't notice me or that I was talking to Leeanne.

When I thought the coast was clear, I snuck Leeanne a suggestive grin and she shot me a quick, admonishing glare that, to my trained eye, looked like a promise.

I liked pushing her like that, testing and teasing her in public, gauging her real response and how close it might come to the surface of her tempered expression. Right now, under her mock scowl, she looked about ready to jump my bones. I couldn't wait to get into the dark theater with her upstairs.

"I'm not late, am I?" my dad asked as he came between Leeanne and me.

I had been so consumed with her, I hadn't noticed him entering the exhibit space.

She checked the watch on her slender wrist.

"You're early."

Dad pulled her in and planted a big, fat kiss on her mouth.

That was new.

I felt the blood drain out of my face as he released her and said, "Let's head on up."

If the color had rushed out of my face, it bloomed into Leeanne's. She turned away, touched her red cheek with her hand, and the way she averted her gaze from either of us gave me a very bad feeling.

In the theater upstairs, I wasn't able to pull off sitting next to her, but rather got stuck in an aisle seat beside my dad, Leeanne sitting to his left.

I tried to concentrate on the play, but even Trip Turner's antics couldn't hold my attention.

Dad had laced his fingers with hers. Leeanne had crossed her legs towards Ron and was leaning into him.

What the hell was going on?

THE FOLLOWING THURSDAY, Dad made the trip up to Lake Placid with me to meet Coach Rappaport and discuss his plans for my Olympic future.

I should have been thrilled. I should have been thinking about how eager I had been to show my dad how easy it was for me to stick my landings now. I should have been proud to give him a tour of the facilities. And I should have enthusiastically reinforced every argument that Rappaport was making to have me train hardcore with him for the next five years.

But all I could think about was that kiss between my dad and Leeanne. I was boiling with it. I tried not to seem distracted when Coach showered me with compliments for my dad's benefit, buttering him up to sign on the dotted line, but I was somewhere else entirely and couldn't seem to pull myself out of the blackhole that was sucking me deeper and deeper into obsessing that something might have happened between Dad and Leeanne.

She wouldn't, would she?

She couldn't have.

She wouldn't do that to me.

"I'll be straight with you, Scotty," Dad said as we drove home.

I was brooding, staring out the passenger's side window of his pickup truck, the summertime hills and mountain landscape nothing but a green blur I didn't care for.

"This is a lot to take in," he went on. "I want you to know I'm gonna have a good, long think on it, and we can talk more about everything Rappaport said, but I just don't know about us moving to Lake Placid."

"You don't have to move," I told him. I was stuck in a dark mood. "I can go myself."

"Now, hang on a minute. I already lost your mother. I'm not going to lose my son."

"You wouldn't be losing me, Dad." I glared at him for a beat, tore my eyes away, then scoffed, "Besides, you've replaced Mom, so it's not like you'll be alone."

That got his attention.

"Listen here, Scotty, no one can replace your mother. That's just the long and short of it. But things have gotten serious with Leeanne, I won't lie. I would have thought you'd be happy for me. You seem to like Leeanne."

"What do you mean, 'serious'?"

He chuckled.

"Remember when I told you about the birds and the bees?"

My stomach dropped.

"Leeanne and I have finally made a little *honey*."

What the hell?

Horrified, I barked, "Stop talking," and Dad chuckled and chuckled from the driver's seat, delighted with himself and phenomenally unaware of exactly why I couldn't stand to hear another word.

My mind was racing. My pulse pounded in my ears so hard I couldn't tell if Dad had shut the hell up about it or not. I could feel my bowels liquifying. I felt like I was jumping out of my skin, every inch of me hot and prickling, enraged.

My heart had leapt up my throat.

I was choked.

Crushed.

Just like that, Dad had destroyed me and he didn't even know it.

But the only person I was mad enough to kill was Leeanne.

It was a very long ride back to Liberty.

SHERIFF JUDY KAVLESKI

Monday, January 8, 2018

SCOTTY HAD CONFESSED to having had a sexual relationship with his former teacher, which placed Leeanne at the center of a love triangle between father and son, but it didn't spell murder, not yet.

The snow was really coming down.

I couldn't feel my toes and Scotty's head and shoulders were dusted white with fluffy flakes as he stood, shoulders hunched against the bitter wind, in front of me.

His eyes were rimmed pink all around and glassy. He had broken down with strangled, emotional sobs more than once as he had described the affair he'd had with Leeanne, but he just looked drained now. Completely spent.

Ron, on the other hand, looked furious, but his anger didn't seem directed at his son.

And then there was Pamela de Barra.

She had peeked out through the curtains at us several times. A hard woman, toughened up by life, that was who Pamela was, having vanished from Liberty. She had abandoned her family and had returned one day last summer from out of nowhere.

Could Scotty have killed Leeanne, the love of his teenage life?

Or had Ron flown into a rage after discovering what his own girlfriend had been up to with his son, and murdered her?

Then there was Pamela. The fact that she had returned provided a solid enough set up. Did she have it in her to kill Leeanne to get the woman away from her husband, or perhaps to protect her kid?

Each of them had a motive to want Leeanne Hessinger dead, but getting one of them to admit it wasn't within my immediate reach.

"I never meant for it to happen," Scotty repeated.

He hadn't been able to lift himself out of the mile-long stare that had come over him.

"You never meant to kill her?" I prodded.

"Hey, now," Ron objected. "He didn't kill Leeanne."

"Did you, Scotty?"

"I *confronted* her," he choked out. "We fought. She would be alive if—"

"Inside!" Ron barked. "Now, go on. Get inside." As he ushered his son with hard shoves up the snowy walk, he told me, "This is over."

"He'll need to sign a statement," I called out. "You both will."

"He was victimized by a predator!" Ron informed me. "It was statutory rape and it has nothing to do with your murder investigation. Leave us alone."

I watched Ron stomp through the snow, his large hand clamped over Scotty's shoulder, Scotty shuffling heavy-footed. The kid might have wandered off into the woods if his father wasn't steering him up the walk, that's how dazed and despairing he was.

I thought he could have killed her, any one of them could have, but I needed a hell of a lot more if I wanted to pressure the correct individual into a confession.

When they disappeared inside the house, I started through the thick snow to my pickup truck and hoisted myself up behind the wheel.

I didn't have the stomach for sandwiches or peanuts. When the baby kicked, I did nothing to acknowledge he had. And as I drove south towards the P.A.C. at Bethel Woods, I couldn't get the image of Leeanne's blue body lying dead in the entryway of her rented house out of my head.

The guilt was getting to be too much.

Guilt that I had the audacity to go on breathing when Leeanne's life had been cut brutally short.

Guilt that I had married a man, who by any woman's standards, was perfect, while Leeanne had struggled to find a shred of love and had only come close with a teenage boy.

Guilt that I still hadn't put anyone behind bars, when the whole town was counting on me to catch the murderer in our midst.

WHEN I ARRIVED at Bethel Woods, I stopped in Mitch's office first.

I was at sea, and though my husband hadn't felt like an anchor for a while now, he was still my guiding light, a lighthouse on the shore to lead me back.

His office smelled like him. His aftershave faintly filled the air. Scents of sandalwood and bergamot smoothed over his leathery, shaved face. I found it comforting as I stepped inside.

"Judy," he said, surprised to see me. He jumped out of his chair, rushed to me, and placed his hands around my stomach like he always did. "Do you need to question the T.A.s again?"

As he helped me to the leather couch, taking my winter coat and easing me down, I reminded him, "I'm not an invalid. I've been getting around just fine, Mitch."

"Why won't you let me take care of you?"

"I am, I do," I protested, "but I don't like being treated like I'm incompetent."

"No, Judy, you're *very* competent," he bristled.

I hadn't fought with my husband in ages. He had been consistently avoiding intimacy, both positive and negative, and though I wasn't a fan of getting into heated spats with anyone, I was itching to surge into a full-blown argument with him, anything to bridge the rift I had been feeling between us. I would do anything to feel connected to my husband again, anything to keep him from offering appeasing crumbs only to hide away in his office at Bethel Woods or in his study at home.

"What's that supposed to mean?" I snapped, provoking him. "Do you have a problem with my competency?"

"You know what, Judy? Maybe I do," he returned hotly without holding back. "Maybe after all these years, it's finally gotten to me, but I wasn't able to see it until I saw how stubborn you can be despite the pregnancy."

"All these *years?*"

"Yes, actually," he said as if deciding right here and now that the revelation was accurate. "You insist on handling *everything.*"

"Excuse me?"

He began listing on his fingers, "You insist on paying half the mortgage, you insist on paying half the taxes, half the groceries, half of everything, and you know what? Maybe I didn't notice it bothered me, even though I'm really not sure what in the hell I'm providing for you since you insist on proving to me you can handle everything. Fine. I've let it all slide. Every time a bill comes, we both sit down with our checkbooks so that you can, what? Assert your competency? Remind me day in and day out that you don't need anything I've built? I don't have to provide for you, because we're partners, is that it? I even let it slide when you lord over me and correct me, nitpicking every last damn thing I do as if you know better than me. I can't even park my car in the garage or put dinner together without you inspecting it for all the mistakes you assume I must have made."

I was aghast. I never knew Mitch minded our separate checking accounts. And frankly, I didn't know where any of this was coming from.

Mitch showed no signs of slowing down.

"But I've lived with it. Christ, I feel like I'm married to a man," he snorted, taking a surreal breath before barreling further into his rant.

"But I can't believe, Judy, I honestly can't believe that you won't let me take care of you now that you're pregnant. You haven't softened. You haven't leaned on me. You've gotten worse. You're actually offended when I try to lift things for you or help you sit down. You were furious that I painted the baby's room yellow, that I had actually made a decision without your input. Where am *I* in all of this, huh?"

I didn't know what to say and stammered, brain-boggled to realize his question hadn't been rhetorical.

"You don't need me," he pointed out.

"I *do* need you," I insisted. "You haven't talked to me at all in the past few months. I miss my husband, Mitch."

"How am I supposed to talk to you, Judy, when you constantly emasculate me?"

I stared at him, slack-jawed and horrified

"I don't know what you want me to do here," I said after a long, baffled moment. "Quit my job? Walk around barefoot and pregnant? Stick my hand out and ask for money like I'm a little girl and you're my father?"

"Oh, that's rich," he scoffed. "Nice. Bring out the sarcasm."

"Well, I don't know what to say, Mitch!"

"I should've known," he said, more to himself than me. "I should've known when you asked me out on our first date and you picked the restaurant and you took charge, making the first move every step of the way."

I sprang to my feet, fully incited, and gasped, "You've had a problem with me since our first date? Where the hell is all of this coming from?"

"I told you! I couldn't see it until I saw how exacerbated your 'I can do everything, I don't need your help' attitude became once we got pregnant! You barely let me take your coat just now. You resented me as I helped you sit on the couch a second ago. You think I can't *feel* the, I don't know what to call it, 'resentment?' rolling off of you? You despise being in a position where you might need me, *really* need me. What am I supposed to do with that?"

"First of all, I don't resent you. Second of all, why do you need me to need you? Thirdly, I *do* need you. I need connection and support, and you're getting mad at me because the kind of support you want to offer me is physical and financial? You've been withholding true emotional support from me because you think I emasculate you just because—sorry Honey, but every time you park your car, you leave me zero room to get in and out of mine, and I'm helping you with dinner, not lording over you. That's not emasculating you, it's *teamwork*."

"This is why I've held my tongue. You don't get it."

"No, I guess I don't," I told him as I pulled my winter coat off the rack. "I thought I could come to you to talk about my case, because I'm falling apart!"

I choked up, felt a sting of tears blur my vision, and pressed my mouth into a fortifying line while I fought to pull it together.

"But I guess I was wrong," I growled out as I made my escape.

I composed myself before finding Carol Patterson, who I asked to show me the archives of the Spring 2017 Creative Writing Workshop final projects.

Carol led me down into the bowels of the P.A.C. where all of the stored archives were kept boxed on shelves that lined a windowless room.

Once she found the correct box and set it down on a folding table for me, she left me to dig through it.

I wouldn't go so far as to say that maybe my deputy, Curt, was onto something when he had attempted to sort through Leeanne's fiction in order to glean kernels of what might have happened, but he had been right that there was a story there.

I had caught a glimpse of the same story, myself. Ron, Scotty, and Pamela de Barra were evidence of that, and I needed to find out for myself if Scotty had been perhaps so obsessed with Leeanne Hessinger that he had planted clues about the affair and possible plans of murder into his novella.

But as I poured over page after page, reading in-between the lines and stretching my imagination to the brink, I couldn't get the argument I had just had with Mitch out of my head.

I had come too far.

We'd built too much.

There wasn't a thing I wouldn't do to keep him.

❋

THREE HOURS LATER, I had learned the intimate details of how Scotty de Barra felt about his vanished mother, and it wasn't good. He regarded her as a selfish, unemotional homewrecker, a cruel woman who had carelessly destroyed his father the day she had walked out. She had shattered the family, driven an icy wedge between father and son, and the way Scotty had told it in his story, Pamela had done all of it with cold, calculating, and almost diabolical intent.

The ray of hope that ran through the novella was a through-line centered on a character that could have only been Leeanne.

By the end of the story, however, Pamela's character returned and inserted herself back into her broken family, which made her, ironically, a homewrecker, since her return drove Leeanne's character away.

It felt like a premonition, as though Scotty de Barra, by some intuitive fear, had predicted within the fiction of his short book what could have very well resulted upon his real-life mother's return.

Had it?

And could that threat have turned into murder?

Pamela hadn't come out to talk to me in the snow earlier today, but she had been watching from the window.

I wanted to know what had really happened when she had come back to Liberty.

So, I made the public library my next stop.

Pamela de Barra was a tough woman who, prior to her disappearance, had been known around town as a petty gambler capable of drinking just about any man under the table. It had been something of a party trick and had earned her a little extra cash come tourist season when out-of-towners would place bets against her, figuring that pint-sized-Pam would have to be a lightweight. She cleaned up pretty good, didn't spend too many nights in the drunk tank as far as I could recall, and had never failed to get to the farm she managed, on-time and ready to work the next day, no matter how much hard liquor she had shot down her gullet the night before.

Thinking back, it was impossible to reconcile that Pamela was Scotty's mother, though she seemed to make a degree of sense as Ron's wife.

Pamela was loose and sloppy, brassy and loud-mouthed, more than a little rough around the edges, and yet her son had grown into an All-American type, a football champ and sports hero, clean-cut and wholesome. But then again, I supposed his 'wholesome' image hadn't turned out to be exactly true, all things considered.

I still didn't know where she'd taken off to all those years ago or how she had spent her freedom. All I knew was that upon her return to Liberty, she had gotten a job as a librarian at the local library on Main Street, which was where I found her after I parked my truck in the slushy lot and waddled my way inside.

But when I reached the front desk where she was scanning returned books into the computer system, I was met with an attitude that I should've seen coming.

"Not talking to you."

"I think you ought to reconsider," I suggested. She wouldn't even look at me. "I know Ron was seeing Leeanne for a time." I leaned in and kept my tone low and amicable as I added, "I know about Leeanne and Scotty. That must have been a lot to discover when you came back."

"You're one to talk," she sneered, meeting my gaze but I could tell it disgusted her to do so. "Isn't your husband the dead lady's boss? All that crap happened right under his nose, and under yours." She lifted her eyebrows to her frizzy hairline, letting me have it. "As far as I'm concerned, you're all a bunch of baby rapers, looking the other way when my son is being molested by some so-called teacher. Why would you care about that, when you can go on acting like the only crimes happening in Liberty are pot smoking and shoplifting!"

"I'm investigating a murder," I reminded her, "and if I'd had even the slightest whiff that Leeanne was behaving inappropriately towards a student, I would've investigated it, as well."

"Yeah, right," she grunted, entirely unconvinced.

"Do you know who killed Leeanne?" I pushed.

I didn't expect a confession, but I trusted that instincts would serve me as I gauged her reaction.

Pamela looked me square in the eye and said, "Do *I* know who killed Leeanne? *You* did…"

My heart lodged in my throat until she added:

"…for all I know."

She tried to turn away, but I asserted, "We aren't done here."

"You want to hear about what went down when I came home and found that tart in my bed?"

"I would, yes."

She snickered and asked, "How much time do you have?"

LEEANNE HESSINGER

Wednesday, August 29, 2017

SCOTTY HAD BEEN CLOSED off and withdrawn for weeks. Brooding. He hadn't met me for bike rides or spent the afternoons away with me at my rented house.

I was once again in-between seasons at Bethel Woods, embarking on another fifteen days to myself, but I wouldn't spend them wrapped around Scotty. He knew. He had found out.

I couldn't say why I had slept with Ron except that it had been out of necessity rather than interest. If I hadn't, then I would have begun to feel terrible about stringing him along. I would've had to face the fact that I had been using him. Ron had kept food in my belly and gas in my car—when it was actually running. He had given me a key and the chance to sit on a couch, and also full access to his son, though he remained innocently in the dark about that. He was kind and generous within his means, and the truth of the matter was that he was a good man and I liked him.

Sleeping with him had been awkward then boring, but my years with Ian had trained me to lie still and make noises when the time came. Scotty had crossed my mind several times during the act, and I was painfully aware, while Ron had moved over me in the bleak darkness, that he was in the midst of driving home from Lake Placid, somewhere on the interstate, due at the house in an hour or so.

Maybe it had been wrong to let Ron have sex with me. It had felt wrong, or like a strange, adult compromise I had made with myself. Maybe I should have broken up with Ron instead of going to bed with him, but I had been functioning with the counterintuitive sense that continuing to see him was the only thing keeping Scotty in check. It forced Scotty to maintain the secret and prevented him from shouting from the rooftops how he felt about me and all that we were in the habit of doing together in the privacy of my rented house.

Looking back, it wasn't lost on me why my sleeping with his father had crushed him.

I expected Scotty to confront me and when that didn't happen, I feared he would retaliate. Destroy me in some unrepairable way. Tell Carol or Mitch about our affair. Get me fired or thrown in jail. Perhaps detail some horrifying story to his father about coercion and rape. But I suppose what he ended up doing was far worse.

He found his mother.

One day he was as sullen as he had been for weeks and the next day Pamela de Barra was back in town.

Just like that.

I didn't know how he had tracked her down or what he had said to convince her to return, or why she had come easily and willingly, but she did.

Ron and I were cozying up on the couch, passing a pint of ice cream back and forth as reruns of a mindless comedy program had played on TV.

Ron had been laughing, not at the jokes, but a split second after every corny laugh track kicked up, in a kind of Pavlovian response he had been trained into over the years.

All humor clipped out of him, however, when Pamela entered the house with Scotty following in.

"Look who I found," Scotty said casually without looking at me.

Ron lurched, bolt-upright, in slack-jawed disbelief.

The melty pint of ice cream we had been working on slipped from his loose fingers.

I picked it up, as the sturdy, windblown-looking woman planted her fist on her hip and glanced around.

"Well?" she asked Ron. "You're not gonna say nothin' to me?"

Befuddled, he stood and couldn't seem to figure out how to hug her, as Scotty plopped down on the couch, cut his eyes at me, and, pointing to his mother, said, "They're going to want to talk. Bye, Hessinger."

TO SCOTTY'S CREDIT, it was a brilliant plan.

Ron and Pamela got back together.

I had no way of knowing how those conversations went or the arguments it must have taken to reconcile and pull their estranged relationship into one that resembled a marriage, but they did it.

Ron didn't have to break up with me or even explain himself. When I left their house that night, I never spoke with him again, and I only occasionally saw him around town.

Having driven me away from his father, Scotty had me right where he wanted me. But he had overlooked one critical factor. Pamela was a bloodhound when it came to sniffing out precisely what her son was up to when he wasn't at home.

When he resumed his habit of swooping in on my bike rides, Pamela found ways to keep tabs on him, pumping gas at 52 Pickup along our route or watching deer graze from the side of the road in time to spy us bicycling by.

When he snuck off and met me at my rented house, Scotty and I having navigated our own reconciliation, his mother became keen to that as well, crawling along Old Loomis Road in her clunky sedan and squinting out at the house even though Scotty never parked in the driveway if he drove his Jeep over at all.

She grilled him at home, which he often complained to me about, she attended all of his practices and games, and even began driving him up to Lake Placid.

Hers was suspecting, obsessive, suffocating behavior, but Scotty had a sense of humor about it and, on the whole, didn't seem to mind.

I, on the other hand, felt strangled.

My paranoia was through the roof and this time it was completely justified. I couldn't laugh it off or find Pamela's relentless circling endearing like Scotty had.

Getting caught was inevitable so long as we kept this up, but he wouldn't take the situation seriously.

He refused to cool off, and I couldn't stop him from showing up at my rented house at all hours of the night.

He reminded me time and again that his seventeenth birthday was right around the corner, as if our relationship becoming suddenly legal would hold up in the court of his mother's suspicion.

I wasn't nearly as optimistic. If anything, it felt like I was living in a constant state of anxiety. I was jumpy. My stomach always felt sour. I feared for my job at Bethel Woods and for my reputation. I couldn't eat and could barely sleep.

And Pamela was getting bolder.

Her maternal stalking evolved into veiled confrontations.

She stopped by at Bethel Woods to chat about Scotty's classwork as if it hadn't been months since he had attended my workshop. She sidled me at ShopRite, commenting on the cooling weather and nearly giving me a heart attack. She once knocked on my door and asked to use the telephone, mentioning the tire she had popped up the road. I suspected she had slashed her own tire if it was even flat at all, as she used my phone, sniffing for Scotty's scent and glancing around for signs he had been there.

But all of that was nothing compared to what she did at Walnut Mountain Park when Trip and I had just crossed the field after our hike.

"I want you to stay away from my boy!" she warned me out of nowhere, as Trip took his turn at the water fountain near the restrooms after a pair of pudgy kids wiped their mouths and heaved breathlessly away.

Pamela was standing near the line of kids with her arms folded. Her frizzy hair was pitched on end, she was so pissed. Staring and glaring, she tapped her sneaker against the asphalt like I needed to hurry up and either admit it or deny it.

I couldn't believe this was happening with Trip looking on.

Was my secret life slamming into my professional one at the hand of an impulsive, mysterious woman who I had once identified with to the point of obsession?

"I don't know what you're talking about," I managed to squeeze out.

I had only incited her. "You like to play hanky-panky with all of your students?"

Trip screwed his face up, but directed his shock at me. "What is she talking about?"

"I'm talking about my son, Scotty," she informed him, sized him up a bit too just to make sure he wasn't cut from the same molesting cloth as me. She concluded her assessment with a grunt, narrowed her angry eyes at me, and threatened, "He's sixteen years old. You think I won't throw you in prison? He's a boy!"

Trip's entire expression loosened and he breathed, "Leeanne——?"

"Stay away from my son!" she barked. "Stay away from my husband. I know where you live and if I so much as suspect that you haven't backed the hell off, I will kill you!"

She stuck it to me, locking those fearless eyes of hers on me, drilled the point as deep into me as she could, as I quaked with panic.

I never thought she would kill me, but the danger I had been terrified of for months—getting caught and exposed and losing the life I had built—had just been orchestrated and put into motion by Pamela de Barra herself.

Now Trip knew.

I realized I had been holding my breath when she stomped off towards the parking area, leaving me to explain myself to my friend and colleague.

I exhaled unsteadily and felt an incredible weight crush my chest, as a wall of tension shot up between me and Trip.

I couldn't look at him and didn't know how to begin.

"Leeanne?"

Petrified, I said nothing.

"Did something happen between you and Scotty de Barra?" he asked.

"Please don't tell anyone." My voice was wind over reeds. "I can fix this."

"Christ, Leeanne."

Trip ran his hand down the entire length of his face and stared, wide-eyed and unseeingly, at the green field and colorful landscape.

"I'll break things off with—"

"I don't want to know," he bristled, cutting me off as the magnitude of it all crashed over him. He let out an exacerbated snort of laughter, sobered up so suddenly I thought he might vomit, then said, "I could have given you everything. I would have. I thought I was in love with you. It made no sense to me why we never started dating."

My composure was under siege. He wasn't disgusted by me. He was hurt and jealous of a teenage boy. But I didn't have a shred of audacity to defend myself or indulge his wallowing assessment.

"That's your problem, Leeanne. You don't want something real that might last. No one is ever going to get close to you, are they? You'll go after a child to avoid anything that might become real."

"It felt real," I breathed.

"Wake up, Leeanne. It's not. It's a secret. It's a fantasy, and it's going to cost you a lot."

Everything inside of me was screaming, on a cellular level, to beg him to keep this quiet. But I couldn't. I felt like I was a million miles away from opening my mouth.

All I could do was stare at him and wait for him to decide my fate.

"If I were you," he said, after a moment of repulsed consideration, "I would end it. Immediately. Make sure Scotty doesn't say a thing to anyone ever. Then deny, deny, deny as much as you can."

"Okay," I agreed.

"I mean it, Leeanne. What you've done is insane."

"I know," I breathed so quietly that I could barely hear my own voice.

"And I would avoid Scotty's mother at all costs," he added. "Don't approach her, and don't let her confront you again. She seems crazy enough to do something to you."

I watched as Trip started across the grassy field for the parking area.

I knew what I had to do and it felt like my body was tearing in half because of it.

✳

TRIP WAS RIGHT. I had enough of an outside perspective of myself to understand that what Scotty and I had wasn't real and would likely never be.

But at the same time, it felt perfect and the feelings he brought out in me were real. Our relationship might have been cocooned from the world, but everything inside of our bubble was as real to me as the air I breathed and the sun on my face.

I couldn't deny, however, that Scotty had also been a beautiful distraction.

Whenever I was with him, I felt suspended from financial stress, and the haunting mess that had become my marriage couldn't touch me. Ian hadn't come back, but I also hadn't divorced him. Life at Bethel Woods felt rote and stale by comparison, and though my fears about our secret relationship becoming exposed had become a new blade of stress to endure, I still welcomed my time with Scotty. I craved him and needed him, but now that Pamela had confronted me and Trip knew, I was able to see the affair for what it truly was and had always been.

Desperate. Delusional. And dangerous.

Scotty and I had no future. I wasn't going to move to Lake Placid with him if he ended up there.

He wasn't going to provide for me. We weren't going to start a family or a life together. The bottom line was that he wasn't a man, and for some reason I hadn't been able to see it until now.

Breaking things off with him felt like both a hard and easy choice, and I was dreading it, as dusk bled over what had been a sunny, summer day and the darkness of a very black night pressed in.

I waited in my kitchen, steeping Earl Grey and reminding myself to memorize every painful emotion I had coming to me. It was safe to imagine this would not be a smooth conversation, but every experience had the potential to live a second—honest and perhaps even purer—incarnation in my novel, which was starting to feel as unreal and distant from coming into actual existence as my romance with Scotty.

I couldn't for the life of me comprehend why I had been procrastinating so badly. I had blown two fifteen-day stretches in-between program seasons and was beginning to wonder if I was suffering from some kind of fear of accomplishment—or failure. Something had been holding me back and it wasn't because I hadn't invented a strong enough title.

It seemed every time I forced myself to sit down in front of my laptop with the aim of finally starting, my mind was torn in a hundred stressful directions and concentration was impossible. I had gotten so fed up with myself, in fact, that I had saved a Word document specifically entitled, 'The Novel That Needs No Name,' hoping the declaration would jumpstart a creative flow.

It hadn't.

Maybe ending things with Scotty would be a good thing. I would nurse the pain, allow the passage of time to turn my emotions into mulch that I could use to fertilize the mood of my novel. I would certainly have free time to myself again. No distractions. No excuses. Determining as much did little to console me, however.

I heard sneakers crunching faintly over gravel outside and opened the front door of my rented house in time for Scotty to slip inside.

Bare-chested in a pair of green jogging shorts, his sculpted physique was glistening with sweat, his hair was windblown and damp, his complexion glowing, as he took a lap around the kitchen and caught his breath.

I had intentionally worn long jeans and a bulky androgynous tee-shirt to keep covered up, but he saw right through the garments, settling a smoldering gaze over me and taking me by the hips.

I urged him back and slid away from the counter.

"We have to stop."

He grinned.

"Yeah, right."

As he angled in, I urged him back again.

"Your mother confronted me."

The smile slipped off of his face as he registered the severity of the situation.

"Trip was with me when she did this. He heard everything. Two people know about us," I sternly informed him then reiterated, "We have to stop. Completely. This can't happen anymore."

Disbelievingly, he tried to brush off what I was telling him. He reached for me, as his mouth tugged into a pleading grin. "You can't be serious."

"I am."

"Are you listening to yourself? Can't you hear your own voice? You think we have to stop, but you don't want to."

"What do you want me to do here, Scotty? Your mother threatened to go to the police! She threatened to kill me, for God's sake!"

"I'm literally two weeks from turning seventeen," he reminded me.

"That does me no good," I snapped. "You think that Carol Patterson or Mitch Kavleski are going to give a damn that you're of legal consenting age? No, they aren't. They're going to look at me like I'm some kind of predator—"

"I'll tell them you aren't."

"No, you won't. We aren't going to confirm any of this to anyone. We're going to end it and never speak of it again. If anyone asks you, especially your mother, you have to deny it."

Scotty was hurt like I've never seen another human being look.

His light eyes rounded, pained, and as he slumped, his broad shoulders slouching and chest sinking, I saw him as the naïve, innocent teenager that he was.

Oh, God, what had I done?

He reached for me and I didn't have the heart to ease him off.

"But I love you," he protested, depressed, his tone low and miserable, as he nuzzled his cheek into my hair.

"I'm sorry."

He stiffened in my arms, and when he released me, stepping back, brow furrowed, eyes glaring down at me, I knew he had just gotten a second wind, and I was in for a serious fight.

"You did this!" he pointed at me, seething. "You slept with my dad."

"Scotty—"

"That's why this is happening. You ruined everything!"

"Would you calm down?"

He was pacing, boiling over with emotion that both enraged and choked him. His voice was hard but cracking as though every blameful accusation was scalding his throat.

"Why did you do it, huh? Everything was fine! You didn't have to sleep with my dad! Do you think I would have dragged my mother into this if you hadn't? God, you're so messed up!"

"I know that!"

"How could you…?" he stammered, coming apart at the seams. "I love you!"

I thought he might punch a wall, or me, but he broke down in furious tears instead.

"What about after I graduate?" he implored.

I didn't have it in me to say a word.

But my silence was enough of a confirmation that there was no hope for us at any point later down the road.

Scotty sunk into what appeared to be a despairing delirium realizing that, and was very quiet as he said, "She *will* kill you. She has it in her. I won't say anything."

I wanted to rush to him and hold him and never let go, but all I did was stare at him, as he saw himself to the door.

When he looked back at me, I felt my heart shatter.

I didn't know it then, but I would never again look Scotty de Barra in the eye.

SHERIFF JUDY KAVLESKI

Monday, January 8, 2018

MY IMPRESSION OF Pamela de Barra wasn't good. She hadn't meant to reveal her controlling, stalking nature or paint herself as an obsessive, potentially murderous parent, but that was how I now viewed her based on her account.

Pint-sized-Pam was larger than life, her indignation and self-righteous rage having blown her up to gigantic proportions from where she stood across from me at the front counter of the library, her palms pressed to its surface so hard that the backs of her hands looked leathery and ropey with veins.

But I couldn't wrap my head around why a woman who had abandoned her family would care one way or the other about her son's sexual escapades.

I was honestly surprised that Pamela had followed Scotty around town closely enough to even find out about Leeanne and the affair. If she gave a damn about her son, why had she taken off one morning in the first place?

"I know what you're thinking," she said, fixing her distrusting eyes on me and sizing me up.

"I doubt that," I countered. "Why did you skip town back in 2011?"

She cocked a single brow, and the light behind her eyes darkened, as she asked, thoroughly skeptical, "That's what you want to know about?"

"I wouldn't have asked if I didn't."

For the first time since I entered the library, she didn't bark at me, as if her tone alone could convince me to believe whatever she was saying, if only she growled hard enough.

Instead, she stared off across the quiet library where middle schoolers were plopping their colorful backpacks down on tables and attentive parents were wrangling toddlers, picking up picture books almost as soon as their kids had flung them.

After a thoughtful beat that seemed to pull Pamela so deeply inward that she couldn't climb out, she confided, "I left in 2011 because I snapped."

I waited for more as she came back into herself.

"The mental breakdown was gentle. A quiet feeling, like there was all this space inside of me where I used to be. I think it was a revelation, like the kind of thing Oprah always talks about. You know what it was?"

I had no idea.

"My insides had been all crowded up with Ron and Scotty and the house and the farm, all this stuff that isn't me, isn't the *real* me. Like life had crushed me under it and I was trapped somewhere inside of myself. But then, one morning, it was all gone from inside of me. I don't know why, I just wasn't crowded or crushed anymore. I was pure *space*. Like glowing emptiness. And I just... *left*."

"You didn't think about your son, how it would affect him? What it would do to Ron?"

"I had lost myself," she explained. "I didn't exist." She glanced down at the ball of my huge, pregnant belly, and assured me, "Just you wait. You'll see."

After a breath, she added, "If you've felt lost for long enough, like life has swallowed you whole, and then one day all the crushing weight you've been under suddenly lifted, and you felt the kind of freeing space that I did, you would leave too. You'd start walking and wouldn't stop either."

"Why come back, then?"

She shrugged.

"I snapped out of it, then when I saw my son, I snapped back into it. I had no idea he would be doing so well. He's going to the Olympics, you know? When he sits down with Oprah on that fancy couch of hers years from now, I don't want him to tell the story of how his mother abandoned him."

A sheepish, almost embarrassed smile came over her.

"I want him to have good things to say about his life, and me. Besides, things are different now than how they were. I was doing way too much before. Now that Ron has been doing everything for years, it's like there isn't that pressure on me anymore. I can breathe. I can feel myself in here," she said, rubbing her chest.

"Leeanne did the same thing, you know. She ran away."

I hadn't meant for the comparison to be insulting, but that's how Pamela took it.

"You know what I *wasn't* doing over in Pennsylvania? Sleeping with underaged boys."

"That's not what I meant—"

"Look, Sheriff," she said, leveling with me. "I didn't kill Leeanne. I would've had no reason to. I told her to back off and she did. There would've been no point in killing her, because she listened."

"Great. Then you should have no problem giving me a DNA sample," I told her, pulling a kit from my purse.

"That's not going to happen."

"I have three suspects at this point and all three of them are de Barras. But that doesn't have to be the case. I could clear all of you. Easily. I just need your samples."

She refused to cooperate.

"Leave me and my family alone or I'll sue you and your department for harassment."

TWENTY MINUTES LATER, I was seated on Leeanne Hessinger's chair, having returned to Bethel Woods.

I had let myself into her office on the lower level without stopping in on my husband.

I still didn't know what to do about our fight, how to proceed or reconcile, and it was starting to dawn on me that marriages that got complicated often broke under the weight of a baby.

Pamela and Ron de Barra had been evidence of that, their marriage bending to the point of collapse by the time Scotty had turned ten.

Then there was Leeanne and Ian Hessinger, whose relationship echoed the same theme and had shattered after the unexpected loss of their unborn child.

I knew mine was the opposite dilemma.

Where Leeanne and Pamela had snapped under the strain of doing too much, I was faced with the downright laughable challenge of doing less in order to appease my disgruntled, emasculated husband.

It wasn't in my character, however, to sit back and not lift a finger, and quite frankly, I was still functioning in a state of numb shock having discovered that behaving that way was precisely what Mitch would like from me.

The office smelled faintly of lilacs and honey.

A thin film of dust had collected across the desk, in-between keyboard keys, along the lip of the computer screen, and over the framed photo resting beside it.

The faculty hadn't touched the room and by the looks of it, no one had been in here since Leeanne's murder.

Since the investigation began, I'm not sure I had ever imagined what it might have been like to be her. But sitting at her desk as I was and idly glancing around her office, I found myself wondering how she might have tackled wrestling with her secrets and demons, while keeping up appearances for people like Carol Patterson, Trip Turner, and the rest of the T.A.s and students.

It must have been an excruciating, exhilarating, maddening burden.

But her affair with Scotty and the fact that Pamela de Barra had found out couldn't have been what had gotten her killed.

That much I knew.

The de Barra's timeline in connection with the murder, like Ian's, was far too delayed.

The framed photo beside her desktop computer was of Leeanne all dolled up in a way I had never seen her look in person around the P.A.C. or in town.

As I studied it, smearing away dust, I determined she was wearing false eyelashes and lipstick. She wasn't so much smiling as smirking. The row of glowing neon slot machines behind her complimented the magenta sequined dress that clung to her frail figure.

It gave me pause.

I examined the ceramic mug next to it. 'Live Dangerously and Write About It' was branded in white letters across its black face. There were a handful of pens and pencils inside the mug, but when I looked deeper, I found a casino chip. I studied it closely then scrutinized the framed photo a bit more.

The purple casino chip was good for one hundred dollars should it ever be cashed in.

Resorts World Catskills.

Leaning back on Leeanne's chair, I asked myself, had Leeanne Hessinger hidden a whole other secret that centered on the new casino in Monticello?

And if so, would I be able to handle the truth?

MITCH KAVLESKI

Friday, September 15, 2017

THE MORNING I SAW a bear lumbering through the backyard of the estate I shared with my wife, I knew my life was about to change. Irreversibly.

The black bear—pure muscle and slack-jawed, backlit by the orange blaze of dawn—was a sight I had never seen from home, if that was what this place was anymore. I couldn't tell. It hadn't felt like home for a good long while, but rather like a prison, one which my very own vows had trapped me within, quite unlike the bear who was traipsing through unencumbered…

…and free.

From the grand deck, with a mug of coffee in hand, I watched it, mesmerized, as dew sparkled across the grassy landscape and crisp, autumn breezes rustled my pajamas.

I imagined the bear was male, a loner, hungry, and driven as I had once been. How had I arrived at the sense I was lost after a lifetime of ambition had compelled me to accomplish so much for this town and county? But that was what I had become, unmotivated and uninspired, a king who had conquered the world and had nothing left to do but die.

I didn't recognize myself anymore. Not the face staring back at me in the mirror. Not even my own thoughts, which had become predictable if not depressing. Every day felt the same, a rote routine I barely cared for. My responses were canned, it didn't matter who asked what. My duties had become so well-practiced that I performed them effortlessly on autopilot. I was practically sleepwalking through a life that felt more like a waking nightmare than a dream. Joyless at best, but more often than not just plain miserable in its unsurprising tediousness.

I had politicians in my pockets, but it no longer excited me. Mine was the final say with the planning commission, but it rarely mattered. My own private kingdom at Bethel Woods felt meaningless. All of Sullivan County respected and revered me, but the woman who I had married didn't…

…and there I stood in the quiet wake of dawn, envying a black bear who reminded me of the man I had once felt like and hoping that my wife wouldn't wake up and find me on the deck of our magnificent house.

I had been trying to make my unborn son my everything, but it didn't feel like enough. He, too, was trapped within the prison of my wife.

If I didn't recognize myself, my perception of Judy was even worse.

The doe-eyed woman with apple cheeks and an air of levity to her personality that I used to find uplifting; the one who had been humbled to work at the police station—*Larry still calls me Peanut but he's been giving me cases!'* The woman who had been demurely charmed to dine with me at the finest restaurants in town; the girl I had fallen in love with and proposed to and had promised to share a life with 'for better or worse' had been replaced by a glowering faultfinder who had abandoned her sense of grace in favor of pointing out my mistakes, no matter how insignificant.

I had backed the mayoral campaigns to the tune of three consecutive reelections, but those victories didn't outweigh my apparently imbecilic attempts at layering wood, kindling, and crumpled newspaper in the fireplace.

I had implemented grant funded after school programs throughout the county that served at-risk kids, keeping them off the streets and helping them graduate high school, but all of that was forgotten the second I loaded the dishwasher incorrectly.

The night after I had filmed a segment for Channel 7 ABC Local News, an endeavor I had been pushing for nonstop for upwards of six months for the purposes of outreach, and one that had almost immediately resulted in an unexpected spike in private donations, Judy had offered a tight, acknowledging smile beside me in bed, then she immediately mentioned the icy walkway and how I hadn't laid down enough salt, as she had angrily rubbed lotion onto her ashy arms. What if the mailman slipped and broke his neck? We would be sued. Hadn't that occurred to me?

In fairness to my wife, she wasn't cruel or heavy-handed with her incessant complaints that may have been pouring out of her unconsciously.

In fact, I honestly doubted she was being deliberate or intentional with those mild, ill-timed criticisms of hers, but the effect was like water trickling over stone.

Throughout the years, she had worn me down into a brittle version of myself that now felt on the brink of cracking.

I knew that was what the bear in our backyard represented, an omen of the fault line inside of me, the inevitable splitting to come.

But I didn't know that Leeanne Hessinger would be the catalyst to cause the crack until I found myself knocking on her closed office door at Bethel Woods later that morning.

I couldn't say what had compelled me to veer down to the lower level of the P.A.C. instead of heading straight for the elevator that would have brought me upstairs to my office, only that the fog I had been joylessly functioning within had cleared and I had become, by some animalistic magic, like the black bear I had observed that morning—hungry and driven.

She called out, "Come in," and I entered to find a friendly, casual smile greeting me that I soon realized was meant for someone else.

"Oh! I thought you were Trip! Good morning!"

Instantly nervous, Leeanne stiffened on her chair and seemed to shrink, those dark eyes of hers staring wide as I eased in, closed the door behind me, and breezed right up to her desk.

"How's the novel coming along?"

In that moment, she looked as bright and vulnerable and intrigued as Judy once had the night I had sat across from her on our very first date.

After some breathy stammering, she said, "I admit, I might be researching it to death."

"You haven't started?"

"The story feels too precious to begin," she waffled, but recovered with a delicate smile—that wide, dramatic mouth of hers pressing sheepishly in such a way that told me she wasn't about to elaborate.

"Perhaps I could lend an ear?" I offered, as I picked up and eyed the framed photo on her desk.

"That's an old high school friend of mine, Theresa," she blurted when I couldn't make sense of why she hadn't removed the black and white stock photography image that the frame had come with and replaced it with a personal picture. "When I came across it in Walmart, I couldn't resist."

It sounded like a lie.

She took the frame and returned it to her desk with care.

"If you'd like to discuss all the research you've been doing—"

"I would!"

A thrill unlike anything I had ever felt swelled in my chest, but I tempered my excitement, straightened the grin that was threatening to curl the sides of my mouth, and mentioned:

"Are you familiar with the new casino in Monticello? Meet me at Bar 360, let's say 10pm?"

"Yes! Okay, yes, definitely!"

"Good," I said, turning for the door.

As I made my way up the stairs, heading towards my office, I questioned whether or not I was losing my mind.

Maybe I was, but a man couldn't argue with hunger, and I had been starving for years.

❄

RESORTS WORLD CATSKILLS clashed with the mountain views and rolling landscape, but I wouldn't go so far as to describe it as an eyesore.

I had been privy to its development and had even voted for its location when the head of the planning commission proposed that the massive, steel structure be situated at the end of a brand-new five-mile road paved specifically for the casino to hide it from town and anyone who might be offended by the prospect of having gaming in their otherwise serene neck of the woods.

Unless a resident chose to travel along Resorts World Drive, that individual could easily forget the casino even existed. Though few had, since the job opportunities were abundant and a considerable chunk of the unemployed population in Monticello and the surrounding towns had quickly garnered work there.

The casino and its corresponding hotel had also boosted the economy and would continue to do so as tourists with a penchant for Black Jack and Craps were expected to drift in from all over year-round.

Naturally, the spouses and children of gambling addicts had protested, but their voices were drowned out when a portion of the gaming advertising budget focused on gambling Twelve Step programs where they could deposit their struggling loved ones so that they wouldn't dart off, crazed and jacked-up at the prospect of winning big on the casino floor.

In three days time, the politically active portion of Monticello would, with any luck, file into the local high school gymnasium to vote in favor of the athletic field drainage project, an effort I had been working towards all year which would require approximately $250,000 of the district's capital reserve fund with no additional impact to the taxpayers.

This was my reason for being at the casino, to attend an awareness event, which smartly offered an open bar to all who came; and to support Gordon Jenkins, the Mayor I had helped get reelected, though recently I had been dissatisfied with the controversies that had been blooming all around him.

A man's secrets should remain precisely that—hidden and unjudged.

I was a born schmoozer. I had discovered long ago that it didn't take much so long as I wore an impressive suit, seldom smiled, and asked good-natured questions to whomever I was engaging with, while gently nudging the person in the direction I intended them to vote. If I could treat them like an old friend, and also like royalty, it wasn't too difficult to earn their trust. Then I would move onto the next cluster of wary residents and warm them over with the same method.

But tonight, I wasn't feeling it. My spiel felt clumsy and badly rehearsed. I couldn't get into the flow, and working the room had fast become a chore I didn't care for, not that Jenkins noticed. He often raised his glass at me from across the room in praise of what must have appeared to him to be a successful event.

Perhaps it was, but I didn't feel especially invested.

If I was focused on anything, it was the hour, which had been slowly crawling towards 10pm. I checked my wristwatch and was pleased to realize that Leeanne would filter into the casino at any minute.

Excusing myself from the dull conversation I had initiated, I weaved my way through the crowded gaming floor and found a vacant table in the lounge of the 360 Bar that was tucked in the back.

I tried not to think about the bristling quarrel I had survived with my wife earlier that day during lunch. If I was being honest with myself, the argument that had set her off this time was exceedingly stupid. It seemed our spats these days tended to revolve around the same grievance—my persistent coddling, which I refused to give up.

Judy was over six months along. I had respected her wishes and had held my tongue throughout her first and second trimesters, but this was getting ridiculous. She had been in denial about her limitations long enough. There were some things that pregnant women shouldn't do, and when I took issue with the sashimi lunch she had brought to Bethel Woods for us, for example, I freely spoke my mind, knowing full well it would incite a terrible argument.

At least I had gotten rid of her horrible cat.

Why she couldn't accept that the health of our unborn son was more important than her own health had consistently been lost on me, but she really didn't appreciate it when I had confiscated her raw fish and had dumped it in the trash receptacle outside of my office.

By comparison, I foresaw Leeanne would be a much-needed breath of fresh air.

Maybe I wouldn't smooth this one over with Judy. Or maybe—and this was my highest hope—I would so thoroughly enjoy my time with Leeanne that apologizing to my wife would be the easiest thing in the world.

I saw a flash of yellow through the crowd and recognized Leeanne in the dress she had worn last spring at the final project presentations in the theater of the P.A.C.

From the lounge where I had been waiting, I watched her approach.

She struck me as timid and out of her element. As soon as I got her attention with a wave, she let out a breathy smile and politely cut through the casino floor in a way I instantly found endearing.

"You made it."

Standing, I shook her limp, cool hand, and as soon as we sat across from one another, a cocktail waitress swooped in with exceptional timing as they often did for me.

"Can I interest you in a drink?"

"Yes," she replied with enhanced enunciation. She told the waitress, "Pinot grigio," then offered me a pinched, nervous smile.

It looked like she was holding herself together. She immediately began fiddling with the hem of her yellow dress.

"A scotch for me, on the rocks." When the waitress left us, I asked, "Have you been here before?"

"I have not."

I sensed warming her would be like coaxing a fox out of its hole. The wine should loosen her up, and I hoped our drinks would arrive without further ado.

"I can't thank you enough for your help with all of those grants." The compliment earned me a genuine smile from Leeanne, but not a response. "I'm tempted to broaden your duties at Bethel Woods so that I can benefit from your obvious grant writing skills, but I wouldn't want you to have less time and energy for your own writing."

She was a deer in headlights—a stunned, beautiful doe—so I kept talking.

"We're lucky to have you. I had been meaning to include a creative writing course in our afterschool programs, but we couldn't seem to interest any of our preexisting T.A.s. When your proposal reached my desk, it was a no-brainer."

"*You* hired me? Thank you!"

I chuckled as our drinks arrived and tried to sound modest as I mentioned, "I have the final and sometimes first say when it comes to hiring."

Leeanne scooped her wine glass with both hands and nervously gulped it down, then a look of horror came over her, realizing she had drained her glass.

I would've preferred to sip and savor my single-malt, but I shot it back like a college frat boy so that she wouldn't die of embarrassment.

"Excuse me!" I called out and our cocktail waitress circled back. "Another round?"

The girl took the empty glasses and promptly started off through the bar-restaurant.

I shrugged as if in cahoots with Leeanne and offered:

"I needed that. It's been a long day."

"Me too, I guess."

"This function," I began explaining with an air of confidentiality as I leaned in, "has been uncharacteristically boring."

She leaned in as well, but then eased back on her leather chair, nodding and smiling and perhaps hunting for a witty response that seemed to be eluding her.

"Tell me about this novel you've been working on," I prompted.

As she delved into giving me the broad strokes of the storyline she had developed, I didn't even notice our waitress placing our drinks on the table until Leeanne took the stem of her glass between her slender fingers.

This time, she was reserved and tempered with each small sip she took, as she went into further detail about the characters and conflicts she hoped to weave into a gripping book. The plotline she had crafted both excited and stumped her. She highlighted some sticking points, at times lighting up. At others, her brow furrowed with thoughtful consideration when she questioned the believability of certain plot points.

She warmed to me, loosening up, and I found her creative ideas, and also her expressive mannerisms, captivating.

When it seemed she had shared as much as there was to share, I said, "I like the title."

The light behind her dark eyes brightened and she beamed a huge smile. "You do?"

"<u>Dusk on the Heart</u> has a nice ring to it."

She groaned with relief and confided, "I can't tell you how great it is to hear you say that! Finding the right title has been excruciating!"

"Well, I think you've found it."

"Good," she determined, as she sank into deep thought as if expecting some kind of literary revelation to emerge. I couldn't tell if one had touched her brain or not, but after a moment she sighed and mentioned, "I'm not good at dividing my daily life between working and writing. I thought I could tackle the novel on the weekends, but it hasn't happened."

"You're not married," I pointed out, and she grew tense. "No distractions at home."

"Right," she breathed, softening from whatever had just come over her.

"No kids," I went on.

"No kids," she confirmed. "I always seem to be battling some form of distracting stress, however." She made a strange, cringing sound and rolled her eyes. "It's my car."

"Your car is preventing you from writing?"

A mile-long stare swept over her and she squinted, unseeingly, into her glass of white wine, then allowed, "In a manner of speaking, yes. It's always something with that damn car."

I figured she was referring to financial stress. "Have you considered applying for a grant yourself? You could certainly take a season off from Bethel Woods if you were awarded one."

"That's not a bad idea," she agreed as she took a thoughtful sip of wine. "But grants take time. Even if I submitted one tomorrow, I wouldn't hear back for half a year at least."

"Don't I know it," I commiserated. "It's impossible to focus on even the simplest tasks when you feel crushed by financial burdens."

A skeptical look spread across her face.

Qualifying my statement, I assured her, "I'm no stranger to ramen noodles, though I admit it's been awhile."

"I find that hard to believe," she teased.

"That sounds like a compliment. I'll take it."

I grinned and polished off my scotch.

Our eyes locked. The conversation lulled. And some daring beast inside of me took over.

Maybe it was the scotch, or her dress, or the possibility that the rising tension between us in that moment felt distinctly sexual, but something inside of me—something hungry and driven—compelled me to take two, crisp one-hundred dollar bills out of my wallet.

At first, Leeanne glanced away as ladies often do in the presence of a gentleman handling the check, but that wasn't what I was doing, and she understood this the moment I placed the cash on her side of the table.

She stopped breathing and stared at it.

"If financial hardships are the only thing holding you back…"

Her wide eyes snapped up and met mine. She looked thrilled and terrified and poised on the edge of her seat.

"I can be very philanthropic," I told her.

Her lips parted ever so slightly, but her jaw didn't fully drop until I rose from the table and mentioned:

"I'll be in Room 516."

I left her and felt darkly powerful as I made my way through the casino floor.

This was what it meant to be alive, and I was zinging with anticipation that Leeanne Hessinger might be brave enough to join me upstairs.

ROOM 516 OF the casino's hotel had been the hub where select members of the mayor's council, school board, along with Gordon Jenkins, myself, and a host of administrators had organized and executed the event, using the room as an office all evening prior to the start of the function.

It was hardly your run-of-the-mill hotel room, but rather an executive suite replete with a lounge space, tables and desks, a full bar, and sizable bedroom beyond a marble bathroom that boasted a jacuzzi and bidet along with the basic features one might expect.

But as I entered the suite, it hardly felt the same as it had earlier in the night.

The stacks of pamphlets and flyers that had covered every inch of the countertops were no longer there. The poster boards had all been removed, and housekeeping had returned the space to a pristine condition, cleaning away the takeout containers and smattering of plastic cups that had once littered the desks.

It wasn't an oversight that I hadn't returned my keycard to the front desk earlier, but in all fairness, I had expected I might use the room to unwind alone and fortify the strength it would take to drive home to my overbearing wife.

I had never cheated on Judy before. The idea had never so much as crossed my mind. If and when a knock came on the door, I knew I would be embarking into uncharted territory. To say that I was anxious would be the understatement of the century. I felt downright petrified...

...and also revitalized.

I imagined this could possibly be what snorting cocaine was like.

Livened with razor-sharp alertness, I was bursting with excitement and pacing the carpeted room like a man who had just fled the scene of a crime.

Only the slightest pinch of guilt stabbed my stomach——sleeping with another woman was a low thing to do, but I hadn't yet committed adultery and there was a chance I wouldn't.

I rounded to the business side of the bar and fixed myself a stiff drink to calm my frayed nerves.

I managed to get half of it down when the knock I had been anticipating finally came.

Had I hallucinated it?

I froze, listening out until I heard the soft rapping of another knock.

We might simply talk, I reasoned. Continue the conversation in this more intimate setting. But who was I kidding? If I found Leeanne on the other side of that door—and I surely would, housekeeping had already tended to the suite—her arrival would imply sexual interest if not consent.

Setting my drink down on the bar top, I started for the door, knowing that once I opened it there would be no turning back.

And there wasn't.

Leeanne said nothing as she stared cautiously up at me, nor did I say anything when she stepped inside.

I glanced up and down the corridor, checking for any witnesses or prying eyes, because I figured that's what smart adulterers did, but there were none.

After closing and locking the door, I watched Leeanne wade shyly into the suite.

I didn't advance on her or set rules, which I supposed was what married men first did with their mistresses to ensure their home life wouldn't become collateral damage in their blind quest to feel alive and valued.

Rather, I eased towards the couch, keenly observing her from behind, as she touched the thick curtains hanging in front of the windows and then slowly pulled them aside, peeking out at the darkened landscape.

"I don't know what I'm doing here," she confessed without looking at me.

"Neither do I."

Finally, she glanced over her shoulder at me and didn't look away as I produced another $200 cash from my wallet and set it down on the coffee table between us so that there would be no mistaking my expectations or the boundary that this wouldn't be a romantic courtship. It would have to be an even exchange, one which benefited both of us equally, but in very different ways.

I wasn't thinking about the myriad consequences that could befall me. The fact that we worked at the same organization didn't cross my mind, and Leeanne couldn't have been concerned either.

She slipped one strap over her shoulder then the next.

The yellow dress fluttered down the lines and curves of her body until it pooled around her high-heeled feet on the carpeted floor.

What transpired next was savage and possibly depraved, but it felt extraordinary. We were primal. I was rough, Leeanne submissive, as I tore into her on the couch then the bed in raw fits of unbridled lust.

I never thought myself capable of paying for sex, but quickly realized it was better.

I did whatever I wanted to her without asking for permission, and she moaned and panted and took all of it until I had nothing left to give even if she would have been able to handle more.

She looked sore and spent by the time I was done with her.

I should've felt dirty or remorseful afterwards, but I didn't.

I showered, dressed, and tossed another hundred-dollar bill on her nude stomach as she lay on the bed, dazed and grinning eerily at all the cash I had given her.

The only thing I said to her before leaving was, "There's more where that came from."

And there would be.

WHEN I GOT HOME later that night, I found Judy upstairs in the baby's room. She was sanding down the hard patches of putty I had spread over seams in the drywall.

The baby's room was an ongoing project, one that I obviously hadn't completed fast enough.

She wasn't wearing a dust mask, only work gloves and a handkerchief that held her brown hair off of her face, but this time I didn't correct the hazard she was selfishly inflicting against our unborn son.

I was too satisfied and relaxed to be bothered.

Judy on the other hand, was not.

She urged me back, annoyed when I tried to take her in my arms and kiss her deeply, my appetite for Leeanne having bled into my marriage.

"What's gotten into you?" she asked, but I had already redirected my affection towards her round belly to greet my son.

"The function went well."

"I'm glad," she allowed, the rough seam of the wall distracting her. "I'm worried the room won't be ready in time."

"We have three months."

"At the rate you're going, we would need a year," she complained with an air of humor I didn't find especially funny.

I moved in for another kiss, but she turned away and selected a sheet of sandpaper with a smoother grain, rejecting me.

For the first time ever, I didn't mind.

LEEANNE HESSINGER

Tuesday, September 26, 2017

FIVE HUNDRED. CASH. Two hundred in the bar, another two hundred in the suite room before the act, and one hundred after. It was more money than I made at Bethel Woods in a week. Actually, I had done the math, and it was as much as I earned every eighth business day at the P.A.C. after taxes.

For the past ten days, I had been grappling with what felt like violently mixed emotions, my heart and head at war, my morals and sense of decency under the siege of an answer I had been persistently searching for all year—how to stay afloat, how to rise so far above financial strains that I would be able to calm down and write, how to make my life work in the exact way I had imagined when I had twirled in the snowfall at Walnut Mountain Park and felt limitless, unstoppable, and blessed.

But the answer that had presented itself in the form of Mitch Kavleski was ugly. Or perhaps I was for having blindly accepted his cash and for having floated, with eyes wide shut, into the hypnotizing spell he had effortlessly cast over me.

Mitch struck me as the type of man who would know what to do with a body, should he discover he had accidentally killed a hooker. He probably had people for that. He was untouchable, and I—desperate and bird-brained—had been easy prey.

That's how I felt—weak and simple and easily manipulated.

I could see myself objectively, and the outside perspective wasn't good.

I didn't feel victimized, however. I felt uniquely empowered, but that was the crux of the internal conflict that had been raging in my chest since our encounter.

Having received so much money for an act so straightforward was darkly liberating. I had gotten a taste of what the most important man in Sullivan County had to offer.

I knew I was already addicted, but what did that make me?

Complicating matters, or possibly tipping the scales, was my attraction to Mitch. He was devilishly handsome, exuded confidence, and had hinted at changing my life. I had felt intimidated by him all year, but also drawn to him, curious about him, magnetized at times. He had the power to destroy me. He could fire me at any time if he wanted to forget the line we had crossed at the casino. And yet, despite all of this or maybe because of it, I was dying to see him again.

For reasons I had failed to figure out, he had chosen me. He had ravaged me. He had ignited in me a carnal craving I had never known was lurking on the dark side of my psyche, one which my time with Scotty de Barra hadn't stirred.

In fact, by comparison, what I had done with my student now seemed strangely innocent, like a dirty dream, hazy and far away and beyond my responsibility, though the reality of it had been thorny and torturous, undoubtedly my biggest mistake.

With Mitch, there hadn't been an exchange of emotions. I didn't fear or even sense he would love me. He would never come to the door of my rented house or sneak in through the window to be with me. He had the means to make my life easier, the means to provide me with the kind of time and space I needed to write my novel. There was so much potential there, potential that hadn't existed with any other person I had ever been with.

I knew Mitch was married, his wife was pregnant, but the pangs of guilt I felt seemed reasonable, very adult, and manageable.

Did that make me a horrible person?

Whether it did or didn't, one thing was painfully clear.

The money was already gone.

I had filled my cabinets with food, the refrigerator as well. I had stopped at Walgreens and picked out eye shadow, a shade of lipstick I thought I could get away with, blush and mascara and even liquid eyeliner that I was fairly certain I would make a mess of. I had even made the long drive down to the mall in Middletown where I bought skirts, blouses, and dresses, all with Mitch in mind.

After loading up my sedan with my new wardrobe in the parking lot of the Crystal Run Galleria, feeling giddy and fantasizing about the stolen glances Mitch might slide my way around the P.A.C., I had been met with an awful grinding sound when I had turned the key in the ignition that quickly sputtered out into an alarming whine. For a flickering moment, I saw myself rotting to death in the driver's seat, that was how stubborn I was about calling my mechanic.

The forty-mile tow ate up half of my Mitch money, and the estimate at Sam's Auto Body Shop had nearly given me a heart attack.

With my car stuck at the repair shop, Trip started giving me rides and was both complementary and skeptical about my improved appearance.

Avoiding conflict was my top concern. It hadn't been easy redeeming myself in Trip's eyes after the Pamela debacle at Walnut Mountain, but I had gradually succeeded.

I also knew what he was thinking, that I was dolling myself up for Scotty, and though I was careful to never address his assumption outright—I couldn't bear to be sucked into a direct conversation about the student I had lost my mind with—I responded in guarded ways meant to assertively dispel his curiosity.

"I'm just *saying*, you look nice," he told me as we pulled into the parking area at Bethel Woods one morning. "No need to get all prickly about it."

"I'm not getting prickly."

"You seem prickly," he maintained as we climbed out and walked through a flutter of falling leaves towards the entrance.

I shot him a warning smile that he was all too familiar with, and he threw his hands up in mock surrender then caught the door as I trailed into the lobby.

"Lila's back in the city," he mentioned, jogging to catch up with me. "The breakup was implied."

"Are you doing okay?"

"These things never last beyond the final performance," he shrugged, but I could tell he was glum about it. "How about a beer at McCabe's after work? It's been awhile."

He tried tempting me with his signature, boyish grin, as we reached the corridor of the lower level, but I wasn't a 'beer' type of girl anymore.

In a single hour, Mitch had transformed me into a stilettos and martinis type of woman, not that either had made an appearance in that hotel room.

"I wish I could. I have plans," I lied.

"Is that why you're all dressed up? I like the skirt, by the way."

I opened my office door and angled another warning smile up at him, but instead of turning for his own office, he leaned on the doorframe and caught my arm.

"Why don't you let me take you out?" he suggested. I wasn't sure how to respond, and Trip must have taken my silence to mean he ought to thrust a little clarity into his insinuation, because he quietly said, "I think we should go on a date."

"Do you?" I questioned.

"Why not?"

"I'm not going to be your rebound girl," I teased.

But my humor was lost on him.

"I would never make you a rebound girl. If anything, Lila was a distraction girl."

"I'm sure she would appreciate that," I deflected, hoping he would drop his year-long effort that had only strained our friendship. "I have a lot of work to do."

As I slowly shut the door, nudging him out, he told me, "You look really pretty."

"Bye, Trip."

Leaning against the door, I sighed and hoped I could turn my lie into the truth by the end of the day.

❄

"COME IN!" MITCH called out, his deep voice quickly falling into a murmur.

He was in the throes of a telephone conversation as I slipped inside of his office on the top floor of the P.A.C., one which I had never had occasion to venture up to. I had felt like I was trespassing and had used brisk, careful movements to cross the corporate level, listening out for and dodging employees who might sniff out my scandalous motive.

Mitch froze behind his desk, mid-sentence, and a rousing look came over him when he saw me, those light eyes of his traveling down the length of my body as though he was drinking in the sight.

His grin was subtle and my breath hitched in my throat, but I gently recovered, as he dove back into his phone call, wrapping up some important matter that demanded his input.

As I approached, certain that my feet weren't touching the ground, he returned his desk phone to its cradle and a thrill surged through me so terrifying and electric that I thought I might faint or black out.

Thankfully, I did neither, as I sat across from him and boldly dared to instigate a second rendezvous at the casino hotel.

"I can't stop thinking about you," I confessed.

"The feeling's mutual."

My spine tingled, and I couldn't feel my hands, but he saved me from having to fumble in terms of taking the lead.

"Same place, same time." He opened his wallet and as he thumbed through crisp bills, he added, "Same amount," and set five hundred dollars cash on the desk in front of me.

"Thank you," I breathed, taking the money, as a zing of wild arousal bloomed over a twinge of disgust. I hadn't expected it. The low feeling had caught me off guard, the sense that I was small and pathetic, but almost as soon as it had touched me, it was gone. As I rose from the chair, I said, "See you soon."

"Leeanne?"

I turned before opening the door.

"Don't come up here again."

Slammed with embarrassment, I apologized, but Mitch was already telling me:

"Wear something sexy. Something red."

The project of fulfilling his instructions was how I spent the early evening since I owned no lingerie, all the while I wrestled with both hope and fear that I was spiraling—perhaps downwardly so—into a twisted version of independence I might not be able to live with.

❆

I COSTED FIVE-HUNDRED dollars. That was the value of my sex. I had always wanted to be valued and I could have never anticipated this would be the form it would take.

Hard, cold cash.

I honestly couldn't say whether it pleased or revolted me, but it would get my car out of the shop.

I met Mitch in Room 516 at 10pm as we had arranged. I wore red, lacy lingerie under a black dress and heaps of makeup, which had garnered more than a few looks from guests and the front desk staff alike as I had walked swiftly through the grand hotel lobby, my high-heels clicking over polished marble.

Mitch was tender and sensual with me, nothing like the man who had roughly taken me ten days before, and to my surprise he gave me even more cash as well as a strong warning against breathing a word of this to anyone.

I left the suite with the clear impression that should anyone find out about us, especially his wife, I would probably be murdered, my bones found years later in some uncharted, Catskills wilderness.

The threat had landed hard.

It was a risk I was willing to take, however. I knew myself. I could keep secrets and could live a lie. I would do anything to ensure I would write, and Mitch's money felt like more than a promise. It was practically a guarantee.

As I crossed through the lobby on my way out, suddenly self-conscious about my mussed hair and smudged makeup, one of the hotel guests stepped in my path.

At first, I thought I might dance with the man in an awkward attempt to get around him, but soon realized he had intentionally stopped me.

"How much?" he whispered, assuming I was a prostitute.

Appalled, I stammered some breathy retort about him having the wrong idea. Then I fled the hotel as quickly as I could.

But as I stepped out into the chilly night, I felt eyes on me, turned, and was sickened to discover two members of the hotel staff pointing and staring at me as they whispered.

I knew then that getting myself killed was a very real possibility.

SHERIFF JUDY KAVLESKI

Tuesday, January 9, 2018

THE LAST TIME I had been to Resorts World Catskills was for its opening night gala. Mitch had invited me, even though as his wife it was implied that I would attend, and I had honestly enjoyed the event. This was before the pregnancy, before Mitch had turned into an elusive stranger in our house, before I had lost my figure and by temporary extension, my looks.

I remember the night like it was yesterday. I had worn a slinky, red dress at my husband's suggestion, even though I ordinarily avoided drawing attention to myself.

Mitch had escorted me around all evening. I had felt as sparkling as the bubbling champagne in my hand, as I had held my husband's arm. That night, Mitch had been proud to show me off.

I was hardly a trophy wife, but at the gala, he had made me feel like one, often whispering naughty suggestions in my ear he probably knew I would never go for, like texting him a photo of my panties from the ladies' room or sneaking off with him to one of the suites upstairs for a quickie.

All he had gotten out of me that night was a cell phone video he had taken of me gracefully descending the stairs in our home before we even left. He had watched the clip several times, grinning down at his phone as I had fetched our coats—'This one's for my deathbed,' he had told me, 'I'll die a happy man.'

Something had gone terribly wrong between us since we had gotten pregnant, but I was having a hard time accepting that Mitch's complaints were the reason.

Conducting myself competently, paying bills on time, and boorishly—according to my husband—asserting how he ought to park his car in the garage didn't feel like enough of an answer to address the question of why he had been aloof for months or why he had reached a boiling point with me in his office earlier that day.

I wouldn't have thought my intelligent, socially responsible husband—a man who not only recognized the importance of gender equality but actively advocated for closing the pay gap and shattering the glass ceiling—would be capable of pulling away just because I had gradually expanded from a size 4 into a shape that even Lane Bryant couldn't accommodate, but that's what I was beginning to suspect.

My arms felt like sausages. I had lost all definition in my face, which I didn't bother dolling up anymore, and I had taken to waddling around like a stuffed penguin.

If my faltering appearance had literally repelled him, well, then, how Neanderthal of Mitch, I thought as I slid carefully out of my pickup truck into the slushy parking lot and started for the casino, as thin snowfall fluttered down, twirling all around me in the blustery darkness of night.

It seemed an odd twist indeed that Leeanne had gone from engaging in an illicit affair with her most athletically gifted student to frequenting a casino, but that's where the story of her mysterious life had taken me, so here I was, waddling onward—as I had no choice but to do—towards the sleek entrance of Resorts World Catskills.

I paused just shy of the sliding glass doors however when I felt my cell phone vibrating in my winter coat, and spied droves of reporters clustered on the other side of the entrance.

It was my deputy.

"Wilcox?"

"Sheriff," he urgently greeted me. He sounded breathless and distraught. "The press got a hold of the Leeanne–Scotty affair—"

"Damn."

"It's a real zoo at the station."

"I'm at the casino," I informed him, implying he would have to handle matters on his own. Though it was dark out, it was barely six o'clock, which meant Curt might have hours of harassment to contend with. "Arrest anyone who enters the station," I advised, "and be forceful about it so that the rest of them don't make the same mistake."

He agreed but sounded dubious about it then asked, "Why are you at the casino?"

"The Scotty affair ended nearly half a year before the murder. It couldn't have been the de Barras."

"Can I tell the press that to get them off our backs?"

"No," I barked. "It'll only encourage more questions. They can wait for the press conference."

"Can I tell them when that will be?" he pleaded, which gave me the sobering impression that the reporters camping out outside of the precinct had grown far more aggressive in my absence.

"No."

I hadn't answered his question, so he pushed, "You're following gossip leads? That's why you're at the casino?"

"It might not be gossip," I argued, though it wasn't lost on me that the press had sunk their teeth into a scoop about Leeanne prostituting at Resorts World before I had even taken a serious look at the possibility. As soon as the notion dawned on me, I ordered, "Go to Leeanne's house."

"Sheriff?"

Bitter winds nipped at me sideways, causing my nose to run and fingers to stiffen, as I elaborated.

"She might have hidden cash somewhere. The warrant is still good, if the landlord, George Miller, questions you. I want you to hunt. Look for loose floorboards, pull the refrigerator out." Recalling Leeanne's calendar—'You have everything you need! This is your year!'—I added, "She might have been squirreling cash away in a hole in the wall. Tear the place apart if you have to."

"Reporters are going to follow me over there and wait outside the door," he grumbled.

"They'll have to wait in the street. Curt," I reminded him. "You arrest anyone that sets foot on private property, you hear me?"

"Yes, Ma'am," he promised through the line. "You think she was killed by a 'John'?"

"I think if I don't put someone behind bars I won't be Sheriff for much longer."

Hanging up, I slipped my cell phone into my winter coat and braved my way through a thick huddle of reporters after stepping through the parting glass doors.

Reporters bombarded me.

"Was Leeanne Hessinger a working girl?"

"Sheriff, is that why you've come to the casino?"

A padded microphone hit me in the mouth and I glared at the reporter on the other end of it, as I pushed through. It was like pollen sticking to a bee. I was covered in them.

"What does it mean for Liberty that a teacher was a secret sex addict?"

"No comment!" I growled out, spilling past the invisible line that separated the lobby from the casino floor and breaking out of the madness.

Two casino employees dressed in black slacks and maroon suit jackets urged the reporters back, thrusting their hands up to cover flashing cameras and barking threats that the reporters had to keep clear of the carpet that marked the gaming floor!

I felt unusually hot as I made my way up the main aisle, a row of Black Jack tables to my left, Baccarat to my right. The sound effects *binging* and *ringing* from the slot machines were incredibly chaotic, but I was focused on a lone reporter who had managed to sneak past security.

Instead of a cameraman over her shoulder and a microphone in her hand, she held a single notepad and furiously ran her ballpoint pen over it, jotting down every word the casino employee in front of her was saying.

"Out!" I ordered, coming between them. "You know the rules. Behind the line!"

The employee looked more ashamed than she did.

"Mandy Vaughn, Jezebel Online," she announced.

Christ, a national tabloid was here?

She demanded, "What can you tell me about Room 516, Sheriff?"

"I can tell you that if you don't get behind that line I'm going to arrest you," I promised, getting right up in her pretty face.

She frowned like I had just kicked her puppy then started off at a reluctant pace towards the lobby, at times peeking at me over her shoulder to see if she might get away with veering in another direction.

I watched her with my glaring eyes until she had deposited herself where she belonged.

Turning my attention to the red-faced casino employee who looked young enough to have just graduated community college, I insisted, "Tell me everything you just told her."

"I didn't talk to her, I swear."

"Then tell me everything you were about to tell her," I prodded. "Starting with Room 516."

"I don't know anything about it."

I narrowed my eyes and reminded him, "A woman has been killed."

Pulling the slick photo of Leeanne all dolled up and posing in front of a line of slot machines from my pocket—I had taken it from her office—I thrust the bent image in his face and stated, "This woman was murdered. Have you seen her around?"

He went pale, cowered, and admitted he had.

"Well?"

"I don't know that she was a prostitute—"

"I don't care what you think you know. What did you see?"

"She came through the hotel lobby. I only saw her a few times when I used to work the front desk, but as soon as I finished my dealer training, they moved me to the tables."

He knew that wouldn't be enough for me, the way I was staring expectantly up at him.

"She looked like a hooker, I guess," he allowed. "But she never cruised the gaming floor. Look, if you work here long enough, you can spot them. They might dress like that," he admitted, referring to Leeanne in the photo I had lowered, "but they hang around the 360 Bar or linger near the high rollers at the tables. That lady, the few times I saw her, came straight through the hotel lobby like she knew exactly where she was going."

"To Room 516?" I surmised. "Thanks." As I turned, I warned him, "Don't talk to the press."

I had to round through the line of reporters to get to the hotel lobby, which wasn't pleasant, but the hotel staff were doing an equally controlled job of keeping the press and cameramen off the marble floor.

At the front desk, I presented my badge and the woman behind the counter looked intimidated.

"I need a list of every guest who has stayed in Room 516 since..." Thinking off the cuff and knowing that Leeanne's affair with Scotty had ended around the late summer, I told her, "September of last year."

"Let me get a manager."

"Do it quickly," I called after her, feeling weirdly thrilled.

I doubted Leeanne would've had any kind of rapport with the hotel that would've emboldened her to book the same room, time and again, in her own name. Though my gut told me that she had in fact been prostituting, I wondered if she might have had only one John. If that had been the case, I could think of a million reasons why he might come after her.

I would have my killer.

A manicured-looking, middle-aged man approached from the opposite side of the long counter and did a cordial job of greeting me:

"Detective—"

"Sheriff," I corrected.

"I understand you would like to see a guest list?"

"Right now," I confirmed.

"Unfortunately, I'm not at liberty to give out that kind of information."

"Are you kidding me?" I blurted. "Then get me whoever can."

He composed himself, determined to remain professional in the face of hostility, and barely regretted to inform me:

"I'm afraid you'll need a warrant."

"You think I can't get a judge on the phone at this hour?" I challenged.

"I'm sure you can," he smugly agreed.

To hell with this prick that he had called my bluff.

I couldn't even begin to imagine what political channels his managerial position at some lousy casino had made him privy to, but he obviously knew as well as I did that I would be hard pressed to get anyone on the phone so close after the New Year, even if my call had come during business hours, which it hadn't.

"I'll be back," I promised, as I shoved off from the front desk and made my slow, furious way towards the exit.

The best retaliation I could think of was to loiter around the lobby, question every guest that passed about the hooker in my photo, and do my damnedest to smear a black stain across Resorts World Catskills in their collective eyes.

As I did just that, catching guest after guest whether or not they were alone or with their spouses and families, the uncooperative manager watched me, but couldn't do a damn thing about it.

I wasn't the press, and I wasn't a ruthless reporter.

I was the Sheriff and I was married to a very powerful man who, if all else failed, would do for me politically what would need to be done in order to promote my investigation.

If the pissant man behind the counter only knew…

…I could have him fired by this time tomorrow.

When next I questioned an Hispanic woman wrapped in a thick winter coat—she was wearing the kind of orthopedic sneakers that only the housekeeping staff would—all of the raging ambition that had filled me swelled to astronomical proportions in my pounding chest.

I showed her the photo of Leeanne.

"I seen her," she guardedly murmured, as she glanced back at the front desk.

"Let me walk you out."

In the falling snow where the casino staff couldn't spy us, I asked, "What can you tell me?"

She clamped the collar of her coat closed against the bitter wind.

"I clean her room. Five floor through ten, those my floors. I interrupt once by mistake."

"You walked in on her with a man?"

"Si," she nodded, then stammered through stuttering broken English before getting her bearings. "Some time December."

"Can you tell me anything about the man?"

"Si." She used exceptional pronunciation to tell me, "George Clooney."

"Come again?"

"She with George Clooney."

I didn't know what to say and my heart dropped.

"So… this woman," I began, lifting the photo for her to see, "was in Room 516 with… George Clooney?"

As if it made all the sense in the world, she said, "Si."

"Thanks for your time."

I slumped, heart sinking and defeated, and felt a mile-long stare come over me as I watched her trek out through the snow towards her parked car.

Christ.

I needed this baby out of me so I could have a drink.

BACK AT MY house, I wriggled my wet boots off and hung my winter coat, vaguely aware of my husband's movements on the other side of the foyer. I was familiar with his sounds. He was in the midst of ensuring he wouldn't run into me. I didn't know whether to blame him or feel relieved. Our argument had been ugly, and I sensed its resolution would not come easily, if at all.

In the kitchen, I found cold spaghetti in a frying pan on the stove, teeming with bacteria no doubt, but I knew better than to confront Mitch about it. I tried not to let the crusted splatters of tomato sauce across the burners and countertops bother me, as I grabbed a carton of orange juice from the fridge, chugged it down, and pulled a large bowl of egg salad out.

As I peeled the dewy cellophane back, found a spoon in the drawer, and began wolfing down the favorite meal that I had denied my unborn son all evening, I tried to fathom why in the hell an Hispanic woman would have been convinced she had seen George Clooney of all people in that hotel suite.

Mitch drifted into the living room, keeping his distance, but staring at me.

"We should talk," he suggested.

"Not now. My brain is fried." I couldn't look at him, as I dug a heaping scoop of egg salad out of the chilled bowl and lifted it to my mouth. Before shoveling it into my face, I mentioned, "The casino was a circus."

The energy wafting from Mitch's side of the house changed instantly, and when I looked at him, curious about what I might have done this time, his handsome face went long.

"You went to the casino?" he hazarded to ask.

"Yup," I sighed, bristling with an edge of resentment. He hadn't given an honest damn about my investigation since its onset. "Leeanne was up to something in the hotel. I'm close."

"What do you think she was up to?" he breathed, stealing my attention from the bowl I had nearly polished off.

"According to one of the maids, she was sleeping with George Clooney for cash," I snorted.

Mitch didn't so much as crack a smile.

I studied him.

Studied the way the soft, tungsten light of the living room illuminated his chiseled features.

Studied the shape of his mouth.

Studied his strong jawline and those easy, bedroom eyes of his, his salt-and-pepper hair, the slope of his broad shoulders and firm chest and how his sweater clung to him…

…and I wondered why he suddenly looked like he had something to hide.

As nonchalantly as I could, I asked, "Have you ever seen Leeanne around the casino?"

"Of course not!" he blurted, startling me. "Why would I?"

"You have ties to the casino and the hotel," I reminded him and he relaxed, but only by a fraction. "Don't you swing by from time to time?"

"No," he answered darkly, his expression clouding over with what—from where I was standing in the low light of the kitchen—looked like veiled aggression. "I haven't been there since last fall. You know that."

"Do I?" I challenged. "You've been a ghost. I don't know where you go or what you're up to."

"Give me a break."

"That's all I want, Mitch," I threw in his face, "to eat egg salad and not have a fight. I told you, I'm exhausted."

"I shouldn't have lost my temper with you."

I stared dead at him. "But you did."

He sighed and ran his large hand down his face, but didn't defend himself or justify his perspective or even say another word to me.

Instead, he did what he always did these days. He turned for his study and left me with a squashed appetite.

"I'm seeing Nance tomorrow!" I called out. "Final prenatal appointment at 7am!"

But I was met with the sound of a closing door, Mitch having given up as he tended to do.

❄

IT DIDN'T MATTER how thoroughly I braced myself for it, the freezing chill of clear gel against my bare stomach never failed to shock me.

Mitch had decided to join me for my ob-gyn appointment, but he sat sullen, despondent, and in unsupportive proximity to the table I was reclining on as Nance moved the transducer back and forth in tight circles over my tremendous stomach. He wasn't even looking at the sonogram monitor. He might as well have been a million miles away.

My obstetrician, Nance, was a sprawling, almost disheveled-looking woman in her late forties who had never made it as a midwife, though she had tried in the early 2000s. Her appearance was deceiving, however. My experience with her taught me that she was a terse, economical woman and rarely nurturing, which was likely why midwifery hadn't suited her.

I appreciated her attitude. Unlike the other technicians that had administered my sonograms earlier in the pregnancy, Nance never annoyed me with gushing compliments meant to inspire excitement in soon-to-be parents. She never patronized me in a flighty sing-song voice as if I might not recognize the miracle I was growing in my own body without someone shining a big, fat spotlight on it.

Mitch, on the other hand, thought her bedside manner left much to be desired, but I was coming to understand that my husband might not be quite as feminist as he had originally let on.

Nance leaned towards the monitor and examined the shadowy image of our unborn son like a scientist scrutinizing a Petri dish for abnormalities in cell division. She seemed objective and unemotional in her duties.

But then, as if she might get away with bringing the subject up casually, she asked, "How are we doing with the possibility of a c-section?"

"It's not going to happen, Nance," I warned.

To my utter horror, though I should've been smart enough to see it coming, Mitch voiced the unthinkable.

"We should seriously consider it, Judy."

"We should what?" I hissed, glaring at him.

Nance reminded me, "Like I said, Judy, you might not have a choice."

"Forget it," I asserted. "No one is going to cut me open and extract my son out of me."

Mitch hotly confronted, "Why can't you put him first for once in your life?"

Nance corrected my husband's point as I gaped, jaw-dropped and seething at him.

"A c-section would actually be in *Judy's* best interest. It's her health I'm concerned with. There could be complications at your age and those complications could put you at risk for serious difficulties during labor," she told me.

"I'm thirty-eight, not fifty!"

Mitch asked her as though I wasn't in the room and hadn't already fiercely objected, "Could we schedule a c-section?"

"You son of a—"

"You can't control everything, Judy!" he shot back. "You can't control nature! You aren't a doctor! We have to consider the possibility that—"

"I'll obviously have a c-section if it comes to that and I have no other options in the delivery room, but I'm not going to sit here and let you schedule a damn c-section! This is childbirth, not a trip to the dentist!"

We would've torn each other's throats out if Nance hadn't calmly interjected, "Judy, Judy, that's perfect. That's all I needed to know. If it comes to it, we'll do one. That's all I wanted to hear."

Mitch was breathing heavily, and my stomach squeezed like a tightening belt, but as I groaned with a sudden, alarming contraction, sounding guttural and raw, I wasn't fooling anyone into thinking my husband's combative attitude had caused it.

"Breathe," Nance instructed, coming to stand at the foot of the table.

She made quick work of unfolding the stirrups and fitting my bare feet inside, as Mitch stood and panicked, "What's happening? What's wrong?"

"Let's make sure you aren't bleeding."

"Is she going into labor?" he demanded.

"A contraction or two isn't uncommon," Nance allowed.

"Does that mean she's going into labor?" Mitch yelled, brain-boggled on the brink of hysteria. He paced a tight circle, biting his thumb, and muttered, "We didn't pack the baby bag."

"I'm fine," I assured them. "It passed."

My cell phone began vibrating faintly from inside my purse, so I grabbed my bag from the chair beside me and answered it.

Appalled, Mitch blurted out, "What are you doing?"

"Curt?"

As my deputy's voice came through the line, Mitch was horrified and asked Nance the same question. "What is she doing? She's taking a call? You're taking a call?"

I held a finger up, not that it would silence my irate husband, as Curt told me, "You were right. I found cash. A little over two thousand. There was a loose floorboard under her makeshift bed."

"I'll be right there," I told him, struggling to swing my legs off the table, as Mitch stared at me in abject disbelief. "I have to get dressed."

"This is ridiculous!" he yelled. "You're being ridiculous! You're due any day now! The baby is coming, don't you get that?"

Nance assisted me, as I soldiered through putting my clothes back on, all the while my husband spat out insults that implied I wasn't going to make a very good mother.

The last thing he said to me as Nance walked me out was, "I can't believe how selfish you are!"

I turned and snapped, "You did this!"

He fell deathly silent and didn't dare utter a single word, as I withdrew my pointing finger from his face and left him to think about what he had done.

LEEANNE HESSINGER

Wednesday, October 18, 2017

THE ROULETTE BALL bounced around its spinning wheel.

As I watched from the side of the table with my shoulders back, pinot grigio in hand, and a serene smile fixed on my heavily made-up face—the gentlemen beside me having gladly made room for the elegant woman in the flashy, magenta dress—the ivory ball plunked into one of the tight slots.

The tailored man to my right chortled, which told me the tides had turned in his favor. The man to my left however, sighed and signaled the croupier to swap out his chips before he could lose any more. The croupier obliged him, raking the gambler's green chips off the complicated table then handing him colored ones that he could cash in at his leisure.

I had gotten to Resorts World early, thanks to my genuine curiosity about the various tables and an inclination to turn my tenth rendezvous with Mitch into a full-blown adventure.

I wanted to start the night early and make it last.

I had never ventured into the actual casino or onto the gaming floor in the month we'd been meeting here, but as I had gotten ready for my secret encounter I had felt gorgeous and lucky.

By observing the table, I had come to understand that Roulette had a high house edge, which meant that a player could lose his money faster here than at any other game in the casino.

I got the croupier's attention, offered my modest $5 chip, and placed what I knew was a risky, inside bet on Red 36, knowing that if I lost, my secret lover would easily replenish the amount.

Mitch had been making good on his philanthropic promise, and despite my cranky sedan, his generous donations had pulled me out of the blind panic that had been constantly burdening me. I had managed to save and I had also been spending—adding to my wardrobe on an almost weekly basis and stocking up on things like false eyelashes, which I went through quickly and which weren't cheap. But concerning my prior financial struggle, I was out of the woods.

The croupier announced that bets were closed, spun the Roulette wheel, and dropped the ball in.

Crossing my fingers, I braced the polished edge of the table, leaned forward, and held my breath, as the ivory ball bounced and bounced and finally settled into...

Red 36!

I shrieked and threw my arms in the air, forgetting my glass of wine and drenching my neighbor who was immediately furious with me.

"Red 36," the croupier announced.

"I won!" I exclaimed loud enough to alert the entire gaming floor.

The croupier suppressed a congratulatory grin and I breathlessly asked to swap out my chips.

I couldn't believe I had actually won! But that was me. My luck had changed. I felt like I was finally winning at life and it was all because of Mitch Kavleski.

Riding my high, I breezed across the gaming floor with two casino chips in my hand. The purple one had a value of $100 should I ever cash it in, and the blue one was for $85.

So buzzing with excitement was I that I didn't even know where I was going.

I stopped at the slots and found my cell phone in a sequined clutch that nearly matched my dress in color.

I texted Mitch to meet me there on the casino floor, giving him my precise location, and got the fun idea to exchange the lesser chip for a ticket.

Then I cruised the first row of blinking, ringing slots, feeling like a kid at an arcade. Selecting one that I sensed would be *hot*, I sat, placed the ticket into the mouth of the machine, which sucked it right in, and rubbed my hands together.

I pulled the lever, watching different varieties of fruits whirl in columns on the screen.

It didn't take long to gamble away the eighty-five-dollar ticket, but I hardly minded. I would forever keep the purple chip I had tucked into my clutch as a token reminder of my daring adventure.

Once again, I felt like the optimistic girl who had twirled in the snow at Walnut Mountain, and in that moment, I promised myself I would hold onto that feeling and hold it dearly no matter what.

Mitch was exactly who I had always wanted, and if I held onto him as well, entertaining and satisfying him, there would be no limit to what I could accomplish or who I could become.

It was a dangerous feeling, however.

I had come to depend on him, and though he had warned me to maintain secrecy, with our every encounter in Room 516, I could tell he had been growing more and more attached to me. Lingering in bed with me after the act instead of stealing away into the bathroom to shower. Opening up to me about the particular trials and tribulations of his difficult marriage. Needing me to nurture and restore him in a way no man I had been with ever had. He depended on me.

I had begun to view Mitch as isolated. A man antagonized by his domineering wife. I viewed him as someone who craved freedom as badly as I had before escaping Ian and fleeing to a town I had chosen for its name alone, which to me had sounded like a promise—Liberty.

I didn't feel like a prostitute when I was with him, even though it wasn't lost on me that I had become one, but only for him.

What we were doing together didn't feel wrong anymore. It wasn't dirty or depraved. It was starting to feel natural and right. We made sense, and I was beginning to hope, since we were both adults and hadn't been coy about what we wanted, that somehow, someway this might eventually become real...

...yet I knew that was the danger.

"There you are."

Mitch eased against a neighboring slot machine and gazed down at me, a veiled glint of admonishment in his otherwise seductive eyes, as I told him, "I just lost."

"The house always wins."

"I'm still in the black," I boasted. "I won big at Roulette."

Though it was guarded, he grinned. "Won *big*, huh?"

"It was big for me," I maintained.

"Come on," he said, glancing up the aisle to check we weren't being spied on. "You know you shouldn't be down here."

I stood, squeezing myself against the firm length of him and giving him a kittenish smile, as I sidestepped out from the row of slots.

Discreetly, he handed me his keycard.

"I'll be up momentarily."

"You don't want to be seen with me?" I playfully sulked as I pulled my cell phone from my clutch.

"Go on."

"Take my picture?" After queuing up the camera app, I gave him my phone and posed in front of the neon machines. "Just one?"

He didn't look especially pleased, but he obliged me, tapping the screen as I held still with what I hoped was a sultry expression for the bursting flash.

"I'll see you up there," he told me, as he returned my phone.

"What do you have to do?"

"If you really must know," he chided. "I'm covering our tracks with the front desk so that this won't bite us in the ass later down the road."

"My hero," I teased.

I would have preferred to hear that he wanted to order champagne or arrange some other romantic gesture at the front desk, but I didn't say a word as I made my way through the gaming floor, heading straight for the hotel lobby where stunned glances and ogling eyes would surely follow me.

IN BED, DRAPED over Mitch, my head resting on his sculpted chest, fingertips tracing the dips and ridges of his slick stomach, the afterglow of our sex lingering and tingling across my skin, I felt the words clawing up my throat. I was bursting with emotion. Brilliant, uncontainable emotion that was coiled tightly in my heart and threatening to spring out of me.

I begged myself not to speak of it, not to let the dangerous, delirious confession leap out into the space between us; not to jeopardize this magical, wild thing we had.

But I had been losing control of myself, the spell of Mitch having thrown my rationale further and further off kilter with our every postcoital caress. The axis of my world drastically tipped sideways whenever I was with him, making it far too easy to forget myself.

So I, mentally composing the subtlest way to ease into the idea to safeguard that he wouldn't be alarmed, made certain to come off sounding very casual and uninvested.

"Are you happy?"

"With you? Yes," he said as he stroked my hair.

It made me smile, encouraged me. I breathed in his scent—the natural musk I had come to love—and asked, "Do you ever think about being with me... in a real way?"

I felt his body stiffen beneath mine. His hand stopped mid-stroke, his fingers deep in my hair.

As I waited anxiously for his response, trying not to cringe that I probably seemed insecure or immature or some damning combination therein, my mind raced for a witty comment I might use to change the course of the boneheaded error I had just been foolish enough to make.

"Leeanne," he breathed but then admitted, "I think about it."

Lifting up and searching his light eyes, I asked, "You do?"

"You know I can't do anything about it—"

"You could," I blurted. "It could work. People leave their spouses all the time."

"They do," he allowed.

"Is it so crazy that I might want that?"

"We shouldn't be talking about this."

"Why?" I challenged. "Because it's against the rules?"

"Because…" he trailed off, but I knew what he would've said if he hadn't.

He wasn't going to leave his wife. He wasn't going to turn his life upside down for me. Wasn't going to abandon a commitment that had been making him miserable for years even though that was precisely what we both knew he wanted and needed.

His spirit had been wilting. Couldn't he see that if he didn't get out of his loveless, thankless, useless marriage, one morning he would wake up and realize that he was fully dead inside?

He urged me away and sat with his back to me on the edge of the bed.

"I need you, Leeanne, but I need you to let this be what it is."

MITCH KAVLESKI

The Months of November and December, 2017

WHEN I TOLD LEEANNE I needed her, I wasn't lying. I did. What we had was more than just sex. Those hours we spent, stolen away in Room 516, had the power to recalibrate my entire outlook on my marriage and attitude towards my wife.

The affair was making my strained and oftentimes tenuous relationship with Judy easier. My tolerance of her inclination to nitpick my every mistake and shortcoming improved. Our communication was better, and the unspeakable rift that had gradually risen between us over the years finally mended. It was all thanks to my mistress, a woman so opposite my wife that she single-handedly empowered me to remember myself and reconnect with the person I used to be.

It might have been antiquated or even chauvinistic, but Leeanne needed me, and because she did, I felt like a real man.

A provider.

Someone who she relied upon to protect her with his wallet.

She was so greatly appreciative of the role I had volunteered to play that I imagined she wouldn't dare criticize me or so much as correct even the slightest inaccuracy should I make one. She never did. It wasn't a partnership. We didn't have equal standing within the secretive confines of our affair. I handled select areas, making her life not only easier but possible, and in return, she gave me her body and admiration and respect, trusting my leadership and obeying my rules.

If only Judy would look at me the way Leeanne did, with need for me and confidence in me, instead of the judgment I was often met with. Those days were long since passed and I didn't have delusions of grandeur that Judy would, by some tragedy or miracle, revert to the vulnerable, dependent woman she had once been.

But again, with Leeanne quenching that very thirst for me, I didn't need my wife to be who she had once been. I didn't need my wife at all.

For months, I met Leeanne at the casino hotel, as autumn froze over with snow and winter swept in with brutal force.

The stale, lackluster rhythm of my life had been replaced with enthusiasm. I never failed to look forward to my trysts with Leeanne, which soon struck with almost nightly frequency. Having a mistress at my beckon call—a precious, thrilling lover—thrusted invigorating adrenaline spikes into the pattern of each week.

I recognized my face in the mirror and also my behavior with my wife, which became attentive, supportive, and husbandly as Judy deserved. I was patient and kind towards her. I permitted her incessant criticisms without complaint. Where once the water of her continuous gripes had worn me down, it now rolled off my back. I was able to be a modern, model husband. Engaging with her during dinner. Allowing her non-stop suggestions as we worked on the baby's room. I even managed to initiate affection so that she would feel desired, though she usually stopped me well before intercourse, claiming her fluctuating hormones had made her too irritable.

She never questioned my late nights, and I never had to explain myself.

To the outsider, our marriage looked intact and our partnership persisted. We appeared to be the same "power couple" as we always had, presiding over the town and running the county.

But the fact of Leeanne having attempted to cross a clear line that I had drawn between us was worrisome.

Though I might not have been happy with Judy for quite some time, I had no intention of ever leaving my wife. If it weren't for the troubling state of my marriage, I wouldn't have needed Leeanne in the first place, and she didn't seem to understand that, no matter how much cash I threw at her.

She continued to test the waters with me, bringing up the prospect of us being together, as we lay in bed at the hotel.

I tried to tow the line between indulging her fantasy—I couldn't afford to lose her, I would never survive my marriage if I did—and shutting it down, but I eventually realized I had phenomenally misjudged Leeanne. I had thought, despite her inherent innocence and the beautiful optimism she seemed to breathe into everything she touched, that she wouldn't fall in love.

It had been the error of a lifetime.

She didn't grasp the importance of maintaining what we had without trying to turn us into something that we were never designed to be, namely real and lasting.

I had been soft with her. Too gentle whenever I discouraged or combatted her hopes. I was weak, perhaps. I avoided inciting an argument at the risk of stimulating her pipe dream, but doing so only stoked the fires of a far more dangerous risk, that she would grow frustrated and take measures to expose our affair.

From a very dark place inside of myself, I knew what I would do if she ever defied me.

As the option began to take form in that exceedingly wicked part of myself while the weeks rolled onward, it occurred to me that waiting until she damaged my life would amount to an even worse miscalculation than having trusted Leeanne to keep quiet about us in the first place.

If I wanted to solve the growing problem of Leeanne, I might have to succumb to a criminal solution.

It would be unsavory, but also necessary. After all, she had come to Liberty from out of nowhere. She could disappear just as abruptly as she had arrived and no one would be the wiser, or so I was starting to convince myself.

But it wasn't until the Thursday before Christmas that I decided I would need to fully commit to the idea if I wanted to safeguard the life I had built. Though I wished it wouldn't have to come to it, I began devising a plan, praying all the while that Leeanne would settle down and accept the limitations of our relationship so that I wouldn't have to bloody my hands.

Her behavior at the Bethel Woods holiday party however, was fast becoming far too much.

I had warned her against dolling herself up for work. I had forbidden her to dress provocatively at the P.A.C. And I had expressly told her not to hit the white wine too hard during the party.

She had disobeyed me on all three counts that night.

Donning a slinky, red dress that barely covered her bottom, she swayed and wobbled in front of the Christmas tree, sloshing wine from her glass, talking loudly, and drawing uncomfortable attention to herself in her effort to perhaps get me to notice her.

Her black heels were much too high, and from where I was standing beside my wife, it seemed Leeanne was batting her lashes so that everyone would know they were false.

If she had been alone with me in Room 516, I wouldn't have found her trashy and garish, but that was how she looked in the festive lights amongst colleagues, donors, and the parents of kids she taught—like a lewd hooker trying to work a corner.

It made me furious.

Trip seemed to be enjoying the show, however. He laughed at her noisy jokes and caught her falling dress strap before she accidentally flashed her breast to the room at large.

But he was also enabling her embarrassing performance, refreshing her glass when it was low, and whispering what I could only assume were instigating compliments into her ear. He probably thought she would go home with him if he stuck to her all night, and quite frankly, if any scandal was destined to come out of her disgraceful display, I hoped that would be it.

"Someone's enjoying herself," Judy snidely commented to me as she stared at Leeanne from across the room.

It was the kind of acknowledgement I could use to finally intervene.

"Let me see if I can convince her to call a cab," I offered, but Judy stopped me.

"Oh, let her have her fun," she said, grabbing my arm. "What harm will it do?"

A lot, I thought, on edge that my drunken lover might proclaim to all of Bethel Woods that she had been prostituting for me at the casino hotel for nearly four months. I wouldn't put it past her at this point.

"She'll be mortified if I don't send her home," I reasoned, and Judy released my arm, admiring my compassion, though confronting Leeanne would only be an act of self-preservation. "Excuse me."

But as I weaved my way through the crowd of festively dressed guests, Leeanne left Trip in favor of stumbling towards the ladies' room where I hoped she might vomit herself into a sober state if she didn't pass out on the toilet, anything to put an end to this waking nightmare.

I didn't like the look on Trip's face when I joined him at the Christmas tree.

"Any plans for the New Year?" I asked good-naturedly.

"I might make it down to the city," he offered. "I'm due for a crazy holiday. It's been years, but those Manhattan hotels will gouge you."

How Trip Turner spent his time off wasn't even in the ballpark of anything I gave a rat's ass about, so I promptly cut the crap.

"I think we both know your coworker has been making a fool of herself."

"I'm sorry?"

"If you're even remotely good to drive, I would like you to get her out of here," I told him.

"Leeanne?"

I tried not to look exceptionally annoyed by how dense he was being, and confirmed, "Yes. Leeanne. Call a cab if you have to, just get her out of here. Do you need cash?"

"Ah, no," he said, puzzled. "I have cab money. I didn't think she had gotten that bad. She only—"

"She has—" I snapped as my gaze locked on the devil we had been speaking of.

Leeanne wobbled with each step, making her unsteady way back to Trip and the Christmas tree.

When she realized I was also standing there, she oozed and the smile she directed at me was outrageously suggestive.

"Hey, Mr. Mitch," she breathed, and Trip's eyes widened.

From the other side of the room, a guttural groan emanated, and I was shocked to find my wife keeling over and holding the ball of her pregnant stomach.

Carol Patterson caught her, and they rushed into the ladies' room as I cut through the crowd and barged in to find Judy bracing the messy sink and moaning in pain.

"What's wrong?"

"I'm bleeding!"

"Breathe," Carol advised as she held my wife's shoulders.

"Something's wrong with the baby!" Judy cried.

I stole her purse, found her cell phone, and immediately called Nance, as Carol ushered her into one of the stalls to sit on the toilet.

"No," I barked at Carol, as I heard our ob-gyn's voice come through the line. "I have to get her to the hospital. Nance?"

Carol redirected my wife through the bathroom, and I followed them out, explaining to Nance at a frantic pace what had just happened to my wife, as the three of us made our way through the party where I sensed Leeanne's bleary eyes on me. But soon we were outside in the snow.

Nothing put the whole of life into perspective like the terrifying possibility of losing my unborn son, and as I helped Judy into the passenger's seat of my Lexus, I knew without question that it was time to get rid of Leeanne.

I HAD NEVER before shown up at Leeanne's rented house, had never knocked on her door in the blustery dead of night, but desperate times called for even more desperate measures.

I was still adamantly praying I wouldn't have to go the far length of executing the plan I had devised, as I started up her icy walk, bundled against the bitter wind.

When she opened the door, she was sober but still wearing that slinky dress, standing barefoot and surprised to see me.

"Mitch—"

"We need to talk," I said, pushing past her through a dingy entryway and into an even dingier kitchen.

"Is she okay? Is the baby…?"

"They're fine."

I turned to face her as she folded her arms and a look of concern came over her, whether it was in response to the health of my wife and unborn son or the precarious state of our affair, I couldn't decide.

All I knew was that now that Judy was safe and sound at home, having received a clean bill of health from Nance at the hospital, I needed everything to go back to the way it had been before I had invited an employee to Resorts World Catskills for a social drink and paid sex.

"Your behavior tonight was unacceptable."

Cringing, she admitted, "I know. It will never happen again."

"What were you thinking?"

Pained, she tried and failed to explain herself then sighed.

"I'm sorry."

"I'm sorry, too," I said, and her dark eyes went dead as she realized what was coming next. "This affair is over."

"No! It can't be!" she protested, advancing on me.

"Judy is going to have the baby in a matter of weeks. I can't have this kind of complication in my life."

"I'm not a complication," she pleaded. "I don't have to be. I was out of line at the party," she groveled then desperately repeated, "I promise, it won't happen again."

"No, it won't," I agreed, "because I won't be inviting you to the hotel again."

"Mitch, don't do this."

"It's already done," I told her, feeling heartless but knowing there was no turning back.

I pulled a thick envelope out of my woolen overcoat. I had withdrawn two thousand for her, which I trusted she would take as hush money in agreement to leave me and my family alone.

"Here."

"I don't want it."

"Take it."

"You can't give me cash and send me on my way, Mitch," she warned.

"That's exactly what I'm going to do," I assured her. "This whole situation has gotten wildly out of hand."

She refused the envelope, so I set it on the kitchen counter and turned for the door, determined not to murder her with my bare hands.

"I'll tell her!"

I turned on my heel, charged at her, and grabbed her by the throat, bending her backwards over the sink.

I hissed, spitting each word through clenched teeth, "If you do that…"

She tried to turn my anger into arousal, but I shoved her away, sending her flying across the floor.

I threw the door open and slammed it shut behind me before I could do anything I would most certainly regret.

But in the days that passed, I lived in the shadow of her threat and feared that I wouldn't be able to hold myself back for much longer.

LEEANNE HESSINGER

Tuesday, January 2, 2018

I WAS DEVASTATED. Sick to my stomach. Crushing depression had swallowed me whole, yet I could barely sleep and rarely sat still, as a series of merciless storms swept through, burying Liberty and cutting the power, as though my world wasn't cold and dark enough already.

I felt too panicked to write and I hadn't eaten—I was convinced a three-day fast would clear my head, but so far depriving myself had only frazzled my already frayed nerves.

I had slipped into such a state of ruin that even showering was impossible. I had taken to bathing myself in the sink, wearing the exact same sweater and jeans day in and day out, and pacing the vacant living room of my rented house when I felt another hot swell of anxiety bubbling up in my pounding chest.

Mitch had used and discarded me like yesterday's trash, but the fact of his cruel treatment wasn't heavy enough to touch me. He still represented all of my dreams coming true, and I couldn't annihilate the scalding desire in my heart to win him back, though I didn't see how I ever would.

He was a king amongst kings, commanding and powerful, and what was I?

A pauper, some sad peasant girl who had sold her body for a small, insignificant amount of cash. A hungry mouse with such little regard for herself and so low a personal value that she had chased through a maze of smoke and mirrors only to find she might never escape…

…and it wasn't just Mitch.

It was life.

Life had teased me with grand possibilities and had taught me that they were never meant to come true. Not for people like me. Not for those who slept on stacks of sleeping bags, too dumb or lazy or uneducated to figure out how to improve their income and buy furniture, even if it meant putting their greatest aspirations on the back burner, buckling down, and growing the hell up.

I had never accepted my lot in life and that was the pathetic tragedy of it all.

I knew I was being self-pitying, that wallowing wouldn't help, but I could feel the full scope of my story. It was harrowing. Devoid of victory and redemption. I was a badly written, bird-brained character who, time and again, had blindly thrown herself—headlong and blissfully—into damaging affairs that anyone with a shred of self-awareness would've steered clear of.

I was naïve, easily manipulated, and motivated by arrogant if not egocentric pursuits, which was probably why even the smallest dangling carrot sent me galloping off in dangerous directions.

My self-hatred made me furious but not more so than the fact that I knew—I could *feel* it deep down—I was still clawing at the walls that separated me from realizing my dream.

Wanting to become a published author had compelled me to literally sell my body. My God, I would've sold my soul for the chance, that's how terribly I yearned for greatness, and why my lust or love for the idea of Mitch had tangled me up in an almost strangling web I couldn't break free from.

Desperate and determined, I refused to give up, but the oscillations between wanting to fight to make my dreams come true and wishing I would be satisfied as a teacher with no ambition to write were maddening.

I couldn't ground myself.

My car broke down for the millionth time, and I fully lost it in the driveway as my landlord looked on.

Christmas day would've been suicidal if I had had the gumption or means.

The stress of my miserable life reached a boiling point, and soon it felt like there was nothing left but blistering steam.

As an act of willful defiance, one morning I decided to document my every warring emotion, all of the pain and hope and fury and optimism and self-hatred and relentless, unwavering self-love that had been violently roiling through me since the night of the holiday party into the clearest, most honest detail I could muster, typing vigorously on my laptop and finally feeling as though the suffocating weight that had befallen me was divinely lifting by some merciful stroke of God or perhaps a very stubborn inclination to rise above.

I would use all of it.

Every choking squeeze and elating wave.

I would pour each and every tortured feeling that had come over me into my novel, and I would write it.

No more procrastinating, no matter what.

I didn't need time and space. I had always had both. I didn't need money. I had even pried one of the floorboards up in my bedroom, creating a nook to hide my cash.

I wouldn't squander a single dime, and had even asked Trip to give me rides to the grocery store and laundromat, which he had been doing, so that I wouldn't have to sink money into getting my car fixed.

I would make the money stretch. I would hunker down, and I would force my goal of drafting a contemporary American novel to come true. Because that's what it was and what it should have always been.

A goal, not a dream, but a long-term effort that would have to be whittled, not wished, into existence.

It would be work, a job, and it was time to get started.

Feeling imbued with a new, stronger sense of self, I bounded into the kitchen, set my ballpoint pen against the calendar that I had gotten from Sam's Auto Body Shop that was hanging on the fridge, and scrawled the most important intention I ever would across the start of the New Year.

'Start novel, 3k words a day! You have everything you need! This is your year!'

Then I saw the month of January's image and gasped.

It was a photograph of Walnut Mountain Park!

'Remember the miracle!' I wrote across the upper edge of the calendar as all of the buoyancy I had once felt filled my soaring heart.

❄

"WHERE DO YOU want these?" Trip asked once he reached the kitchen.

"The counter is fine," I said, and he placed the four bursting grocery bags he had carried for me on the space beside the sink.

"Thanks."

"Anytime," he returned as he opened the refrigerator. "Power's back on."

"Finally," I sighed and flipped the light switch on. A wash of tungsten light brightened the room as sleet ticked against the windows. "It'll probably take a few hours for the fridge to recover."

"Want me to dump this?" he asked, having sniffed a carton of soy milk creamer I used for my tea.

As I began filling the cabinets with the food I had bought at ShopRite, I told him, "I can do it."

He watched me as I darted around the kitchen, stocking canned beans and bags of rice where I always did. My stomach growled just handling the foodstuff, but I still had a little over twenty-four hours before I would let myself eat.

"What?" I asked him with an apprehensive smile.

"You okay?"

"Why wouldn't I be?"

"No reason," he said but quickly added, "You look a little thin, is all."

"Trip," I warned.

"Don't get me wrong. You look good, just thinner."

"I'm fine."

"Are you?"

I gave him my full attention, having crammed the empty plastic bags into the cupboard beneath the sink, and assured him, "Yes."

He sized me up then asked, "Did you do anything special for New Year's?"

Perking up—the mere thought of my novel had me beaming reflectively—I mentioned, "As a matter of fact, I did."

"Oh?"

"I outlined my whole book. I'm going to do it," I grinned. "And if I stick to my writing schedule, I'll have a full draft within thirty days."

"That's great," he complimented as he edged towards me and opened his arms in a way that took me by surprise. "Bring it in for the real thing."

"Huh?"

He answered my confusion when he pulled me into a hug.

He didn't release me.

"Trip?" I breathed into his shoulder.

"You smell good," he said softly, and I got a weird feeling.

I tried to urge him back and twist out of his embrace, but he was holding me too tightly.

That's when panic surged through me.

"You have to let me go now," I said, keeping my tone light and unalarmed.

I was probably reading this wrong, wasn't I? But my fear about the situation I hadn't seen coming was confirmed the second he took firm hold of the back of my head and leaned in.

I jerked away before he could kiss me, shoving him off, and yelled, "What are you doing?"

"Come on, Leeanne," he said in a strange voice that sounded both condescending and threatening. "All the car rides? The holiday party?"

He stepped in again and tried to take hold of me, but I shoved him off as sudden terror ripped through my gut.

I fought for composure as I said, "Thanks for your help. I have a lot of writing to do."

"You've been teasing me all year," he accused and the next thing I knew he was all over me.

I slapped him—hard—across the face, but he overpowered me to the kitchen floor, wrestling me to my stomach as I wriggled and twisted, making shocked, grunting cries that I barely recognized as coming from myself.

"You think I didn't see you at the casino?" he sneered.

He went on to detail, using insulting language I would have never thought him capable of, how he had followed me to the hotel, knew what I was up to, how this should be easy for me, this was what I did, wasn't it?

Disgusted with me and enraged, he didn't stop, and what he was doing to me, against my will—murdering my soul—caused my rattled brain to shut down.

Pinned down, I went numb.

My vision blurred with tears.

And when he was finished, he left me on the floor.

I could hear his heaving breathing as he got up, zipped his fly, and sucked snot back into his face.

"What do I owe you? Forty?" he sarcastically guessed. "Great doing business with you."

Though I heard him leaving and the distinct click of the front door closing next, it was a very long time before I scraped myself off the floor.

When I finally did, mind scrambling and cheeks damp, I was mad enough to kill.

I wanted revenge.

Wanted to retaliate against every last one of them!

Against Ian and Mitch and Trip. Against every boy in high school who had fingered me and blabbed about it. Every man who had hurt me in the name of his own gratification even if it was at my expense; every single one who had no regard that I was human and already so badly broken that I might not survive.

I didn't call the police, which I was smart enough to know would only invite blame. I wouldn't be able to deny I had been prostituting if Trip mentioned it, and I doubted anyone in this town would buy that I had only had one John and it was Mitch Kavleski.

Instead, with shaky hands, I did my worst, carefully composing a letter to Mitch's precious wife, Judy.

Using my best penmanship, I explained the affair I had been having with her husband.

I detailed our encounters graphically, but never mentioned the location of our countless rendezvous.

I made it sound like a plea, like I was begging her to understand, to let Mitch go, to let us be happy, knowing full well that as soon as she read it, she would turn on her perfect husband, and his life would be destroyed.

I decided to address the envelope to Sheriff Judy Kavleski's attention and mail it to the police station where Mitch wouldn't be able to intercept it.

As I tucked the letter into my mailbox and lifted its red flag, I envisioned a billion outcomes…

…but not one of them was my own murder.

I didn't know it then, but I had just sealed my fate.

SHERIFF JUDY KAVLESKI

Wednesday, January 10, 2018

THE NIGHT AFTER my last prenatal visit when I finally got home, I closed the door of the master bedroom I shared with Mitch and eased onto my side of the king-sized bed, alone.

Icy sleet, the kind that could scratch your face, ticked and tapped against the large picture windows, but the gusty wind outside wasn't strong enough to rattle the panes. I liked the sound. It relaxed and zoned me out, which was the only place I had left to go, coming hot off the heels of the day I'd had.

I allowed myself a moment to simply breathe, listening to the nasty weather and trying to feel my body, though my legs felt constricted in these maternity pants I had come to hate, and the sweater I wore had been causing me to break out in both hot and cold sweats. I could use a shower, but didn't see myself getting off the bed any time soon.

While Leeanne had lived in an old, rickety, one-story house that at one point in time had likely been a detached garage, I had been calling a virtual castle my home.

While she had made do with sleeping bags to rest her head at night, lying low on the floor and refusing to feel badly about it, I had been curling up on a quality mattress, cozied under a warm comforter, my bed so high off the ground that even now as my legs dangled over the edge, my socked feet didn't touch the carpet.

While she had scrimped and saved and began turning tricks to get ahead, I had been sitting on checkings, savings, and asset accounts with such fat balances there was no need to log online and check them before I made purchases both big and small.

We couldn't have been more different, and yet I felt so close to her that I almost couldn't stand it.

I had been investigating her murder for a full week, learning about each and every sordid character who had made a perplexing, if not menacing, appearance in the story of her life, and I had also uncovered what I could only regard as her fearless, albeit misguided, conviction. I had gotten a taste of her spirit…

…and it broke my heart…

…because in the midst of her determined effort to find freedom, this town unknown to her had eaten Leeanne Hessinger alive.

I felt hollowed out over it, like smoky sorrow was scratching through my chest. I welcomed, then willed myself to cry—anything to relieve this heaviness—but tears wouldn't come.

I was depleted.

So deep in thought was I that I barely recognized the vibration of my cell phone in the front pocket of my stretchy pants.

"Sheriff Kavleski," I said, answering the call, though the number that had lit up the LCD screen was unfamiliar to me.

It was a technician from the forensic lab we had been using in Monticello.

"We ran the hunting knife for fingerprints and also Touch DNA," I was told. "But it was wiped clean. No prints or DNA. I can fax the report over."

"Please do," I said, barely finding my voice. "Thank you."

I set my cell phone down on the nightstand.

It didn't surprise me that there wasn't a shred of evidence on the knife.

I didn't have a prayer of obtaining a warrant for Room 516, but I didn't need one.

I knew who Leeanne's John was.

I had been hoping that I was wrong about it being Mitch.

But I had been correct.

I wasn't going to be able to put Trip Turner behind bars for this, wasn't going to be able to strongarm Scotty into confessing, or Ron de Barra or his brassy wife. Ian Hessinger might have had the most motive to kill Leeanne, but I knew I would never succeed at getting him to admit as much.

There was no one to pin this on. No one to wear down for hours at the station and coerce into a false confession, like I had been angling for, having hunted through the dark secrets of the beautiful and enigmatic teacher's life.

I pulled open the nightstand drawer and stared at the handwritten letter Leeanne had addressed to me.

I must have read it one hundred times since I had first received it at the station house and had been blindsided by its contents.

The final sentence jumped out at me like it always did—*Let us be happy.*'

I never told Mitch about the letter, never confronted him about the affair, which I feared would shatter our delicate marriage. I never sought to confirm the graphic elements she had severely detailed to hurt me or perhaps provoke me into leaving my adulterer husband.

So long as I lived, I would never tell Mitch that I knew. I would do anything to save us, and I trusted that as soon as the baby was here, our son would patch things up between us and bring us together as we had once been.

I heard footfall nearing the closed door, folded the letter, and returned it to the nightstand drawer.

Mitch peeked his head in.

"I made a bowl of egg salad for you. It's in the fridge."

"Mitch?" I said, catching him before he could retreat into the hallway. "I love you."

When he said it back, I knew Leeanne Hessinger hadn't broken us…

…and that nothing ever would.

SHERIFF JUDY KAVLESKI

Thursday, January 11, 2018

I NEARED THE LECTERN and stood in front of a bouquet of padded microphones, setting my printed statement down as cameras flashed.

It had taken all morning, but my deputy, Curt, had rearranged the bullpen of the police station to accommodate the dozens of reporters who had been crawling all over this town, pursuing gossip and rumors, and presenting to the public all kinds of enthralling angles that had cut dangerously close to the truth.

Curt had been slow and labored in his effort, the weight of having learned what I would be announcing at the press conference cracking the very foundation of his faith in morality.

It had pained me to deliver the blow. I knew he wouldn't recover easily, if at all.

Curt had always believed that the truth of what had happened to Leeanne was within our reach if only we dug deeply enough to uncover it.

The fact of the matter was that it *was*, and that had always been my greatest fear.

I had decided to promote him with the title of 'Chief Deputy' and had even offered him a pay bump for his valiant police work on the case as he had planted folding chairs in rows across the station house floor, but the accolades had been lost to his bitter indignation that a woman who so represented the glory and tranquility of Liberty could, after her brutal murder, receive not even one merciless shred of justice.

I had let him be, but even now, as I prepared to convey to the journalism community at large the disturbing result of our department's thorough—and though I would absolutely never admit it, corrupt—investigation, I could feel my deputy's acrimony consuming him though he stood off to the wayside, pink-eyed and crestfallen, behind my view.

Curt had taken full moral responsibility for the failures of the police station he worked for, taken it completely to heart, and he had no intention of shirking the cross he had volunteered to bear.

My husband, Mitch, stood stoically beside him, as did a wealth of detectives and police officers that comprised our simple precinct.

Mitch had fixed an appropriate expression on his face, and the uniformed men and women poised among him had cast their eyes downward, holding still and solemn in a way I knew would paint the right kind of picture to convey our collective loss.

I cleared my throat, and after touching eyes with my husband, I began.

"Early Thursday morning, on January 4th of this year, a thirty-four-year old woman, Leeanne Hessinger, was found dead in her house by a colleague. The cause of death was undoubtedly a homicide. Hessinger was stabbed in the sternum of her chest with a long-blade hunting knife. This murder weapon was collected from the scene of the crime."

I took an unsteady breath as the cameras clicked, flashes bursting and assaulting me with blinding light.

"After exhausting all possible leads…" I went on after composing myself.

My hands were trembling badly and I felt a cry of clawing emotion tightening my throat. But the crippling regret I felt had no place in my official statement.

"The Liberty police department has determined that the crime was a robbery gone wrong."

My unborn son kicked from within the round ball of my belly, a trilling series of taps that reminded me life would in fact go on.

"And unfortunately, our investigators were not able to connect her murder to a suspect."

The sea of reporters immediately confronted me with so many overlapping questions that it sounded like a roaring engine, but I pushed onward.

"Leeanne Hessinger was a valued member of our community. She was, first and foremost, a dedicated teacher at the Bethel Woods Performing Arts Center, and the loss of her life has, and will continue to, affect us all."

I intentionally ignored an onslaught of questions that were being shouted about Leeanne's alleged prostitution at the Monticello casino as well as her illicit affair with an underaged student.

Instead, I turned from the lectern, as reporters shouted all kinds of unanswerable questions at me, locked uneasy eyes with Mitch, and deeply hoped he understood that he must never duplicate the same mistake.

❇

THAT SAME NIGHT, I sat across from Mitch at our elegant dining room table, a plate of glazed chicken between us.

As we worked on our salad, wine glasses filled to the brim with merlot since Nance had advised a glass of wine might be advantageous in terms of inducing labor, I stole glances at my adulterating husband, studying him for all he was worth.

I had thought it nearly fifteen years ago, and I still thought it now:

Mitch was the most dashing, handsome, confident man I had ever encountered. I was as madly in love with him tonight as I had been the first day I had ever laid eyes on him. The greatest miracle of my life was that he had chosen me, had gotten down on one knee, and had proposed.

If he needed me to soften, I would. If he wanted me to loosen the reins of my competence, I could do that for him. I would do anything to preserve the magic of us, regardless of the fact that he had strayed, disgustingly so, from the vows we had promised one another. Mitch was my everything, and I would be damned if we wouldn't quickly and efficiently recover from the plague of Leeanne Hessinger that had marred our otherwise impeccable marriage.

But, as I watched him handsomely sip wine and pick at his salad, I couldn't stop myself from wondering…

Would history repeat itself, or had Mitch learned his lesson?

Did he admire me for the great lengths I had gone for us?

Or was he stewing in resentment that I had once again corrected a problem he had unwittingly created in our lives?

"I think it was someone from the casino," I said, meeting his troubled gaze across the table.

"But I don't know who," I gently added with the aim of giving him hope.

"Best to stay away from that place," I warned, heavy-handedly smashing what I hoped my husband would interpret as thick, undeniable subtext into my comment.

In that moment, the implication that I knew my husband had been sneaking off to Resorts World Catskills with Leeanne landed squarely in his brain. I could see it in his elongating, paling face.

"I feel badly for her, but she asked for it," I said.

I watched as Mitch swallowed hard, forcing down some lump of remorse or responsibility I felt he ought to choke on.

He stiffened knowingly, but was cool and mild in his agreement.

"I have no reason to ever go to the casino again. Judy, I'm telling you, I won't go there. Any night I had ever spent at Resorts World has only been a horrible waste of time."

Though he had satisfied me, I would have driven my symbolic point home even further if I hadn't felt a pop deep within my swollen abdomen.

My maternity pants were instantly drenched between the legs, and as I pushed my chair away from the dinner table, thrilled and terrified that my water had just broken, I exclaimed:

"The baby's coming!"

Mitch swept in, scooping me out of my chair, and we rushed to the hospital.

❄

NEARLY TWELVE HOURS later, in the wee hours of the morning, our son was born.

Exhausted, yet sparkling with the kind of hormone-induced euphoria that only a new mother could feel, I accepted my washed, bundled infant into my arms, as Mitch leaned in, weeping giddily with emotion beside me.

All was right in the world.

Our son sneezed adorably, taking our very breath away.

I heard some awful commotion coming from the icy windowsill outside of our maternity room.

A nasty cluster of ratty pigeons were squawking and competing for the ledge, making a racket that no new mother should ever have to deal with.

Promptly, Mitch neared the window and drew the blinds, covering the violent fight so that I wouldn't have to watch the dirty struggle...

...and that isolated action set the tone for our entire marriage from that moment onward.

Ours was a world that wouldn't tolerate that kind of ugliness...

...even though that was Liberty.

The price of freedom could come at quite a cost…

…but we were in a position to pay.

We could afford it.

LEEANNE HESSINGER

Thursday, January 4, 2018

THE MORNING OF my murder, as the dawning sun cut through the kitchen window of my rented house, casting the prettiest orange light I had ever seen across the room and marking a brand-new day, I filled a kettle under the running faucet, set it on one of the front burners of the stove, and cranked the dial on high.

After tearing open its wrapper, I dropped a bag of Earl Grey tea into a clean mug on the counter, briefly paused in front of my refrigerator calendar to drink in the exquisite declaration I had written—'*This is your year!*'—and returned to my bedroom where I sat cross-legged on the nest of sleeping bags I had been calling a bed for a little over one year.

Propping my laptop against my folded shins, I dove back into reading one of the many short stories Scotty had written with me in mind. I had scanned and saved them on my computer long ago along with all of my students' work, but hadn't been able to bring myself to reread Scotty's thoughtful and endearingly misspelled prose until now.

I missed him. Missed his friendship and protection. Missed our springtime bicycle rides, those long afternoons we had spent discussing great literature, and cooking dinner together as we had laughed uproariously and made a mess of his father's kitchen.

As I read his story, I realized he always saw me as important, someone special and deserving.

He had treasured and cherished me. He had treated me with care. Had loved me…

…and I had loved him in return.

As I scrolled down, absorbing the dazzling magnitude of how cleverly he had transformed his deep affection for me into heartwarming prose—'She might not have known it, but she held the whole world in her dark eyes. She could do anything, but not until love had breathed life into her, and that's all he wanted to do.'—I felt moved and inspired and also lost.

Where had I gone wrong?

Why had I walked away from someone who meant so much to me?

How could life have handed me a love I wouldn't be able to keep?

There came a loud knock on my front door as I read the final sentences of his story, the hidden message he'd intended for only me:

'He wanted her to be happy.'

My eyes misted over.

'He wanted her to be free.'

Whoever was out there was pounding, and as I closed the scanned document, shut down my laptop, and tucked it under my pillow, Scotty's last words to me echoed through my mind.

'…be free.'

I opened the door and found Mitch's wife standing in the fluttering snow, her jaw clenched, her eyes glaring, my letter to her bent in her balled fist, which she nearly punched into my face as she demanded:

"What is this?"

"It's what happened. You should know—"

All conviction drained out of me the second I saw the hunting knife in her other hand.

I stumbled, backing away from her, white-faced and shocked that this tremendous woman was stalking in after me.

Pregnant and livid, Judy's eyes pierced me with outrage, as I tried to claim more space and pleaded:

"Mitch broke things off! It's over! I swear!"

Her face didn't change as she closed in.

She didn't believe me for a second.

She lunged.

One swift, hard blow and her knife sliced through my chest as we fell.

It took a moment for the incredible sting of pain to reach my brain.

The agonizing pinch exploded and my whole body broke out, on fire with indescribable pain, when she yanked the knife out of my sternum and stood over me, the kettle on the stove suddenly shrieking at a deafening volume.

As I gasped and gurgled, blood spitting out of my mouth and spurting out of the gaping wound, my vision dimming towards darkness, I watched her wipe the handle of the knife and set it on the floor beside me, the horrible sound of the whistling kettle the only thing anchoring me to this world, but even that was hard to hold onto.

I was slipping away and the last thought I had before death stole me was of the student who had once given me a taste of happiness.

And suddenly, I was free…

THE END

Thank you for reading this mystery novel!
If you enjoyed this story, please consider leaving a positive review on Amazon & Goodreads.

ALSO BY MIRA GIBSON

Thomas from the Sea

Who Killed Leeanne?

The Kensington Killers: The Complete Series
Lunatic (The Kensington Killers, Book One)
Crank (The Kensington Killers, Book Two)
Maniac (The Kensington Killers, Book Three)

The New Hampshire Mysteries: The Complete Series
Daddy Soda (A New Hampshire Mystery, Book One)
Rock Spider (A New Hampshire Mystery, Book Two)
Tar Heart (A New Hampshire Mystery, Book Three)

ABOUT THE AUTHOR

I write mystery novels, detective novels, sleuth mysteries, and psychological literary fiction! You can find me most days working on my computer in the sunshine of beautiful Long Beach, NY where I dream up small town characters and write dark mysteries that are filled with unsuspecting tenderness.

Find me on Facebook! **/MiraGibsonAuthor**

Visit MysteryRoyalty.com to learn more.